Private
Arrangements

Private Arrangements

SHERRY THOMAS

BANTAM BOOKS

PRIVATE ARRANGEMENTS
A Bantam Book / April 2008

Published by Bantam Dell
A Division of Random House, Inc.
New York, New York

This is a work of fiction. Names, characters, places, and incidents either are the product of the author's imagination or are used fictitiously. Any resemblance to actual persons, living or dead, events, or locales is entirely coincidental.

Bantam Books and the rooster colophon are
registered trademarks of Random House, Inc.

ISBN 978-0-440-24431-8

Printed in the United States of America
Published simultaneously in Canada

www.bantamdell.com

OPM   10 9 8 7 6 5 4 3 2 1

For my mother. There are few joys in life greater than that of having you as my mother

To the memory of my grandfather. I will always miss you. And to the memory of my grandmother, for loving books as much as I did.

Acknowledgments

Because I'm sure to forget someone, if you are reading this now, let me say thank you. Thank you for everything.

Now on to specifics.

Miss Snark, for her unqualified recommendation of Kristin Nelson via her snarkalicious—and much lamented—blog. Kristin Nelson, for living up to every last one of those recommendations and then some. Sara Megibow, for being the first person besides myself to read this book, and emailing Kristin late at night telling her she'd better get reading too.

Caitlin Alexander, my editor and Fairy Godmother—for making me feel like Cinderella. Everyone at Bantam, for treating me so well and publishing me so beautifully.

All my friends, classmates, and professors at the UT MPA program. It was a great year and I think of you with such fondness—in particular, Professor Fabio, who should have graced my cover.

Everyone at the Harrington Fellowship program, for everything. And putting my picture in the *New York Times* on top of it.

All my friends and sisters from Austin RWA. You guys are the best.

Janine, Jane, and Sybil. Bloggers rock.

Sue Yuen—for her excellent advice on *Schemes of Love* and for all the good times.

Mary Balogh, Jane Feather, and Eloisa James—for their generous praises. I hope to have the pleasure of meeting you and the honor of cleaning your houses.

My husband and sons, three of the cutest and kindest men in the world under one roof. The wonderful family I married in to, everyone unfailingly supportive of my dreams, especially my grandfather-in-law, who backed up his prayers for my eventual publication with donations to that effect. You see, Appachen, it has come true.

Private Arrangements

Chapter One

Only one kind of marriage ever bore Society's stamp of approval.

Happy marriages were considered vulgar, as matrimonial felicity rarely kept longer than a well-boiled pudding. Unhappy marriages were, of course, even more vulgar, on a par with Mrs. Jeffries's special contraption that spanked forty bottoms at once: unspeakable, for half of the upper crust had experienced it firsthand.

No, the only kind of marriage that held up to life's vicissitudes was the courteous marriage. And it was widely recognized that Lord and Lady Tremaine had the most courteous marriage of them all.

In the ten years since their wedding, neither of them had ever uttered an unkind word about the other, not to parents, siblings, bosom friends, or strangers. Moreover, as their servants could attest, they never had spats, big or small; never embarrassed each other; never, in fact, disagreed on anything at all.

However, every year some cheeky debutante fresh from the schoolroom would point out—as if it weren't common knowledge—that Lord and Lady Tremaine lived on separate continents and had not been seen together since the day after their wedding.

Her elders would shake their heads. Foolish young girl. Wait 'til she heard about her beau's piece on the side. Or fell out of love with the man she married. Then she'd understand what a wonderful arrangement the Tremaines had: civility, distance, and freedom from the very beginning, unencumbered by tiresome emotions. Indeed, it was the most perfect marriage.

Therefore, when Lady Tremaine filed for divorce on grounds of Lord Tremaine's adultery and desertion, chins collided with dinner plates throughout London's most pedigreed dining rooms. Ten days later, as news circulated of Lord Tremaine's arrival on English soil for the first time in a decade, the same falling jaws dented many an expensive carpet from the heart of Persia.

The story of what happened next spread like a well-fed gut. It went something tantalizingly like this: A summons came at the Tremaine town house on Park Lane. Goodman, Lady Tremaine's faithful butler, answered the bell. On the other side of the door stood a stranger, one of the most remarkable-looking gentlemen Goodman had ever come across—tall, handsome, powerfully built, an imposing presence.

"Good afternoon, sir," Goodman said placidly. A representative of the Marchioness of Tremaine, however impressed, neither gawked nor gushed.

He expected to be offered a calling card and a reason

Private Arrangements 3

for the call. Instead, he was handed the gentleman's headgear. Startled, he let go of his hold on the doorknob and took the satin-trimmed top hat. In that instant, the man walked past him into the vestibule. Without a backward glance or an explanation for this act of intrusion, he began pulling off his gloves.

"Sir," Goodman huffed. "You do not have permission from the lady of the house to enter."

The man turned around and shot Goodman a glance that, to the butler's shame, made him want to curl up and whimper. "Is this not the Tremaine residence?"

"It is, sir." The reiteration of *sir* escaped Goodman, though he hadn't intended for it to happen.

"Then kindly inform me, since when does the master of the house require permission from the lady to enter into his own domain?" The man held his gloves together in his right hand and slapped them quietly against the palm of his left, as if toying with a riding crop.

Goodman didn't understand. His employer was the Queen Elizabeth of her time: one mistress and no master. Then the horror dawned. The man before him was the Marquess of Tremaine, the marchioness's long-absent, good-as-dead husband and heir to the Duke of Fairford.

"I do beg your pardon, sir." Goodman held on to his professional calm and took Lord Tremaine's gloves, though he was suddenly perspiring. "We have had no notice of your arrival. I shall have your chambers prepared immediately. May I offer you some refreshments in the meanwhile?"

"You may. And you may see to the unloading of my luggage," said Lord Tremaine. "Is Lady Tremaine at home?"

Goodman could not detect any unusual inflection in Lord Tremaine's tone. It was as if he had simply come in from an afternoon snooze at his club. After ten years! "Lady Tremaine is taking a constitutional in the park, sir."

Lord Tremaine nodded. "Very good."

Goodman instinctively trotted after him, the way he'd trail a feral beast if it happened to have made it past the front door. It was only half a minute later, as Lord Tremaine turned about and raised a brow, that Goodman realized he had already been dismissed.

Something about his wife's town house disturbed Lord Tremaine.

It was surprisingly elegant. He had half-expected to see the kind of interior he'd become accustomed to in the houses of his neighbors on lower Fifth Avenue: grandiose, gilded, aiming only to recall the last days of Versailles.

She had a few chairs from that era, but they had held their share of velvet-clad bottoms and looked comfortable rather than luxurious. Neither did he encounter the heavy sideboards and unchecked proliferation of bric-a-brac that were firmly associated, in his mind, with English homes.

If anything, her residence bore an uncanny resemblance to a certain villa in Turin, at the foot of the

Italian Alps, in which he had spent a few happy weeks during his youth—a house with wallpapers of soft antique gold and muted aquamarine, faience pots of orchids atop slender wrought-iron stands, and durable, well-made furniture from the previous century.

During an entire boyhood of decamping from one domicile to the next, the villa had been the only place, other than his grandfather's estate, where he'd felt at home. He had loved its brightness, its uncluttered comfort, and its abundance of indoor plants, their breath moist and herbaceous.

He was inclined to dismiss the echoing similarity between the two houses as a coincidence until his attention shifted to the paintings that adorned the walls of her drawing room. Between the Rubens, the Titian, and the ancestral portraits that occupied disproportionate acreage on English walls, she had hung pieces by the very same modern artists whose works he displayed in his own town house in Manhattan: Sisley, Morisot, Cassatt, and Monet, whose output had been infamously likened to unfinished wallpaper.

His pulse quickened in alarm. Her dining room featured more Monets and two Degases. Her gallery made it look as though she had bought an entire Impressionist exhibit: Renoir, Cézanne, Seurat, and artists no one had ever heard of outside the most gossipy circles of the Parisian art world.

He stopped midway down the gallery, suddenly unable to go on. She had furnished this house to be a fantasy-come-true for the boy he had been when he married her, the boy who must have mentioned, during their long hours of rapt conversation, something of his preference for understated houses and his love of modern art.

He remembered her spellbound concentration, her soft questions, her burning interest in everything about him.

Was the divorce but a new ruse, then? A cleverly sprung trap to re-ensnare him when all else had failed? Would he find her perfumed and naked on his bed when he threw open the door to his bedchamber?

He located the master's apartment and threw open the door.

There was no her, naked or otherwise, on his bed.

There was no bed.

And nothing else either. The bedchamber was as vast and empty as the American West.

The carpet no longer showed depressed spots where chair legs and bedposts had once stood. The walls betrayed no telltale rectangles of recently removed pictures. Thick layers of dust had settled on floor and windowsills. The room had stood vacant for years.

For no reason at all, he felt as if the breath had been kicked out of his lungs. The sitting room of the master's apartment was sparkling clean and fully equipped—tuft-backed reading chairs, shelves laden with well-read books wrinkled at the spines, a writing desk freshly supplied with ink and paper, even a pot of amaranth in bloom. It made the void of the bedchamber all the more pointed, a barbed symbol.

The house might have been, once upon a time, designed with the single-minded goal of luring him back.

But that was a different decade—another age altogether. He had since been eviscerated from her existence.

He was still standing in the doorway, staring into the empty bedchamber, when the butler arrived, two footmen and a large portmanteau in tow. The nothingness of the chamber made the butler blush an extraordinary pink. "It will take us only an hour, sir, to air the chamber and restore the furnishing."

He almost told the butler not to bestir himself, to let the bedchamber remain stark and barren. But that would have said too much. So he only nodded. "Excellent."

The prototype of the new stamping machine Lady Tremaine had ordered for her factory in Leicestershire refused to live up to its promise. The negotiation with the shipbuilder in Liverpool dragged on most unsatisfactorily. And she had yet to answer any of the letters from her mother—ten in all, one for each day since she'd petitioned for divorce—in which Mrs. Rowland questioned her sanity outright and fell just short of comparing her intelligence to that of a leg of ham.

But that was all expected. What made her head pound was the telegram from Mrs. Rowland three hours ago: *Tremaine came ashore at Southampton this morning.* No matter how she tried to explain it to Freddie as something par for the course—*There are papers to sign and settlements to be negotiated, darling. He has to come back at some point*—Tremaine's arrival portended only trouble.

Her husband. In England. Closer than he had been in a decade, except for that miserable incident in Copenhagen, back in '88.

"I need Broyton to come in tomorrow morning to look at some accounts for me," she said to Goodman, handing over her shawl, her hat, and her gloves as she entered the town house and walked toward the library. "Kindly request Miss Etoile's presence for some dictations. And tell Edie that I will wear the cream velvet tonight, instead of the amethyst silk."

"Madam—"

"I almost forgot. I saw Lord Sutcliffe this morning. His secretary has given notice. I recommended your nephew. Have him present himself at Lord Sutcliffe's house tomorrow morning at ten. Tell him that Lord Sutcliffe prefers a man of sincerity and few words."

"That is too kind of you, madam!" Goodman exclaimed.

"He's a promising young man." She stopped before the library door. "On second thought, have Miss Etoile come in twenty minutes. And make sure no one disturbs me until then."

"But your ladyship, his lordship—"

"His lordship will not be taking tea with me today." She pushed the door open and realized Goodman was still there, hovering. She turned halfway and glanced at him. The butler wore a constipated expression. "What is it, Goodman? The back troubling you again?"

"No, madam, it's not. It's—"

"It's me," said a voice from inside the library. Her husband's voice.

For a long, stunned moment, all she could think was how glad she was that she had not invited Freddie home with her today, as she often did after an afternoon walk together. Then she could not think of anything at all. Her headache faded, replaced by a mad rush of blood to her head. She was hot, then cold. The air about her turned thick as pea soup, fine for gulping but impossible to inhale.

Vaguely, she nodded at Goodman. "You may return to your duties."

Goodman hesitated. Did he fear for her? She entered the library and let the heavy oak door close behind her, shutting out curious eyes and ears, shutting out the rest of the world.

The windows of her library faced west, for a view of the park. The still-intense sunlight cascaded through clear glass panes at an oblique angle and landed in perfect rectangles of warm clarity on her Samarkand carpet, with its poppies and pomegranates on a field of rose and ivory.

Tremaine stood just beyond the direct light, his hands braced against the mahogany desk behind him, his long legs crossed at the ankles. He should be a figure in relative obscurity, not particularly visible. Yet she saw him all too clearly, as if Michelangelo's Adam had leapt off the ceiling of the Sistine Chapel, robbed a Savile Row bespoke tailor, and come to make trouble.

She caught herself. She was staring, as if she was still that nineteen-year-old girl, devoid of depth but full of herself.

"Hullo, Camden."

"Hullo, Gigi."

She had allowed no man to call her by that childhood pet name since his departure.

Forcing herself away from the door, she crossed the length of the library, the carpet beneath her feet too soft, a quagmire. She marched right up to him, to show that she did not fear him. But she did. He held powers over her, powers far beyond those conferred by mere laws.

Even though she was a tall woman, she had to tilt her head to look him in the eye. His eyes were a dark, dark green, like malachite from the Urals. She inhaled his subtle scent of sandalwood and citrus, the aroma she had once equated with happiness.

"Are you here to grant me the divorce or to be a nuisance?" She got to the point right away. Trouble that was not confronted head-on always circled around to bite one in the bum.

He shrugged. He had taken off his day coat and his necktie. Her gaze lingered one second too long on the golden skin at the base of his neck. His shirt of fine cambric draped over him lovingly, caressing his wide shoulders and long arms.

"I'm here to set conditions."

"What do you mean, conditions?"

"An heir. You produce an heir and I will allow the divorce to proceed. Otherwise I will name parties to *your* adultery. You do know that you cannot divorce me on grounds of adultery if you happen to have committed the same sin, don't you?"

Her ears rang. "Surely you jest. You want an *heir* from me? *Now?*"

"I couldn't stand the thought of bedding you before now."

"Really?" She laughed, though she'd have preferred to smash an inkwell against his temple. "You liked it well enough last time."

"The performance of a lifetime," he said easily. "And I was a good thespian to begin with."

Pain erupted inside her, corrosive, debilitating pain she'd thought she'd never feel again. She groped for mastery and shoved the subject away from where she was most vulnerable. "Empty threats. I have not been intimate with Lord Frederick."

"How chaste of you. I speak of Lord Wrenworth, Lord Acton, and the Honorable Mr. Williams."

She sucked in a breath. How did he know? She'd been ever so careful, ever so discreet.

"Your mother wrote me." He watched her, evidently enjoying her mounting dismay. "Of course, she only wished for me to fly into a jealous rage and hurry across the ocean to reclaim you as my own. I'm sure you will forgive her."

If there ever existed extenuating circumstances for matricide, this was it. First thing tomorrow, she'd set loose two dozen famished goats in Mrs. Rowland's prized greenhouse. Then she'd corner the market on hair dyes and force the woman to show her graying roots.

"You have a choice," he said amicably. "We can resolve

it privately. Or we can have sworn testimonies from these gentlemen. You know every word they utter would be in all the papers."

She blanched. Freddie was her very own human miracle, steadfast and loyal, loving her enough to willingly take part in all the hassle and ugliness of a divorce. But would he still love her when all her former lovers had testified to their affairs on public record?

"Why are you doing this?" Her voice rose. She took a deep breath to calm herself. Any emotion she displayed before Tremaine was a show of weakness. "I had my solicitors send you a dozen letters. You never responded. We could have had this marriage annulled with some dignity, without having to go through this circus."

"And here I thought my lack of response adequately conveyed what I thought of your idea."

"I offered you one hundred thousand pounds!"

"I'm worth twenty times that. But even if I hadn't a sou, that's not quite enough for me to stand before Her Majesty's magistrate and swear that I never touched you. We both know perfectly well that I shagged you to a fare-thee-well."

She flinched and grew hot. Unfortunately, not entirely from anger. The memories of that night—no, she would not think about it. She had forgotten it already. "This is about Miss von Schweppenburg, isn't it? You are still trying to punish me."

He gave her one of his cool stares that used to turn her knees to pudding. "Now, why would you think that?"

And what could she say? What could she say without dragging up their entire complicated and bitter history? She swallowed. "Fine," she said, as indifferently as she could. "I have an evening engagement to keep. But I should be home about ten. I can permit you a quarter hour from half past ten."

He laughed. "As impatient as always, my dear marchioness. No, tonight I will not be visiting you. I'm weary from my travels. And now that I've seen you, I'll need a few more days to get over my revulsion. But rest assured, I shall not be bound by any asinine time limits. I will stay in your bed for as long as I want, not a minute less—and not a minute more, no matter how you plead."

Her jaw dropped from sheer stupefaction. "That is the most rid—"

He suddenly leaned toward her and placed an index finger over her lips. "I wouldn't finish that sentence if I were you. You will not enjoy eating those words."

She jerked her head away, her lips burning. "I would not want you to remain in my bed if you were the last man alive and I'd had nothing but Spanish flies for a fortnight."

"What images you bring to mind, my lady Tremaine. With every man in the world perfectly alive and no aphrodisiacs at all, you were already a tigress." He pushed away from the desk. "I've had all I can take of you for a day. I wish you a pleasant evening. Do convey my regards to your beloved. I hope he doesn't mind my exercises in conjugal rights."

He left without a backward glance.

And not for the first time.

Lady Tremaine watched the door closing behind her husband and rued the day she first learned of his existence.

Chapter Two

Eleven years earlier ...
London
July 1882

Eighteen-year-old Gigi Rowland gloated. She hoped she wasn't too obvious, but then, she didn't really care. What could the bejeweled, beplumed women in Lady Beckwith's drawing room possibly say? That she lacked becoming modesty? That she was hard-edged and arrogant? That she reeked of pound notes?

They had predicted, at the beginning of her London season, that she would be an unqualified disaster, a girl with no class, no comportment, no clue. But lo and behold, only two months into the season and she was already engaged—to a *duke*, a young, handsome one no less. *Her Grace the Duchess of Fairford.* She liked the sound of it. She liked it tremendously.

The same women who had scorned her had been forced to stand before her and offer their felicitations. Yes, the wedding date had been set—in November, just after her birthday. And, yes, thank you, she already had her first consultation at Madame Elise's for the wedding gown. She'd chosen a lush cream satin, with a twelve-foot train to be made of silver moiré.

Secure in her soon-to-be exalted status, Gigi settled deeper into the bergère chair and snapped open her fan as other, fiancéless debutantes prepared to entertain the ladies with their musical skills—Lord Beckwith being notoriously lengthy with his postdinner cordials and cigars, sometimes keeping the gentlemen for more than three hours.

Gigi turned her attention to more important matters. Should she do something fantastical with the cake, have it done in the shape of the Taj Mahal or the Doge's Palace? No? Then she'd have the layers made in an unusual shape. Hexagons? Excellent. A hexagonal cake covered in gleaming royal fondant icing, with garlands of—

The music. She looked up in surprise. The performances usually ranged from acceptable to execrable. But the creamy, exquisite young woman at the bench was as adept as the professional musicians Gigi's mother sometimes engaged. Her fingers glided across the piano keys like swallows over a summer pond. Crystalline, sumptuous notes caressed the ears the way a good dish of crème brûlée caressed the tongue.

Theodora von Schweppenburg. That was her name. They'd been introduced just before dinner. She was new to London, from a minor principality on the Continent, the daughter of a count, by right a countess herself—but it was one of those Holy Roman Empire titles that went on to all descendants, so it meant little.

The performance ended, and a few minutes later

Gigi was surprised to find Miss von Schweppenburg at her side.

"Many congratulations on your engagement, Miss Rowland." Miss von Schweppenburg spoke with a light, pleasing accent. She smelled of attar of rose underpinned with patchouli.

"Thank you, *Fräulein.*"

"My mother would like me to do the same," Miss von Schweppenburg said with a small, self-conscious laugh, sitting down on a straight-back chair next to Gigi. "She has ordered me to ask you how you accomplished it."

"It is simple," Gigi answered, with practiced nonchalance. "His Grace is in financial straits, and I have a fortune."

It was less simple than that. Rather, it had been a campaign years in the making, waged from the very second Mrs. Rowland at last inculcated in Gigi that it was both her duty and her destiny to become a duchess.

Miss von Schweppenburg would not be able to duplicate Gigi's success. Nor would Gigi herself. She knew of no other marriageable duke with such overwhelming arrears that he'd be willing to marry a girl whose only claim to gentility was her mother, a country squire's daughter.

Miss von Schweppenburg's eyes lowered. "Oh," she murmured, turning the handle of her lace fan round and round within her palms. "I don't have a fortune."

Gigi had guessed as much. There was a sadness to her, the somber melancholy of a high-born woman who could only afford to have a parlor maid come in every other day, who moved in the dark after sunset to save on candle wax.

"But you are beautiful," Gigi pointed out. Though long in the tooth, she thought, at least twenty-one or twenty-two. "Men like beautiful women."

"I don't do it very well, this . . . beautiful woman undertaking."

That, Gigi had seen for herself already. At dinner Miss von Schweppenburg had been seated between two eligible young peers, both of whom had been piqued by her beauty and her shyness. But there'd been something glum about her reticence. She'd paid scant attention to either man and, after a while, they'd noticed.

"You need more practice," said Gigi.

The girl was silent. She drew the tip of her fan across her lap. "Have you ever met Lord Reginald Saybrook, Miss Rowland?"

The name sounded vaguely familiar. Then Gigi remembered. Lord Reginald was her future husband's uncle. "I'm afraid not. He married some Bavarian princess and lives on the Continent."

"He has a son." Miss von Schweppenburg's voice faltered. "His name is Camden. And . . . and he loves me."

Gigi smelled a Romeo-and-Juliet story, a story whose appeal escaped her. Miss Capulet should have married the man her parents chose for her and then had her torrid but very discreet affair with Mr. Montague. Not only would she have stayed alive, she'd have realized, after a while, that Romeo was just a callow, bored youth with little to offer her other than pretty platitudes. *It is the east, and Juliet is the sun* indeed.

"We've known each other a long time," continued Miss von Schweppenburg. "But of course Mama would not let me marry him. He has no fortune either."

"I see," Gigi said politely. "You are trying to remain true to him."

Miss von Schweppenburg hesitated. "I don't know. Mama would never speak to me again if I don't marry well. But strangers make me...uncomfortable. I only wish Mr. Saybrook were more eligible."

Gigi's opinion of the girl deteriorated rapidly. She respected a woman out to marry to her best advantage. And she respected a woman who sacrificed worldly comforts for love, though she personally disagreed with such decisions. But she could not tolerate wishy-washiness. Miss von Schweppenburg would neither commit to this Camden Saybrook, because he was too poor, nor commit to her husband-hunting, because she enjoyed too much being loved by him.

"He's very handsome, very sweet and kind," Miss von Schweppenburg was saying, her voice reduced to a whisper, almost as if she were talking to herself. "He writes me letters and sends lovely presents, things he'd made himself."

Gigi wanted to roll her eyes but somehow couldn't. Someone loved this girl, this utterly useless girl, loved her enough to go on wooing her, even though she was being paraded before all of Europe for takers.

A moment of stark despair descended upon her that she would never know such love, that she would go through life sustained only by her facade of invincibility. Then she came to her senses. Love was for fools.

Gigi Rowland was many things, but she was never a fool.

"How fortunate for you, *Fräulein*."

"Yes, I suppose I am. I only wish…" Miss von Schweppenburg shook her head. "Perhaps you might meet him at your wedding."

Gigi nodded and smiled absently, preoccupied once again with the structural elegance of the cake to be served at her imminent wedding.

But no wedding ever took place between Philippa Gilberte Rowland and Carrington Vincent Hanslow Saybrook. Two weeks before the wedding day, His Grace the Duke of Fairford, the Marquess of Tremaine, Viscount Hanslow, and Baron Wolvinton, after six hours of solid drinking in honor of his upcoming nuptials, climbed up to the roof of his friend's town house and attempted to moon all of London. All he accomplished was a broken neck and his own demise by tumbling four stories to the ground.

Chapter Three

Victoria Rowland was not quite herself.

She knew this because she had just decapitated all the orchids in her beloved greenhouse. Their heads rolled on the ground in beautiful, grotesque carnage, as if she were enacting a floral version of the French Revolution.

Not for the first or even the one thousandth time, she wished that the seventh Duke of Fairford had lived two weeks longer. Two measly weeks. Afterward he could have swilled poison, tied himself to a railroad track, and, while he was waiting for the train, shot himself in the head.

All she wanted was for Gigi to be a duchess. Was that too much?

Duchess—everyone had called Victoria that when she was a young girl. She'd been beautiful, well-mannered, serene, and regal; they were all convinced she was going to marry a duke. But then her father was defrauded out of almost everything they had, and her mother's long, lingering illness plunged the family finances from merely precarious to catastrophic. She'd ended up marrying a man twice her age, a rich industrialist looking to infuse some gentility into his bloodline.

But John Rowland's money had been deemed too new, too uncouth. Suddenly Victoria found herself shut out of drawing rooms where she had once been welcome. Swallowing her humiliation, she swore that she would never let the same happen to her own daughter. The girl would have Victoria's polish and her father's fortune, she would take London by storm, and she would be a duchess if it killed Victoria.

Gigi had almost done it. In fact, she had done it. The fault there lay entirely with Carrington. And then, to Victoria's amazement, she had done it again, marrying Carrington's cousin, heir to the title. How happy and proud Victoria had been on the day of Gigi's wedding, how resolutely giddy.

And then everything went wrong. Camden left the day after the wedding, with no explanations to anyone. And no matter how much she begged, cried, and wheedled, Victoria could not get a word as to what had happened out of Gigi.

What do you care? Gigi had said icily. *We have decided to lead separate lives. When he inherits I'm still going to become a duchess. Isn't that all you've ever wanted?*

Victoria had had to content herself with that while she corresponded with Camden in secret, dropping bits and pieces of Gigi's news between descriptions of her garden and her charity galas. Four times a year his letters came, as reliable as the rotation of the seasons, informative, and amiable to a fault. Those letters kept her hopes alive. Surely he meant to come back one day or he would not bother writing to his mother-in-law, year in, year out.

But could Gigi not leave well enough alone? What was the girl thinking, risking something as nasty and damaging as a divorce? And for what, that all-too-ordinary Lord Frederick, who wasn't fit to wash her drawers, let alone touch her without them? The thought made Victoria ill. The only silver lining she could see was that this was sure to make Camden sit up and take notice. Perhaps he'd even come back. Perhaps there'd be a passionate confrontation.

Camden's telegram the day before, informing her of his arrival, had made her walk on clouds. She dashed off one back to him, scarcely able to contain her jubilation. But this morning his response came, thirty-one words of unrelenting bad news: *dear madam stop please kill your hopes now stop as a merciful act to yourself stop I mean to grant the divorce stop after a certain interval stop yours affectionately stop camden.*

And she had grabbed the nearest garden implement and mangled all her lovely, rare, painstakingly raised varietals. Now she dropped the shears, like a contrite killer flinging away her murder weapon. She must not go on like this. She would end up in Bedlam, an old woman with wild white-streaked hair, beseeching the pillow not to abandon the bed.

Fine, so she could not prevent the divorce. But she would find Gigi another duke. In fact, one lived right down the lane from her cottage here, a few miles from the coast of Devon. His Grace the Duke of Perrin was a rather intimidating recluse. But he was a man of able body and sound mind. And at forty-five years of age, he was not yet too old for Gigi, who was getting dangerously close to thirty.

So Victoria had wanted the duke for herself when she'd been an eligible young lady, living in this very same cottage on the periphery of his estate and his sphere. But that was three decades ago. No one else knew of her erstwhile ambition. And the duke, well, he didn't even know she existed.

She'd have to abandon her duchesslike reserve, forget that they had never been introduced, and barge into his path, which took him past her cottage each afternoon right about quarter to four, in fair weather and foul.

In other words, she'd have to act like Gigi.

When Camden returned to the town house after his morning ride, Goodman informed him that Lady Tremaine wished to confer with him at his earliest convenience. No doubt she meant that he should present himself that very moment. But that would not be at *his* convenience at all, as he was both hungry and disheveled.

He breakfasted and bathed. Giving his hair one last rub, he let the towel drop to his shoulders and reached for the fresh clothes he had laid out on the bed. At that precise moment, his wife, in a blur of white blouse and caramel-colored skirts, burst through the door.

She took two steps into the room and stopped, a

furrow instantly forming between her brows. As promised, the bedchamber had been aired, cleaned, and furnished, an entire handsome redwood set—bedstead, nightstands, armoire, and chest—roused out of long slumber in the attic and pressed into service. Beneath the large Monet that hung above the mantel, two pots of tailed orchids bloomed silently, their fragrance light and sweet. But despite all the buffing and polishing Goodman had ordered, a musty scent clung to the resuscitated furniture, an odor of age and blank history.

"It looks exactly the same," she said, almost as if to herself. "I had no idea Goodman remembered."

Goodman probably remembered when she had last broken a nail. She had that effect on men. Even a man who left her behind never forgot anything about her.

In those days when he'd felt more charitable toward her, Camden had been certain God lingered over her creation, breathing more life and purpose into her than He bestowed on lesser mortals. Even now, with the ravage of a sleepless night plain on her face, her onyx-dark eyes still burned brighter than the night sky over New York Harbor on Independence Day.

"May I be of some assistance?" he said.

Her gaze turned to him. He was quite decent. His dressing gown covered everything that needed to be covered and most of the rest of him too. But she did look surprised and then, faintly but unmistakably, embarrassed.

She did not blush. She rarely blushed. But when she did, when her pale, snooty cheeks turned a shade of strawberry ice cream, a man would have to be mummi-fied not to respond.

"You were taking a long time," she said brusquely, by way of explanation.

"And you suspected me of deliberately making you wait." He shook his head. "You should know I'm above such petty vengeances."

Her expression was a pained sneer. "Of course. You prefer your vengeance grand and spectacular."

"As you like," he said, bending to step into his linen. The bulk of the bed stood between them, the top of the mattress as high as his waist. But this act of dressing was nevertheless a display of power on his part. "Now what's this urgent business of yours that can't wait un-til I'm dressed?"

"I apologize for barging in on you," she said stiffly. "I'll see myself out and wait for you in the library."

"Don't bother, since you are already here." He pulled on his trousers. "What do you wish to speak to me about?"

She'd always been quick on her feet. "Very well, then. I have given some thought to your conditions. I find them both too vague and too open-ended."

So he'd gathered. She was hardly the type to let any-one walk over her. In fact, she preferred to be the one doing the walking over. He was only surprised that she hadn't come earlier with her objections.

"Enlighten me." He tossed the towel on a chair by the window, untied his dressing gown, and dropped it on the bed.

Their eyes met. Or rather, he looked at her in the

eyes and she looked at his bare torso. As if he needed any more reminders of the naughty, cheeky young girl who used to send her fingers out on feats of alpinism up his thighs.

Now their gazes met. She blushed. But she recovered quickly. "Heir-producing is an uncertain business," she said, her tone brisk. "I assume you want male issue."

"I do." He pulled on his shirt, tucked in the bottom, and began to fasten the trouser buttons at his right hip, adjusting his parts slightly to ease the discomfort caused by his reaction to her.

Her gaze was now somewhere to his right. The bed-post, probably. "My mother never managed one in ten years of marriage. Besides, there is always the possibility that one of us, or both, could be barren."

Liar. He chose not to call her on it. "And your point is?"

"I need an end in sight, for myself and for Lord Frederick, who should not be asked to wait forever."

What had Mrs. Rowland said in her irate letter to him? *Lord Frederick, I will cede, is very amiable. But he has all the brains of a boiled pudding, and all the grace of an aged duck. I cannot fathom, for the life of me, what Gigi sees in him.* Camden snapped his braces over his shoulders. For once, Mrs. Rowland's shrewdness failed her. How many men were to be readily found in England who'd faith-fully stand beside a woman in the midst of a divorce?

"... six months from today," his wife was saying. "If by the beginning of November I still have not conceived, we proceed to the divorce. If I have, we will wait 'til I give birth."

He could not envisage an actual child, not even a pregnancy. His thoughts stopped at the edge of a bed and went no further. Part of him revolted at the very idea of any sort of intimacy with her, even the most impersonal kind.

And then there were other parts of him.

"Well?" she demanded.

He collected himself. "What if you present me with a female child?"

"That is something I cannot help."

Was it?

"I can see merits to the concept of limits, but I cannot agree to your particulars," he said. "Six months is too short a time to guarantee anything. One year. And if it's a girl, one more attempt."

"Nine months."

He held all the trumps in this game. It was time she realized that. "I did not come to haggle, Lady Tremaine. I am indulging you. A year or there is no deal."

Her chin tilted up. "A year from today?"

"A year from when we start."

"And when is that going to be, O Lord and Master?"

He laughed softly at her acerbic tone. In this she had not changed. She would go down fighting. "Patience, Gigi, patience. You'll get what you want in the end."

"And you would do well to remember that," she said, with all the haughty poise of Queen Elizabeth just after the sinking of the Spanish Armada. "I bid you a good day."

His gaze followed her retreating back, her efficient

gait, and the dashing sway of her skirts. No one would know, by looking at her, that she just had her head handed to her on a platter, surrounded by her entrails.

Suddenly he was reminded that he had once liked her. Too much.

Chapter Four

Gigi disliked Greek mythology, because the gods were forever punishing women for hubris. What was wrong with a little hubris? Why couldn't Arachne claim that her skills were greater than Athena's, since they were, without being turned into a spider? And why should Poseidon be angry enough to toss Cassiopeia's daughter to a sea monster, unless Cassiopeia's boast was true and she really was more beautiful than Poseidon's own daughters?

Gigi was guilty of hubris. And she, too, was being punished by jealous gods. How else was she to view Carrington's abrupt and senseless death? Other roués lived to unrepentant old age, ogling debutantes with their red, rheumy eyes. Why shouldn't Carrington have enjoyed the same opportunities?

A fierce gust nearly made off with her hat. She rubbed the underside of her chin, where the hat ribbon chafed. Briarmeadow, the Rowland property, was eight thousand acres of woodland and meadows, most of it flat as a ballroom floor, except for this corner where the land rolled and sometimes creased into ridges and folds.

She'd grown up in a house nearer to Bedford. Briarmeadow, her home for the past three years, had been purchased with the express purpose of sweetening the deal for Carrington, since it shared a long border with Twelve Pillars, Carrington's country seat.

Gigi liked to walk the boundaries of Briarmeadow. Land was solid, something she could count on. She liked certainty. She liked knowing exactly how her future would unfold. Marriage to Carrington had promised her something along that line: No matter what else happened, she'd always be a duchess, and no one would ever again snub either herself or her mother.

With Carrington gone, she was back to being just Miss Moneybags. She wasn't head-turningly beautiful, no matter what her mother tried. She had been known to step on a toe or two on the dance floor. And, vulgarity of all vulgarities, she had an abiding interest in commerce, in the making of goods and money.

Overhead, thick clouds hung like giant wads of soiled linen, gray with stains of pus yellow. The snow would come down soon. She really should be turning back. She had another three miles to go before she'd come within sight of the house. But she did not want to go back. It was dejecting enough to contemplate by herself what might have been. It was ten times worse with her mother there.

Mrs. Rowland alternated between shock, despair, and an angry defiance. They'd do it again, she'd hug

Gigi and whisper fiercely when she was in one of her wilder moods. Then she'd lose all hope, because they couldn't possibly repeat it—Carrington having been a rather unique case of debauchery, insolvency, and desperation.

A brook separated Briarmeadow from Twelve Pillars. Here there were no fences, the brook being a long-recognized boundary. Gigi stood on the bank and threw pebbles into the water. The spot was pretty in summer, with pliant green willow branches that danced in the breeze. Now the defoliated willows looked rather like naked old spinsters, all thin and droopy.

Across the brook the land rose into a slope. Suddenly, atop the slope, directly opposite her, a bareheaded rider appeared. She was taken aback. Besides her, no one ever came here. The rider, in a dark crimson riding jacket and buff riding trousers tucked into long black boots, charged down the slope. She was startled into stumbling backward, for fear the horse might gallop into her.

At the bottom of the slope, some fifty feet downstream from her, the rider guided his mount to a muscular, graceful leap, jumping clear across the twelve-foot-wide stream. He drew up his reins, halted, and looked at her. He'd been aware of her all along.

"You are trespassing on my land," she shouted.

He came toward her, nudging the huge black horse with ease, ducking under the denuded willow branches. He didn't stop until he had a clear line of sight to her, about ten feet out. And she had her first good look at him.

He was handsome, though not as pretty as

Carrington, who—poor sod, may the she-devils of hell not use him too hard—had been Byron reborn. This man here had features that were both sharper and nobler, set in a leaner, more masculine face. Their gaze met. He had beautiful, deep-set eyes, the irises a gorgeous green. A thinking man's eyes: perceptive, opaque, seeing much, giving little away.

She couldn't look away. There was something about him that was instantly appealing to her, something in his bearing, a confidence that was unlike either Carrington's arrogant sense of prerogative or her own unyielding obduracy. Poise forged with finesse.

"You are trespassing on my land," she repeated, because she couldn't think of anything else to say.

"Am I?" he said. "And you are?"

He spoke with a subtle accent, not French, German, Italian, or anything else she could immediately think of. A foreigner?

"Miss Rowland. Who are you?"

"Mr. Saybrook."

Was he—no, not possible. But then, who else could he be? "Are you the Marquess of Tremaine?"

Carrington had died heirless. His uncle, the next male in line, had inherited the ducal title. The new duke's eldest son took on the courtesy title of the Marquess of Tremaine.

The young man smiled a little. "I suppose I have become that too."

He was Theodora von Schweppenburg's beau? She had envisioned a man as spineless and ineffectual as Miss von Schweppenburg herself.

"You are returned from university."

He had not attended Carrington's funeral alongside the rest of his family because of his classes at the École Polytechnique in Paris. His parents had been vague about what he studied. Physics or economics, they'd said. How could anyone possibly confuse the two?

"The university lets us out for Christmas."

He dismounted and approached her, leading the black stallion behind him. She tamped down her discomfort and remained where she was. He removed his riding glove and offered her his hand.

"Delighted to meet you at last, Miss Rowland."

She shook his hand briefly. "I guess you know who I am, then."

The first snowflakes began to fall, tiny particles of puffy ice. One landed on his eyelash. His eyelashes, like his brows, were of a much darker shade than the molten gold at the tips of his hair. His eyes, she was sure, were the color of an Alpine lake, though she'd never seen one.

"I was going to call on you tomorrow," he said. "To offer my condolences."

She chortled. "Yes, as you can see, I am inconsolable."

He looked at her, truly looked at her this time, his eyes scanning her features one by one. His scrutiny discomfited her—she was more accustomed to being pointed at behind her back—but it was not unpleasant, coming from such a rivetingly handsome man.

"I apologize for my cousin. He was most inconsiderate to die before marrying you and leaving an heir."

His bluntness took her aback. It was one thing for

her mother to say something along that line, quite another to hear it repeated by a complete stranger to whom she hadn't even been properly introduced.

"Man proposes, God disposes," she said.

"A crying shame, isn't it?"

She was beginning to like this Lord Tremaine. "Yes, it is."

The snowflakes suddenly increased in dimension, no longer icy sawdust but fingernail-size fluffs. They fell densely, as if all the angels in heaven were molting. In the minutes since Lord Tremaine first appeared, the sky had become visibly darker. Soon dusk would cloak the land.

Tremaine looked about them. "Where is your man, or your maid?"

"Don't have one. I'm not out in public."

He frowned. "How far away is your house?"

"About three miles."

"You should take my horse. It's not safe for you to walk that long in the dark, in this weather."

"Thank you, but I don't ride."

He looked into her eyes. For a moment she thought he meant to ask her outright why she was afraid of horses. But he only said, "In that case, permit me to walk you home."

She breathed a silent sigh of relief. "Permission granted. But you should be forewarned that I am disastrous at small talk."

He pulled on his glove and looped the stallion's reins about his wrist. "It's quite all right. Silence does not derange—pardon—disturb me."

The word *déranger* in French meant *to disturb*. He didn't really have an accent. His English, a language that he hardly ever spoke, was simply somewhat rusty.

They walked in silence for a while. She couldn't resist glancing at him every minute or so to admire his profile. He had the classical nose and chin of an Apollo Belvedere.

"I conferred with my late cousin's solicitors before coming to Twelve Pillars," Tremaine said, breaking the silence. "He left us a complicated situation."

"I see." She certainly did, being intimately acquainted with Carrington's financial particulars.

"The solicitors gave me the sum of his outstanding debts, a staggering number. But for four-fifths of the amount, they could not show me any demands from creditors that are less than two years old."

"Interesting." She was beginning to see where he was going with this. How had he pieced it together so quickly? He must not have been in England for more than two or three days or she'd have learned about his presence already.

"So I made them show me his marriage contract instead."

A very shrewd move. "Did you find it soporific reading?"

"On the contrary, I quite admired it. As watertight a legal document as I'm likely to come across this lifetime. I noticed that you'd absolve him of all his debts upon marriage."

"There might have been such wording."

"You are the one who holds the lion's share of his

arrears, aren't you? You bought out his creditors and consolidated the preponderance of his debts to persuade him to marry you."

Gigi looked upon Lord Tremaine with a new, almost warm respect. He was young, twenty-one or so. But he was sharp as a guillotine blade. That was exactly what she had done. She had eschewed Mrs. Rowland's advice to win a duke in drawing rooms and ballrooms and had gone about it her own way. "That's right. Carrington didn't want to marry the likes of me. He had to be dragged kicking and screaming to the negotiation table."

"Did you enjoy the dragging?" He glanced down at her.

"Yes, I rather did," she confessed. "It was amusing threatening to strip his house bare to the last plank on the floor and the last spoon in the kitchen."

"My parents are convinced of your grief." She heard the smile in his voice. "They said tears streamed down your face at his funeral."

"For nearly three years of hard work down the drain, I cried like a bereaved mother."

He laughed outright, a rich sound with all the beguilement of spring. Her heart skipped a beat.

"You are an unusual woman, Miss Rowland. Are you also fair and honest?"

"If there's no disadvantage to me."

She could swear he smiled again. "Good enough," he said. "I'd like to negotiate a deal with you."

"I'm all ears."

"Twelve Pillars generates a decent income, if managed properly. That, combined with the sale of nonentailed properties, should help pay off Carrington's creditors, if you hold off calling in your portion of his debts."

"I'm not infinitely rich. Acquiring Carrington's liabilities was a heavy outlay, even for me."

"I'm willing to cede you an advantageous interest rate if you would let us pay you back in quarterly installments, starting next year this time and finishing in, let's say, seven years."

"I have a better idea," she said. "Why don't you marry me instead?"

Marrying the new duke's heir had always been the first alternative, but she had been unenthused about the enterprise. Carrington had poked everything that moved, but he had no loyalty except to himself, and that was something she could understand and even appreciate, on occasion. She recoiled at the idea of a mawkish husband who pined away for another woman, especially a woman for whom she had so little admiration.

Lord Tremaine in person, however, had already proved anything but useless. She warmed up to the idea of an alliance with him like a pan on a stoked stove. "Upon our marriage I'll cancel seventy percent of the debts."

He gave her a long look, but his response was not the shock and amazement she had anticipated. "Why only seventy percent?"

"Because you are not a duke yourself and probably

would not be for many years." She considered being a bit more demure and giving him time to think. But the next thing out of her mouth was "What say you?"

He was silent a moment. "I'm deeply honored. But my affections are already pledged elsewhere."

"Affections change." Good Lord, she sounded like the devil out to purchase his soul.

"I should like to think that I have some constancy to my character."

Damn Miss von Schweppenburg. Why should that drawing-room ornament be so lucky? "You are probably right. But I do not require your affections, only your hand."

He stopped, putting a hand on the stallion's neck to signal the horse to halt. She stopped too. "You are very ruthless toward yourself, for someone so young," he said, with a gentleness that made her want to clutch his hand and tell him everything that had happened to make her the hard-bitten female she was. "Why?"

She shrugged instead. "I've had to deal with fortune hunters since I turned fourteen. And grande dames who wouldn't give me the time of the day."

"Affection and good opinion—are they not at all a consideration for you in marriage?"

"No. So I would not mind that you love someone else. In fact, you can spend all your time with her, if you like. Once our marriage is consummated, you need only to come back to me when you need heirs."

She probably should not have said it. It was too forward, too indelicate, even for her. In reaction, his gaze dipped briefly, encompassing all of her. And when he looked back at her, his irises darker than she remembered, the back of her mouth grew hot.

"I have a different view of marriage," he said. "I do not think I'm the right person for what you have in mind."

All that beauty and cleverness, why must he possess principles too? The depth of her disappointment was out of all proportion to the casualness of her proposal. "What if I choose to call in the debts, then?" she said churlishly.

"It would be a bad deal for you," he said calmly. "Stripping us of everything we have will at most make up half of what my late cousin owed you. You know that."

They resumed walking, but her mind was no longer on the finances of her social climbing. Instead, she entertained disturbingly angry thoughts about Miss von Schweppenburg. The woman was so insipid, so weak, what hold did she have on this remarkable man? What right did she have toward him, she who would have meekly accepted the proposal of any rich, powerful man who had caught her mother's fancy? Did beauty, elegance, and flawlessness at the pianoforte really count for *that* much?

He noted her sullen silence. "I have offended you."

How could he offend her? She liked everything about him, except the woman he loved. "No. You are not obliged to marry me just because it would delight me."

"I don't know if it is of any comfort to you, but I'm honored. No one has ever asked for my hand in marriage before."

"I suspect it's because you are young and you used to be a bit of an impoverished nobody. Expect the proposals to fly fast and thick now."

"But you'll always be my first," he said.

Was he teasing her? "Well, the first one you turned down, to be sure," she answered glumly.

He allowed her to sulk for the remainder of the trek. She stomped, her boots raucously crunching the snow underfoot. Despite his greater size and weight, his riding boots were as quiet on the snow as she imagined a Siberian tiger's paws must be.

Half a mile from the house, they were met by Mrs. Rowland and a trio of lantern-swinging servants.

"Gigi!" Mrs. Rowland cried. She picked up her skirts and came running.

Gigi could not prevent the mother-hen hug that swooped upon her. Mrs. Rowland kissed her on her forehead and cheeks. "Gigi. You foolish, foolish girl. Where have you been? Look at this weather! You could have frozen to your death out there."

"Mother!" Gigi protested, embarrassed to be so fussed over before Lord Tremaine. "I was not out in Antarctica risking frostbite and gangrene."

"I'm just worried because you haven't been yourself lately. Now, do let us—"

At last Mrs. Rowland noticed the stranger, and the very large horse, next to Gigi. She swung toward Gigi in alarm.

Gigi sighed. "Mother, may I present his lordship, the Marquess of Tremaine? Lord Tremaine, my mother, Mrs. Rowland. Lord Tremaine has graciously deigned to accompany me, to help me grope my way home in the midst of this veritable blizzard we are experiencing."

Mrs. Rowland ignored her acerbic remarks. "Lord Tremaine! We thought you still in Paris."

"My term ended a week ago, madam." He bowed. "I hope you will forgive me. I trespassed onto your land without knowing and came upon Miss Rowland. She kindly permitted me to walk with her."

He turned to Gigi and bowed also. "It's been a rare pleasure, Miss Rowland. I trust you are in good hands now."

"But you cannot mean to go back the way you came!" Mrs. Rowland gasped in horror. "You will surely get lost in this darkness and this weather. You must come to our house instead."

He protested. But Mrs. Rowland was convinced he would perish if he went ahead with his foolhardy plan to return to Twelve Pillars either on foot or on horseback. In the end he acquiesced to dinner and to being taken home in a warm, comfortable brougham afterward.

Gigi was unhappy about it. She was all for sending Lord Tremaine away, the sooner the better. It did not amuse her to see her mother's extremely favorable reaction upon viewing him for the first time in good light. And it hurt—a sharp pinch somewhere deep in her chest—watching Mrs. Rowland shower him with the kind of pampering attention reserved for prospective sons-in-law.

Yet Gigi put on her best dinner gown, a midnight-blue confection of silk and tulle, and had her hair recoiffed three times. God help her, she wanted him to think her pretty and desirable.

Over dinner, Mrs. Rowland patiently, skillfully elicited details of Lord Tremaine's twenty-one years of life. He had led quite the cosmopolitan existence, it appeared, having sojourned in every major capital of Europe, plus quite a few of the Continent's favorite watering holes.

He conducted himself with the poise of a prince but without the arrogance so ingrained in most members of the aristocracy. Yet he was most certainly an aristocrat. Not only was he heir to an English ducal title, but through his mother, who'd been born a Wittelsbach, he was related to the House of Hapsburg, the House of Hohenzollern, and the House of Hanover itself, from cousinship with the dukes of Saxe-Coburg-Gotha.

Worse, unlike Carrington, whose slack chin, wet lips, and vacant eyes became all too noticeable upon further acquaintance, Lord Tremaine's already handsome features, married to his graciousness and intelligence, grew more striking with each passing minute.

Mrs. Rowland was clearly in awe of him. She sent Gigi pointed looks. *Speak more. Enchant him. Don't you see he's perfect?* Gigi, however, was nose deep in misery, a desolation made more unbearable by every minute spent in his painfully enjoyable company.

Her torture did not end there. After dinner, Mrs. Rowland asked him to play for them, having heard from the duchess that he was a fine pianist. He did, with a born performer's flair. Gigi stared alternately at his flawless profile, his long, strong hands, and her lap, fighting a wretchedness that seemed to have seeped into her blood.

The final blow came when he rose to take his leave of them, only to discover that a blizzard had indeed arrived. Mrs. Rowland smugly informed him that in her great foresight, she had already sent off a messenger three hours ago to inform his parents that he'd stay the night because of the worsening weather.

Gigi had counted on his departure, on never seeing him again. How was she to get through the night with him under the same roof and almost within reach?

Camden had trouble falling asleep, but it had nothing to do with being in an unfamiliar bed. He was used to it, having never had a home of his own, always traveling to a different city, a different house, always sleeping in rooms that belonged to other people.

He hadn't lied to Mrs. Rowland. He'd indeed lived in some of the Continent's most glamorous locales. He'd simply omitted the less than glamorous reasons behind this peripatetic life: because his parents hadn't an ounce of money sense between them and could never afford a permanent residence.

So they moved in counterrhythm to the wealthier elites. In summer, when everyone was off to Biarritz and Aix-les-Bains, they occupied some relative's winter villa in Nice. In winter, the reverse. Occasionally, they stayed in one place for a while, when a house stood vacant because its owners had gone off on some wild adventure, such as when Cousin Konstantin left Athens for schemes in Argentina. Or when Cousin Nikolai went to China for two years.

At age thirteen, Camden had taken over the management of the household. By then he was already accustomed to dealing with creditors, handling servants, and learning new languages in an instant so he could haggle with local merchants in order to stretch his family's meager coins further. He didn't mind being poor, but he hated having to lie about it, to dissemble and feign, as he did tonight, so that his parents could continue on in their blissful ignorance of their financial precariousness.

It had been a relief to be with Theodora. They'd met in St. Petersburg, where their mothers shared the use of a troika. He'd been fifteen then, she sixteen. She was as poor as he and, like him, lived in fashionable places in unfashionable seasons. They understood each other's plight without ever needing to speak a word of it.

But it was not thoughts of Theodora that kept him awake. It was Miss Rowland.

Even before their accidental meeting, he had more or less expected Miss Rowland to propose a merger between his future title and her fortune. He had also expected a great deal of regret over turning down those sweet stacks of pounds sterling, after having lived in want of them his entire life.

What he emphatically did not expect was Miss Rowland herself. She was unsentimental, hardened, and cynical beyond her years—but her greatest cruelty was reserved for herself, in her insistence that she would be perfectly fine, thank you, if she could only cosh a duke senseless with his own ledgers and haul him to the altar.

For someone who was otherwise levelheaded and manipulative, there'd been an odd, poignant transparency to her this evening. She liked him. She liked him enough to be not just disappointed over his unavailability, but unhappy.

He liked her too, surprisingly. How could he not like a girl who called him an "impoverished nobody" to his face? Her frankness was refreshing and welcome after the nuanced subtlety and selective narratives that had characterized his exchanges, all his life, with people outside his immediate family.

But what caused his fidgeting at this witching hour was not her overly simplistic approach to things and people, but her brooding sexuality.

She'd wanted to touch him. That desire had been there in every full-on stare and every sideways glance all throughout the evening. *Once our marriage is consummated, you need only to come back to me when you need heirs.* The girl might be a virgin, but she was neither pure nor innocent. She knew about these things.

What she probably didn't know yet, but he already did, was that with her single-mindedness she would be a force of nature in bed. No man could roll out of her bed and walk away. His overriding objective, despite his exhaustion, would be how he could get her to lie with him again.

* * *

Camden dozed fitfully. Then suddenly he was awake. He had left the curtains and shutters open, out of years of habit, so that he could look out and recall in which country, which city he found himself. The blizzard must have passed; a shaft of silvery moonlight drifted through the window and lit the way clear to the door. A woman stood just inside, in a long nightgown, her back against the door. He couldn't see her face but he knew instinctively that it was Miss Rowland, she of the entirely unfitting, too-childish pet name Gigi.

The Rowland manse, while not a cumbersome behemoth like the ducal manor at Twelve Pillars, still had some eighty, ninety rooms. He had been put to bed in a different wing from where his hosts had their bedchambers. She had not accidentally returned to the wrong room after using the water closet. She had to have walked a good two hundred feet to visit him.

And he was naked beneath the covers. The late Mr. Rowland's nightshirt, kindly supplied at bedtime, had been too restricting.

She stayed in that spot, unmoving, for a long time, until he was tempted to tell her either to get on with whatever in the blazes she had planned or leave him to his tossing and turning in peace. Abruptly, she moved, coming toward the bed in long, determined strides, her feet silent on the Persian carpet.

She knelt by the bed, her eyes even with his elbow. Her hair was loose, dark as the fabric of the night; her white nightgown almost glimmered. He could not see her features clearly, but he heard her uneven breaths, a long, slightly trembling inhalation, a few heartbeats of breath being held, and a short rush of exhalation. Repeat. Repeat.

But she remained still. What was she waiting for? Hadn't she yet satisfied herself that he was really, completely asleep? He squeezed his eyes shut, pretending she wasn't there. But her breaths tickled the hairs on his forearm, triggering seismic tremors along his nerves. And her scent, a fine blend of chamomile and cucumber, warm, powdery, and insidious, enfolded him.

What did she want?

She touched him, placing her hand over his curled fingers, straightening them so that they were palm to palm, then she interlaced her fingers with his. Her fingertips were icy. A silent, dangerous thrill coursed through him. He wanted to pull her atop him and show her what awaited a foolish young woman who slipped into a man's bedroom in the dead of the night after having devoured him all evening with those dark, intense eyes of hers, setting his blood to simmer over three long hours.

Her hand moved. Her fingers encircled his wrist, searing him with her cool skin. Two fingertips slowly trailed up his arm, barely touching him. She rose from her crouch to access more of him, and a strand of her hair caressed the inside of his upper arm. He bit his lower lip, nearly undone by the spike of pleasure.

At the top of his arm, her fingers spread out over his collarbone and his shoulder. She hesitated before sliding her palm up the side of his face. He heard an almost inaudible gasp as she snatched her hand away. His stubbles—they had surprised her. Her inexperience excited him almost as much as her audacity. She had not done this before.

Her hand returned, the back of it this time, smooth skin over strong bones, skimming along his jaw. Her thumb found his lips and traced over them. He fought the urge to lick her fingertip. God, but he burned, everywhere. On the side away from her, his fingers clawed into the counterpane. She had no idea what she was doing to him, or she would not dare continue.

She moved again, settling a hip on the bed. As her head bent forward, her hair cascaded, a skein of silk threads unspooling on his chest, all gossamer coolness and teasing chaos.

Suddenly it became too much. A violent upheaval of lust seized him. He grabbed the front of her nightgown and yanked her down. She gasped and flailed. But he subdued her easily, rolling them so that he ended above her, pinning her down with his weight and her fear.

Only her nightgown separated them. And Gigi Rowland was all outrageous femininity: full breasts, soft belly, and lusciously rounded hips. A moan of sweet, terrible pleasure escaped him. He kissed her, her ear, her cheek, her neck, and, through the soft flannel of her nightgown, her shoulder. His hand settled at the indentation of her waist, above the flare of her hips. His fingers dug into young, firm flesh. Other parts of him also wanted to dig in, hard, harder.

She was at his mercy here, having thoroughly compromised herself. There were so many wicked things he could do to her, and she would not dare make a sound—she would be biting her lips to suppress her moans and whimpers, because he'd make her as wild and ravenous as he.

It took all of his willpower and a large dose of shame—shame over his lack of control, his bad faith toward Theodora, and his harsh handling of a girl who was guilty of nothing more than being attracted to him—to let go. He rolled off her, turned his back, and emitted a few grunts, as if he'd been dreaming.

She scrambled off the bed. But she didn't scuttle out of the room. She panted, as if she had been running from a wolf, a werewolf. In the raspy sounds she made, there was both terror and arousal.

He prayed that she would see herself out. Because if she didn't, if she came to his bed again, he would not be able to stop.

She moved, *toward* the bed, her soft footfall as loud to his ear as a shot in the dark. His blood pounded thickly. His erection grew painfully hungry. She took one more step, until she was standing at the edge of the bed again. He balled his hands tight, digging his nails into his palms until he was sure he must be bleeding, afraid that if he didn't hold fast onto some shred of mastery, he'd—

She ran, slamming the door behind her. He listened as she sped down the corridor, feeling the vibration of the floor through the mattress beneath him.

When the house was once again silent, he rolled onto his back and let out the breath he had been holding. His cock stood straight up, hot and unsatisfied. He gave it a mean *thwack*. But it only bobbed, more famished and demanding than ever.

He let out a sigh, put his hand on it, and let his imagination run wild.

Gigi burned, one moment with the fires of hell, one moment with the ecstasy of that other afterworld, but mostly with an earthly amalgam of mortification and raw ferment.

She'd been a hairbreadth away from climbing back into bed with Lord Tremaine. The entire scenario had already unfolded in her mind: the ardor, the consummation, the dismay, and the consequences. In the end, he would marry her, because it was the honorable thing to do, despite his disgust for her and his relative blamelessness in the matter.

Everything in her yearned for him. He would be the equal she had never known, the deliverance from her vast loneliness, the balm to any and all misery. If only she could have him....

But she had stopped herself. Because it was too craven a thing to do, too much beneath her dignity. And she wanted his good opinion, she craved it, she who had never cared what anyone else thought of her.

An eternity passed before it was time to dress and head down for breakfast. She thought she would be alone, but he was already there in the breakfast parlor when she entered. Her face burned again.

He set aside the ironed copy of *Illustrated London News* he'd been reading and rose. "Miss Rowland," he said, all courtesy and impeccable breeding. "Good morning."

She didn't respond immediately. She couldn't. All she could think of was the way he'd shoved her under him, his arousal pressed fully against her, separated from her thigh by only the flannel of her nightgown.

But he had slept through all of it. He had no recollection.

"Lord Tremaine. Did you sleep well?"

His gaze met hers, level, innocent. "Oh, yes, splendidly. I slept like a log."

While she suffered for the want of him. While she alternately berated herself and marveled at what she had done. While she went over each moment of their perilous encounter, recalling his topography, his texture, his scent, and his frightening yet delicious weight as he held her captive.

He smiled at her. And it hit her like a mallet to the temple, the realization that she was in love with him. Stupidly, dreadfully in love with him.

Overnight, she'd become a fool.

Chapter Five

P hilippa!" Freddie cried.

Philippa. Less than twenty-four hours had passed since she'd last heard her name on Freddie's lips. She'd loved the sound of the spirant syllables, loved the slight catch in Freddie's voice that always accompanied their utterance, as if he still couldn't believe that she permitted him to address her so intimately.

But all she could think now was that he didn't call her Gigi. He didn't even *know* that she was Gigi. No other living man thought of her as Gigi.

Only Camden.

"Are you all right, my love?"

She smiled at the man she adored. With his fair complexion, rosy cheeks, and earnest eyes, Freddie was Gainsborough's Blue Boy all grown up. He had a wonderful head of sandy curls, blue eyes the color of Delft chinoiserie, and a gentle, unassuming nature as kind as the sun in May. Her very own Mr. Bingley—everything a young man ought to be.

"I'm fine, darling, I'm fine."

He came forward to take her hands in his but stopped before he quite reached her, the concern in his eyes breaking her heart. "Can we be sure that Lord Tremaine has really left? What if it's a trap, and he returns to spy on you? He can...if he chooses to, he can make things unbearable for you."

How did she even begin to explain that Camden already had an armory of unbearable-making devices at his disposal? That he held her entire future in his not-so-tender mercy?

"Tremaine has been quite civil," she said. "He is not the sort to throw tantrums."

"I can't believe he left town already," said Freddie. "He arrived only yesterday afternoon."

"There is nothing keeping him here, is there?" Gigi said.

They were in the back parlor where they usually took tea together, a room done in shades of lavender: the upholstery amethyst brocade, the draperies lilac velvet, and the tea service white with borders of wisteria. In her youth she had disdained all but the primary colors, but now she appreciated a broader segment of the spectrum.

And so it was with Freddie. At eighteen—or perhaps even twenty-three—she'd have scoffed at an alliance with such a shy, unworldly man. She'd have seen him as an embarrassment, a burden. But she had changed. The only thing she saw when she looked at Freddie was the shining goodness of his heart.

"Where did he go?" Freddie asked anxiously. "When will he be back?"

"He didn't bring a valet, so there is no one to tell us anything. I wouldn't even know he had gone off somewhere if Goodman hadn't overheard him telling the cabbie to take him to the train station."

She was incensed that he made free use of her house and her staff without informing her of his movements—the least courtesy, surely. She was also profoundly relieved by the small respite of his absence.

The way she had ogled him this morning—at his torso, which seemed to have been sculpted by the hands of Bernini himself, smooth, lean, lithe, with long, beautifully sinewed arms like those of a seasoned sailor—could she have done anything more mortifying short of dropping her handkerchief and falling to the floor in a dead faint?

She and Freddie sat down side by side on the chaise longue. "Tell me what he wanted," said Freddie. "He must have wanted *something*."

She had been able to think of nothing but what Camden wanted. Even now, with him miles away, she was still distracted and tense. Disaster, that was what he wanted. For what else could bedding her achieve but somehow, somewhen, calamity on an epic scale?

"He is not convinced that we should be divorced for something as trivial as me wishing to marry someone else," she said. It was beyond her to tell Freddie that her husband meant to invoke his long-abdicated rights and shag her until she showed something for it. Nor could she reveal that she would submit to this connubial copulation, while planning to make use of every device ever invented to block conception.

What was it about Camden that turned her into such a chiseler and now a double-crosser? "But he's willing to be reasonable. If we are still determined to marry in a year's time, he'll let the divorce proceed."

"A year!" Freddie exclaimed. Then he breathed a sigh of relief. "Well, if that's his only condition, then it's not half so bad. We can wait a year. It will be an awfully long year, but we can wait."

"Freddie." She gripped his hand, gratitude inundating her heart. "You are so good to me."

"No, no! You are the one who's good to me! Everyone else thinks I'm clumsy and dense. You are the only person who thinks I'm all right."

On any other day she'd have preened with pride, to think that at last she possessed the depth and maturity necessary to appreciate a diamond of the first water like Freddie, when all about her, men and women were still blinded by superficialities. But today her depth and maturity truly made their presence known. She was more than humbled; she felt unworthy. But she could not say it. Freddie looked to her for strength and guidance. She must not tumble off her pedestal now.

"I am most certainly not. I know for a fact that Miss Carlisle thinks highly of you."

Miss Carlisle was in love with Freddie. She was dignified and self-contained about it, but she could not conceal it from Gigi. Normally, Gigi would not have pointed out such a thing to Freddie. But these were not normal times, and her guilt overshadowed her possessiveness.

"Angelica? Really? She used to laugh at me all the time when we were younger, whenever I fell off my pony or some such. And she used to tell me that I was a veritable idiot."

"People change as they grow older," Gigi said. "At some point we learn to value kindness and constancy above all else, and in that, we cannot find better than you, Freddie."

Freddie smiled in pleasure. "If you say so, then it must be so. Angelica hasn't been feeling quite well lately. I've been meaning to have a bottle of tonic sent to her. I think I'll deliver it in person now, and ask her if I've become less of a dunce over the years."

The mantel clock chimed the half hour. Freddie had been in her parlor for fifteen minutes. She used to allow his calls to stretch for half an hour and more, but that was no longer possible with Camden's return.

"I think I'd better go," Freddie said, standing up. "Though I hate to leave."

She rose. "I hate it too. I wish—oh, never mind what I wish."

Freddie clasped her hands in his broad, warm palms. "Are you sure you are quite all right, my love? Are you really sure?"

No, she was not all right. She felt ill and lonely. And appalled at herself. She was about to undertake a dangerous gamble, lying and cheating at both ends. And here she thought she had forever sworn off fraud and swindle.

She mustered a radiant smile for him. "Don't worry about me, darling. Remember what you yourself have said? Nothing can shake me. Nothing."

Langford Fitzwilliam, the Duke of Perrin, began his five-mile afternoon walk a half hour earlier than usual. He liked a little unpredictability from time to time, as currently his life consisted of all the variety of a mediocre vicar's Sunday sermons. But he didn't mind it, not too much. A scholar needed peace and quiet to delve deep into the Homeric past and the heroic battles before the walls of Ilium.

One of his favorite places along the walk was a cottage located exactly two and a quarter miles from his front door. The cottage itself was ordinary enough: two stories, white walls, red trims. Its gardens, however, were worthy of a sonnet, if not a hoity-toity ode outright.

The front garden was a fantasia of roses. And not just the tight-budded roses he usually came across but full-open, immodest blooms from an earlier, less strait-laced era—big, riotous flowers weighing down bushes and drooping off trellises, ranging from the most pristine blush to a wine-dark, blowsy red.

He was curious about the back garden, where gardeners often concentrated the main of their energy and effort. But a high hedge surrounded the back garden, and all he could see was the ridge of what looked to be the roof of a sizable greenhouse. He did not wish to make the acquaintance of the cottage's residents, so he waited for that inevitable day when someone forgot to put away the ladder after trimming the hedge.

He had no scruples about peeking into a private garden. What was anyone going to do? Call the constable on him? The one thing he had learned from nearly thirty years of being a duke was that, short of actual murder, he could get away with just about anything.

Today, however, there was a ladder, though it didn't lean on the hedge. Instead, it had been put up against an elm tree across the lane from the garden. A woman stood on the ladder, her back to him, dressed in an afternoon gown much too fashionable and ridiculous for such things as climbing fifteen-foot ladders.

The woman was lecturing a cat, a kitten that she was attempting to perch on a branch twelve feet off the ground, a sight that halted Langford dead in his tracks.

"Shame on you, Hector! You are a cousin of the mighty lions of the savannah. You disgrace them! Now stay put, and you will be rescued in time."

The kitten disagreed with her assessment. The moment she removed her hands, it leapt back into her bosom.

"No, Hector!" the woman cried as she caught the cat. "You will not do this again. You will not foil my plan. You will not be yet one more capricious male to stand between my daughter and a coronet of strawberry leaves!"

Langford's interest in the situation escalated dramatically, given that he was the only man in a fifty-mile radius known to possess a coronet of strawberry leaves—the ducal headgear worn at the coronation of a sovereign. He wasn't quite sure where his particular coronet was kept, though, there having been not a single British coronation during his lifetime.

"Listen to me, Hector." The woman lifted the kitten until the creature's eyes were level with her own. "Listen and listen well. If you do not cooperate, I will cut every ounce of fish, liver, tongue, you name it, out of your meals. What's more, I will bring a dog into the house and feed it foie gras right in front of you. A dog, you understand, a dirty cur like Gigi's Croesus."

The kitten meowed pathetically. The woman remained pitiless. "Now up you go, and stay this time."

And damned if the kitten didn't obey, meowing plaintively but staying put all the same. The woman let out a long sigh and slowly descended the ladder. Langford began moving again, tapping his walking stick purposefully on the packed soil of the lane.

The woman turned at the sound. She was beautiful, with jet-dark hair, alabaster skin, and red lips, like Snow White after a few decades of happily-ever-after—and older than he'd supposed. From her voice and her figure he'd thought her somewhere in her thirties, but she was at least forty, likely more.

At the sight of him, her eyes widened to the size of gold guineas, but she recovered quickly. "I do beg your pardon, sir." She sounded breathless, nothing like the tyrant she'd been with Hector. "I don't mean to trouble you, but I can't get to my kitty. He is stuck up high."

He frowned. He had a fearsome frown, the kind that sent people scurrying to the opposite side of a room.

"You have no groom or footman to retrieve the beast for you?"

She was clearly offended by his reference to the fur ball but swallowed it. "I have given them the afternoon off, I'm afraid."

A woman who thought ahead, a rare phenomenon. Although, if he was pressed hard, he'd admit that men who thought ahead were equally rare. His frown deepened, but it seemed to have temporarily lost its menace, for she was not at all deterred by it.

"Won't you be so kind as to retrieve it for me?" she asked, all fluttering handkerchief and feminine helplessness.

A delightful conundrum. Should he rudely refuse and watch her crumple or play along for a bit of diversion?

"Certainly," he said. Why not? His life had become monotonous of late. And he'd been fond of charades and tableaux in his younger days.

Eagerly, she stood aside and watched his approach with such idolatrous rapture that he felt like the Golden Calf itself. If he hadn't known that she was an ambitious mama who had him marked out for her daughter, he'd have thought she was out to ensnare him herself.

He ascended the ladder, a rickety contraption that did not sound willing to hold his weight. The kitten had stopped its meows and regarded him uncertainly. He grabbed it by the scruff of its neck and brought it down. As soon as it could, the kitten jumped free of him and landed back in its mistress's bosom—an ample bosom that strained the front of her bodice very nicely.

"Hector," she cooed shamelessly. "You had me worried, you naughty kitten." Hector, still frightened over a vegetarian future, did not contradict her. "How can I thank you enough, sir?"

"It is gratification enough to be of assistance. Good afternoon, madam."

"But you must let me know your place of domicile at least, good sir!" she cried. "My cook makes an excellent strawberry cake. I shall have one sent to you."

"I thank you, madam. But I am not overly fond of strawberries."

"A cherry pie, then."

"I have nothing to do with cherries." Now he'd see how far she'd go to worm her way into his acquaintance.

She was taken aback, but again, her recovery was quick. "I also have a case of Château Lafite claret, from the forty-six vintage."

This was an offer more difficult to resist. He had acquired a taste for fine wines in his younger years. And '46 was an extraordinary vintage for Château Lafite. He had gone through his last bottle three years ago.

Two things immediately became clear about her. She was much wealthier than he'd guessed from her modest cottage. And this scheme to rope him in for her daughter was no lark. She was prepared to go if not to hell then at least to Jakarta and back.

"Or do you not care for that either, sir?" She played it coy, having already perceived his temptation.

He gave in. "I live at Ludlow Court."

Her right hand detached itself from the kitten, arced in the air, and returned—*smack!*—to her bosom, fingers spread in a gesture that traditionally heralded delighted incoherence. "Surely—oh, dear! You do not—but—goodness gracious me!"

As she was made from sterner, cat-exploiting stuff, she sank not into a faint but into a gorgeous curtsy. "Your Grace. I shall have the case delivered to Ludlow Court before dinner."

As she straightened herself, he suddenly had the feeling that he had seen her before, back when the world was young—or at least when he was. He dismissed the thought and nodded curtly. "Good afternoon."

"Mrs. Rowland," she supplied, though he still hadn't asked for her identity, even implicitly. "Good afternoon, Your Grace."

Mrs. Rowland. The name triggered a new stirring in his mind but nothing strong enough to yield a remembrance. She had the good sense to let him go without further ado—or any mention of her daughter—leaving him mystified and rather too curious for his liking.

Chapter Six

December 1882

Miss Rowland did not skip rocks. She tossed them. Shelves of thin, brownish ice hugged the stream's two banks, but a narrow band of water still flowed free at its center. Into this part of the brook she flung the rocks, *plop, plop, plop.* There was no particular rhythm to it. Sometimes she threw a dozen pebbles in quick succession, sometimes a minute or more would pass between two *plops*. It was as if she underscored her own state of mind, restiveness followed by a stretch of contemplation, only to be overtaken by yet another fit of agitation.

When there were no more stones to be had, she sat down on a tree stump, her chin on her knee, her long, lugubrious blue cape flapping about her ankles in the unrelenting gust. From where Camden stood at the top of the opposite bank, he couldn't see her face beneath the rim of her hat. But he felt the loneliness that emanated from her, a loneliness that echoed somewhere deep within him.

He'd been able to think of nothing else except her.

Years ago, he'd come to accept that courting Theodora—a woman who couldn't make up her mind about him, whom he hadn't seen in a year and a half—opened him up to temptations in the here and now.

Somehow, a young man of reasonable looks and sexual restraint posed an irresistible challenge to a certain subset of women, across class strata, in every capital of Europe. If he had a franc, a mark, or a ruble for every time he had been propositioned from the age of sixteen onward, he could retire to the country and live the life of a prosperous squire.

He'd turned down every last one of those offers, with tact and dignity when possible and ingenuity otherwise. A man of honor did not profess love for one woman while welcoming a host of others into his bed.

It wasn't easy, but it was doable. Being busy helped. Having no moral or philosophical opposition to solitary releases helped. Immersing himself in his chosen field helped—thermodynamic equations and advanced calculus tended to keep one's mind off breasts and buttocks.

But nothing helped now. He was busy all day long, seeing to the beast of an estate that was Twelve Pillars, yet thoughts of Miss Rowland clamored every other minute. Whatever he did in the privacy of his bedchamber only created more fantasies of her to agitate him the next day. Thoughts of *her* breasts and buttocks—not to mention her morosely hungry eyes and her heavy, cool spill of hair—rendered him slow and bungling before simple quadratic equations and utterly impotent in the face of integrals of logarithms.

And yet if it were only a case of simple, rampant lust. That would be perfectly understandable in the case of a young man of robust appetites who stubbornly refused to surrender his virginity. But he wanted more than just to touch her. He wanted to know her.

Theodora's mother, as pushy and determined as she was, had nothing on Mrs. Rowland, the patron goddess of all ambitious mamas. At least Countess von Schweppenburg had the excuse of being poor and needing the security of a well-married daughter, whereas Mrs. Rowland was driven entirely by—he felt— her own unfulfilled ambition, something that cracked a harder whip than did any of Beelzebub's lieutenants.

And yet Miss Rowland did not fear her mother, not one little bit. If anything, Mrs. Rowland was in awe of her daughter, amazed beyond all expectations by this Hannibal of social climbing, who managed to bring her pound-sterling elephants across the figurative Alps of aristocratic disdain to wreak havoc on an unsuspecting London society.

Two days after their accidental meeting, he'd paid a formal call to the Rowlands, in the company of his parents and his siblings, Claudia and a bored Christopher. Claudia, impressed by the Greek marbles, Louis XIV furniture, and Renaissance paintings stretching as far as the eyes could see, begged to have a tour of Briarmeadow.

While his parents continued to converse with Mrs. Rowland, Miss Rowland obligingly conducted the three callers of her generation through the drawing rooms, the library, and the solarium. Christopher became more and more restless and, finally, in the gallery, before a miniature portrait of Carrington that must have been given to Miss Rowland upon their engagement, he lost his company manners and reverted to fourteen-year-old loutishness.

"Mother always said Cousin Carrington was a terrible example," said Christopher. "I guess you'll marry any bounder who has a coronet of strawberry leaves."

She didn't even break her stride. "My Lord Christopher, with your family's depleted resources and your vast personal charm, I predict you'll marry any heiress who would have you, teeth and literacy on her part strictly optional."

Camden's face hurt from not laughing out loud at his brother's dismay. Christopher might be an oaf, but he was still the son of an English duke and the grandson of a Bavarian prince. Another young woman in her place, feeling the inferiority of her station, would have suffered his rudeness or, at best, laughed it off. She, however, smacked the boy hard and put him in his place with the ruthless efficiency of a born predator.

Unlike her mother, who garnished the house with subtle reminders of her erudition—Mycenaean bronze, possibly older seals from the island of Crete, glass-encased fragments of papyrus dating to the time of the pharaohs—Miss Rowland felt no need to prove to the world that she knew Antiphanes from Aristophanes. She was fine, thank you, with being the daughter of a man whose forebears, only a few generations ago, had washed laundry and carried coal for those exalted families into which she intended to marry.

He admired her surety. She knew her own worth and did not pretend otherwise for those who judged her on her parentage. But by refusing to tolerate fools and play nice, she'd condemned herself to a solitary path, both in defeat and in victory.

Camden walked his horse down the incline until he was nearly at water's edge and mounted it to cross the stream. As soon as he reached dry land, he dismounted and tethered the horse. By then she was already standing up, shaking the dust from her skirts.

"Miss Rowland." On impulse he didn't offer to shake her hand but took her by the shoulders and kissed her on each cold, satiny cheek. He was still a foreigner to these parts, and he wasn't above taking advantage of it. "I beg your pardon. I must have thought myself still in France."

Their gazes entangled. Her eyes were a nearly absolute black, the boundary between pupil and iris impossible to discern at any civilized distance. She glanced down momentarily, her eyelashes long and striking against the paleness of her skin. Then she looked back at him. "No need to beg pardon, my lord. It's quite acceptable to flirt with a girl you don't plan to marry. I don't mind."

He should be embarrassed, but he wasn't. "Do you flirt with men you don't plan to marry?"

"Certainly not," she said. "I don't even flirt with men I do plan to marry."

His darling little tigress. All blunt grandeur during

the day. All melting fire at night. "You talk to them about their ledgers instead," he teased.

That elicited a small smile from her. "I prefer the direct approach."

He grew hot from these mere words. Had her approach to him been any more direct that night, he'd have kept her in bed so long, they'd have been discovered by Mrs. Rowland herself.

"It's cold," he said. "You should be inside."

The winter here was nothing like that of the true North, where temperatures plunged to such abysmal lows that she'd need much more than a cup of hot chocolate to warm up: She'd require a bottle of vodka and a man's naked body.

She sighed. "I know. I can hardly feel my toes. But it's the only way I can have a bit of peace, away from my mother. She hasn't stopped talking of you since your stay. And she would not be convinced that I've already done my level best to make you her son-in-law. After my success with Carrington, she thinks I've but to will it and a man will stride forth to offer his hand."

"I could dispel her illusions for you," he said.

She shook her head. "She met Miss von Schweppenburg last season. No offense to Miss von Schweppenburg, but nothing you can say will persuade her that I'm not a better match for you."

It was hard to argue with that. Even harder to remember his nobler intentions standing next to her, knowing that she wanted him with a cynic's hidden ardor, knowing exactly how she'd feel underneath him.

But he must not think only of himself. Theodora

needed him. She was frightened of this world; he could not abandon her to the vagaries of fortune.

Miss Rowland checked the small watch that dangled from her wrist. "Crumbs. It's half past three already. I'd best head back home. Or my mother will be out looking for me high and low again."

She offered him her hand to shake. "Good day, Lord Tremaine."

He shook her hand. But somehow, he didn't let go when he was supposed to.

He didn't want her to leave. He wanted something—not the wild lovemaking of his fantasies, but something reasonable and halfway decent that would keep her with him for a bit longer.

Except his wit deserted him.

He could think of nothing. And he could not let go of her hand.

Gigi's mind was a chaos of hopes and fears in collision. One moment they were both on their best behavior, following the established choreography of decorum to the last dip and turn. The next thing she knew, he either owed her an apology or a kiss.

She received neither. He simply stepped back from her, tilted his head, and grinned ruefully. "That was gauche of me, wasn't it?"

And that was it. No fumbling words of explanation, no awkwardness, no opening for her to demand compensation without coming across as either bumpkinish or hysterical.

She gazed upon him with churlish admiration. This man knew far more of potentially compromising situations than she'd heretofore suspected. The smoothness with which he extricated himself was both impressive and disquieting. Perhaps he *was* only flirting with her after all, a dalliance to entertain him for the duration of his holiday in the backwoods.

"I suppose only you could judge that, my lord," she said.

"You should take my horse," he said.

An expression of horror crossed his face then, as if he'd openly and loudly declared before his mother and hers that he'd like to get under her petticoats and stay there but good.

He'd gone out of his way to be considerate of her fear, walking the stallion at a crawling speed and tethering it far away from her. Yet now he'd forgotten all about it. Her heart soared. Beneath his sleek serenity, he'd been as flustered as she, possibly more.

"I don't ride," she reminded him.

He took a deep breath, the audible exhalation as close an admission of mortification as she was likely to get from him.

"Why don't you?" he asked, once again his cool, collected self. "I can't believe your mother would have omitted equestrian lessons."

She shrugged. "She didn't. I choose not to ride."

"Tell me why. You seem like you would enjoy riding, enjoy the control and freedom it affords you."

Oh she'd enjoyed it, all right. She'd loved riding. Until she'd fallen off for the second time, breaking three ribs and her right arm in two places. "I'm afraid of horses. That's all."

"And why are you afraid of horses? They are far milder and more reasonable creatures than dowager duchesses. You are not afraid of the latter, from what I hear."

He certainly had ways to loosen her tongue, with his gentle, persistent, and—by all appearances—genuine interest in her. Not her money, because she'd already tried to give it to him. *Her.*

"I fell twice. Hurt myself badly the second time."

Still he shook his head. "You'd have gotten back up on that horse before the doctors even let you out of bed. What really happened?"

It was none of his business. None of his concern. At least, not while he considered himself promised to another. She opened her mouth to tell him exactly that, only to hear herself say, "A disappointed fortune hunter. He was infuriated with my mother for keeping him at arm's length and chose to take it out on me. He took what little was left in his wallet and bribed our groom."

And when the first fall did her no damage—having just slowed down when the saddle strap snapped, she slid off and landed on something soft—he tried it one more time. "I was lucky. The doctors said I could easily have broken my spine and been bedridden for life rather than just two months."

Mr. Henry Hyde, Gigi's would-be maimer, had been arrested two days later on unrelated charges. Apparently he was so desperate for fresh funds that he'd attempted to poison his widowed aunt for the few hundred pounds promised to him in her will. He died while imprisoned.

Lord Tremaine listened intently. She couldn't tell by his solemn eyes whether he was disgusted or saddened. She regretted her candor already. What good did it do to burden him with all this ugly history?

"Please wait here," he said. "I'll be only a minute."

He returned, leading his horse behind him. For such a tall man, he moved with an easy grace, his leisurely seeming gait eating up the distance swiftly. His long riding boots reached halfway up his thighs. She had to exercise considerable restraint to not follow the lines of his fawn trousers and stare where she shouldn't.

"Will you walk a little with me?" he asked, with great solicitude that told her nothing.

"Certainly." She didn't understand what he wanted, but it mattered not. She would do almost anything with him, up to and including forfeiting her virginity, if he but asked, with or without a nuptial contract.

Since meeting him, every morning she woke up with a sweet, wrenching pain in her heart—the joy and overwhelming terror of being in love—not knowing how she would get through the day without him, not knowing how she would ever survive another encounter with him.

The land rose and flattened into a meadow, gray and yellow in winter, densely wooded to either side. They walked until they came to a weathered hitching post that hadn't been used in years. There Lord Tremaine stopped, tied the horse, and removed its saddlery, setting everything carefully down on the ground.

"What are you doing?" she asked, beginning to be suspicious. "Is anyone going to ride bareback?"

"Come closer," he requested. "I want you to watch me."

As if she could do anything else while he was near.

He looked into the stallion's eyes and ears, ran his hands down the horse's legs, and raised and inspected each hoof in turn. "We really should sell him," he said. "Carrington had a good eye for horseflesh, too good for his finances."

He picked up the saddle pad, smoothed it, and settled it on the horse's back. Then he placed the stirrup irons over the back of the saddle and folded the girth strap up so that neither would hit the horse while the saddle was being mounted. Only then did he lift the saddle high and set it down on the horse, as softly as he would place an infant in its bassinet, sitting the cantle just slightly high on the withers, so that as the rider swung into the saddle it would slide down into position while keeping the horse's coat in the correct orientation.

She was amazed. She'd never seen gentlemen do anything more physically demanding than lifting a shooting rifle. Yet here he was, performing a groom's work as if he'd done it hundreds of times before. There was a neatness to his motions, an efficiency, every task completed quickly, attentively, and well. She was beginning to understand his poise—it was more than inborn confidence, it was also knowledge and experience.

"Come feel the girth," he commanded her.

She complied. The strap was strong and in good repair. He made her test the billet straps too and verify with her own eyes that everything had been properly fastened to the saddle. Only then did he buckle and tighten the girth, making sure that he didn't cinch the horse too tight, that he could slip his fingers between the girth and the horse's belly. She stared at his hands, so capable, skillful, dexterous—and impossibly erotic in those supple, close-fitting black leather gloves.

He stood by the stallion's head and had it raise each of its forelegs, to settle the saddle and smooth out wrinkles in the pad. When he was at last satisfied that the horse was properly saddled, he rebridled it too, so that she could see every precaution had been taken, every procedure impeccably observed.

"You know what I want you to do, don't you?" he said with a small smile. "You are not afraid of horses. You are afraid of people wishing you harm."

She shrugged. "What's the difference?"

He held out his hand. "I like to see you fearless."

Memories of the fall came unbidden. She felt that unending instant of terror and panic, the flailing, the scream tearing her chest; she felt the desire to never leave her bed again, to coast on and on in her laudanum daze.

It was this incident, more than anything else, that had at last convinced her to marry as high as the sky. She would not be a victim of her fortune. She would hunt, rather than be hunted. Three months later the purchase of Briarmeadow was complete. Scant weeks afterward she'd fired the first salvo in the direction of Twelve Pillars.

She placed her hand in Lord Tremaine's. He gave her a quick squeeze, his eyes never leaving hers. "Ready?"

"It's not a sidesaddle," she said.

"Something tells me you know how to ride astride," he replied, entirely confident in his intuition. "Come. Just fifty yards. A sedate little walk. I'll hold on to the reins."

She knew what he wanted. He wanted her to overcome her fear, and he wanted to be the one to help her reach that laudable goal. Had it been anyone else who'd led her to this point, she'd have risen to the challenge simply because she refused to show that much weakness.

But with him it was different. She wasn't afraid that he'd see her as less than invincible. Before him it seemed permissible, somehow, to be frank, frustrated, and, at times, even apprehensive.

She would mount that horse because she wanted to please him, to make him think that he'd made a material improvement to her life. And perhaps, just perhaps, she could make it fifty yards if she held on tight, clenched her teeth, and prayed to whichever deities had a little compassion for forlorn, uppish females.

"I promise not to ogle your trim ankles," he said lightly. "If that's what you are concerned about."

"You shouldn't mention my ankles. And they are hardly trim." And the balmorals she wore were hardly those lace-frilled, eyelet-spangled fancy boots designed to make a man weak in the knees should he happen to catch a glimpse of them peeking out from underneath the hem of her dress.

"I'll be the judge of that. Now, should we?"

"Fine, then, fifty yards."

The admiration in his eyes almost made the whole mad enterprise worthwhile. He sank down to one knee and cupped his hands together. She expelled a long, ragged breath, took hold of the reins with one hand, the cantle with the other, and placed her left foot on his hands. He gave her a strong boost, she swung her right leg over the horse's rump, and she was in the saddle.

The horse snorted and shifted. She squealed and reached wildly for the bridle. He caught her arms just in time.

"Easy," he murmured, to the horse or to her she couldn't be sure. "Easy."

Then he lifted his eyes to her, the most reassuring eyes she'd gazed into since her father had passed away. "Don't worry. I'll keep you safe."

"I should have asked you to be my groom instead of my husband," she said.

He only grinned. "Hold on."

He led the horse to a slow walk. Mercy, the ground must be fifty feet below her and receding. She'd forgotten what it was like to sit up so high on a great big stallion. She knew the horse's motion was gentle and smooth beneath her, but she *felt* herself perched atop a wild bronco, about to be heaved off any second. An incipient nausea roiled her tummy. She wanted to throw her arms about the horse's neck, clamp her legs around its belly, and hang on for all she was worth. She wanted to get off *this instant*.

"You are not really Lord Tremaine, are you?" she

said, desperate for distraction. "You are a pauper who looks like him, and the two of you decided to switch places, fool everyone, and have a jolly old time."

He laughed. "Well, I am a pauper—an 'improverished nobody' as you so aptly put—except I'm already related to every royal house in Europe. So sometimes I put on my fancy clothes and go out and drink champagne with my noble cousins. Sometimes I change into rags and work in the stable. In truth, we shouldn't even have kept horses. But my father said then we might as well stop wearing hats and shoes. It was one economy I could not persuade him to make."

His answer was so breathtakingly frank that she momentarily forgot her fear of an imminent tumble. "And your parents permitted this...this folly?"

"They turned a blind eye and pretended that somehow I was able to run the house better and for less expense without ever dirtying my own hands. Or running betting games at whichever lyceum I happened to be attending."

"Betting games?!"

"Games that tend to run true to probability. So I could promise a prize of, say, a pound, and charge my fellow lyceans—particularly those who suffer at mathematics—a shilling a try to line up six coins heads up while blindfolded. I always came out ahead."

"Good Lord," she breathed. "Did you ever get caught?"

"For having a few coins in my pocket?" He chuckled. "No. I was the most courteous, virtuous, promising young man any professor had ever seen."

There was such lovely mischief in his voice. He *was* courteous, virtuous (as far as she could tell), and infinitely promising. But he was also clever, cunning, and willing to bend the rules.

Why did the Fates tempt her so? Why must he be so marvelously perfect for her and yet so abysmally unattainable?

"Is there anything you can't do?"

"No," he said, laughing. "But there are things I can't do very well. I'm a terrible cook, for instance. I tried, but my family refused to live on my frugal meals."

The very idea of it shocked her. Even before he became Lord Tremaine, he'd been cousin to dukes and princes. This man, whose blood was so blue it was probably indigo, had worked before a stove and—success or not—produced at least one entire meal. What next? The Prince of Wales laying down railroad tracks with his own bare hands?

An even more shocking thought occurred to her. "Did you plan to work for a living?"

"I did. But lately I've become hesitant. A title does hamper things, even if it's only a courtesy title—for now. I suppose running an estate is a noble and time-consuming task." He shrugged, his sleeve brushing the edge of her skirts. "But it's not what I'd have chosen to do."

"And what would you have chosen?"

"Engineering," he answered easily. "I study mechanics at the Polytechnique."

"Your parents said something about physics or economics."

"My parents are still in denial. They think mechanics sounds too common, too much grease and smoke and soot."

"But why engineering?" Her father had worked with dozens of engineers. They were an earnest and rather single-minded tribe, seemingly having nothing at all in common with the elegant marquess beside her.

"I like to build things. To work with my hands."

She shook her head. Hands. The future duke liked manual labor. "Well, don't tell anyone else what you've told me," she cautioned. "They wouldn't understand at all."

"I don't. I only told you because you spend as much time with your accountants and solicitors as you do your dressmaker. You are pushing to define a new normality as surely as I am."

She'd never thought of herself quite that way. She was more an idiosyncratic ignorer of established boundaries than a glutton for the new and the uncharted. But perhaps they were one and the same, each one implying the other.

She looked at him, at his calm, unhurried progress, his gloved hand holding on securely to the horse's tether. His other hand he extended to the lower branches of the Old Willow, brushing their supple tips.

"I—" she began, and did not finish.

The Old Willow. They were going by the Old Willow. Which was at least a furlong away from the hitching post. She couldn't believe it. Yet as she glanced back, the hitching post in the distance was the size of a matchstick.

"Yes?" he prompted her, keeping up their stately pace.

She looked back one more time to make certain her eyes hadn't cheated her. There was no mistake. She'd come some two hundred yards, her nausea having dissipated somewhere along the way, her hands no longer gripping the reins but holding them loosely, almost casually.

Somehow, in animated conversation with him, the impossible had happened. She'd forgotten her fear and her body had relaxed into a comforting, familiar rhythm.

"We've done more than fifty yards, I think," she murmured.

He looked behind. "So we have."

"You knew we'd gone past fifty yards long ago, didn't you?"

He didn't answer her directly. "Would you like me to help you dismount?"

Would she? Suddenly she felt dizzy again, not with fear but with the exhilarating absence of it, the way simple robust health felt a blessing and a miracle after a long, painful illness. No, she didn't want to dismount. She wanted to ride, to hurtle along in a mad dash.

He stepped back. "Go ahead," he said.

So she did. It felt wonderful, the sensation as new as the first shoots of spring, as weightless as walking on water. She gave in to the moment, to the euphoria of once again being young and fearless. The horse, as if sensing her elation, flew.

If she could distill the sensations that flooded her—the headlong rush, the metrical, earthy hoofbeats pounding away beneath her, the dense evergreen woods tearing by at the periphery of her vision, and the cold wind that was utterly powerless before the fire of her exuberance—she would have the essence of joy.

She heard herself laugh, all breathless, incredulous delight. She urged the horse to even greater speed, feeling its strength and spirit radiate into her every organ and sinew.

Only as the horse sped up the next incline did she rein it to a stop, then turned it around. Lord Tremaine was there in the distance. He set his thumb and forefinger against his teeth and whistled, a piercing note of conspiratorial celebration. She grinned, feeling her mirth spread from ear to ear, and answered his call, galloping back toward him as if she were a medieval knight at tournament and he her striking post.

He ran toward her, as light-footed and swift as a creature of the African savannah, and reached her just as she slowed. She unhooked her feet from the stirrups and threw herself into his waiting arms. He easily took the impact of her momentum and weight, lifting her high in the air and spinning her around.

"I did it!" she yelled, unladylike and thrilled.

"You did it!" he cried at almost the exact same moment.

They grinned hugely at each other. He set her down but left his hands around her waist. She happily let her hands remain on his shoulders. "I couldn't have done it without you."

"Don't encourage me, I'm not so modest to begin with."

She laughed. "Excellent. I hate modesty with a passion."

And loved him to distraction. He had done it. He had cajoled and wheedled and lured her out of her self-imposed exile from all things equestrian and restored a treasured joy to her life.

Her hands crept toward his collar, and then, before she knew it, she was cradling his face in her palms, the tips of her ring fingers brushing at his earlobes. He went still, the laughter in his eyes transmuting to a dark, quiet intensity, almost forbidding if he hadn't momentarily chewed on his lower lip.

She carved a thumb along his cheekbone, tracing its subtle contour, feeling the weight and the heat of his unwavering, unblinking stare. This was—or should be—their moment, the coming together of two kindred souls in an instant of ecstatic camaraderie.

She spread her fingers, pushing her kidskin-clad fingertips into his hair, pulling his head down toward hers. She wanted him. She needed him. They were perfect for each other. One kiss, just one kiss. And he'd know it too, not just deep in his heart but foremost on his mind.

He didn't stop her. He was compliant to the gentle pressure of her hands, his eyes gazing down at her with an almost befuddled wonder. Bliss erupted in her. He'd seen the light. He'd at last understood the unique, rare splendor of their bond.

They came so close she could count his eyelashes—and no closer.

"I can't," he said, his voice barely above a whisper. "I'm pledged to another."

Her bliss turned to cold daggers in her heart. Her limbs froze. But disbelief still reigned, like a mother's denial over a child's abrupt and senseless death. "You *really* want to marry Miss von Schweppenburg?"

"I've told her that I would," he answered obliquely.

"Does she care?" Gigi could barely keep the bitterness out of her voice.

He sighed. "I care."

Her hands dropped. The pain in her chest was her hopes charring to ashes. But still those hopes smoldered, pinpricks of unbearable light in piles of hot cinder. "And what if you hadn't pledged yourself to her?"

"What if my departed cousin had chosen a less fateful way to express his disdain for the great city of London?" His eyes were such raw intoxication, all ruinous gentleness and wistful resignation. "Life is intractable enough as it is. Don't torment yourself with what-ifs."

The opportunities she'd lost with Carrington's death had not beleaguered her, because they were only those of title and privilege, a business alliance fallen through. She was the daughter of an entrepreneurial man. She understood that even the most careful nurturing didn't always yield the fruits one sought.

With Lord Tremaine, she'd lost all detachment and perspective.

"You have already proposed to Miss von Schweppenburg?"

"I will." He was unequivocal. "When I hear from her next."

Slowly, unwillingly, she began to understand that for good or ill, he intended to marry Miss von Schweppenburg. Neither the prospect of riches nor the promise of carnal delight would lure him away from this chosen path.

Her entire happiness—something she hadn't even known she remotely cared about—had hung on his answer. And he'd doomed her. He might as well have shot the stallion out from under her as she galloped toward him in feckless rapture.

"I'm sure you will be very happy together," she said. A lifetime of training under Mrs. Rowland was barely enough to force that platitude past her larynx with any semblance of dignity.

He bowed and handed the reins of the horse to her. "The day flees. You'll return home faster riding."

He helped her mount. They shook hands again as they bid each other good day. This time, he did not linger in his touch.

Half a mile out, it hit Gigi that Lord Tremaine didn't know exactly where Miss von Schweppenburg was.

Last season, Mrs. Rowland, in a mood of largesse, had invited the countess and Miss von Schweppenburg to attend a garden party. They'd declined—with a longish note full of regret from Miss von Schweppenburg—as they'd have departed London already.

Gigi had thought it strange that a team with nothing but advantageous marriage on their mind would leave before the most fruitful time of year for proposals: the end of July. She was, however, not surprised to later hear of rumors that pressing debts had forced the von Schweppenburgs to leave town sooner than they'd wished. Perhaps they'd underestimated the cost of a London season. Perhaps such was their usual practice and this time they misjudged the patience of their landlord and creditors.

She hadn't cared then to find out what exactly was the case. And she didn't now. The important thing was that Lord Tremaine's intelligence on Miss von Schweppenburg's whereabouts and goings-on at any given point in time wasn't much better than Gigi's. And if Miss von Schweppenburg's waffling stance was any indication, he was by far the more reliable correspondent of the two.

Part of her recoiled at the direction of her thoughts. *Beyond this point there be monsters.* But just as a locomotive hurtling at full speed could not be stopped by a mere wooden fence across the tracks, her thoughts rumbled on, to the defiant *clickety-clack* of *if only... if only... if only...*

If only Miss von Schweppenburg were already married. Or if only Lord Tremaine came to believe, somehow, that such was the case.

Do not consider such a thing, begged her good sense. *Do not even think it.*

But her good sense was no match for the wrenching pain in her heart, for her crushing need of him. She could bear everything, if only she could have him for a year, a month, a day.

If he would not offer her this opportunity, then she'd create it herself, by fair means or foul, at whatever cost, come plague or locust.

Chapter Seven

The hansom cab stopped. "Yer house, guv," said the driver.

A long line of landaus and clarences filled the curb up and down from the Tremaine town house. His wife was having herself a party, it seemed, with some thirty, forty people in attendance. Camden had been gone four days to visit his parents. Was she celebrating his disappearance off the face of the earth already?

The butler, though distressed to see his return, hid it well under a layer of huffy solicitude. Milord must be tired. Would milord care for a bath? A shave? Dinner delivered to his room? Camden half-expected an offer of laudanum too, to tumble milord into a quick, insensate slumber, so that milady's soirée could continue unhindered.

"Are more people expected?" he asked. They would be, if there was to be a ball.

"No, sir," Goodman answered stiffly. "It is only a dinner."

Camden consulted his watch. Half past ten. The guests should be in the drawing room by now, both the men and the women, getting ready to take their leave in the next half hour in order to make the rounds of balls and *soirées dansantes*.

He pushed open the double door to the drawing room and saw his wife first, splendid in a surfeit of diamonds and ostrich feathers. Next to her stood an exceptionally handsome man, who, with a frown on his face, seemed to be admonishing her. She listened to him with an expression of exaggerated patience.

Slowly, one by one, then by twos and threes, the guests realized who had come amongst them, even though none of them had ever met him. The hum of conversation faded, until even *she* had to glance at the door to see what had caused the hush.

Her mouth tightened as she registered his presence, but she let not a second pass before putting on a bright, false smile and coming toward him. "Camden, you are back. Come, do meet some of my friends. They are all dying to make your acquaintance."

Such breathtaking insolence. Such cheek. Such bollocks. He hoped Lord Frederick liked wearing skirts. Camden took his wife by the elbows and kissed her lightly on the forehead. He had heard that he had the most courteous marriage known to man. Far be it for him to argue otherwise. "Of course. I would be delighted."

Following her lead, her guests received him amicably, though most of them didn't quite achieve her smoothness. The handsome man from her tête-à-tête she introduced last, by which time he was standing by a tall brunette as uncommonly fine-looking as himself.

"Allow me to present Lord Tremaine," said his wife. "Camden, Lord and Lady Wrenworth."

So this was Lord Wrenworth, The Ideal Gentleman, according to Mrs. Rowland, and Gigi's erstwhile lover.

"A pleasure, my lord," said Lord Wrenworth, with all the creamy innocence of a man who had never cuckolded Camden.

Camden found he was almost enjoying himself. He appreciated a fine bit of farce. "Likewise. You wouldn't be the same Felix Wrenworth who authored that fascinating article on the capture of comets by Jupiter?"

This took everyone aback, especially Lady Tremaine.

"Are you an astronomy enthusiast as well, my lord?" asked Lady Wrenworth, her tone tentative.

"Most assuredly, my dear lady," Camden answered with a smile.

His wife glanced uneasily at her former lover.

The guests, faced with the choice of either being the first to observe and gossip about the Tremaines appearing in public together or attending a ball not so different from the one they went to three days ago, forgot to leave.

Camden did not disappoint. He was a charming host. But better than that, he was candid, to a degree.

How long did he intend to stay in England? A year, at least.

How did he like his house? His house, which he liked exceedingly well, was on Fifth Avenue in Manhattan. But he found his wife's house agreeable enough.

Was not Lady Tremaine looking very fine tonight? Fine was much too tame a word. He'd known Lady Tremaine since she was practically an infant, and she'd never looked anything less than spectacular.

Had he met Lord Frederick Stuart yet? Lord who?

It was past midnight—and after a few pointed reminders from his wife about their subsequent commitments—that their guests finally prepared to depart. Lord and Lady Wrenworth were the last to leave. As Lady Wrenworth exited the front door, Lord Wrenworth turned around, pulled Gigi close, and whispered something into her ear, as if her husband weren't standing only five feet away.

She laughed, a sudden swell of mirth, and literally shoved Lord Wrenworth out the door.

"Let me guess. He proposed a ménage à trois?" Camden asked lightly, as they mounted the stairs side by side.

"Felix? No. He has become a tiresome proponent of home and hearth since his marriage. In fact, he was arguing most tediously against the divorce the whole evening, before you came along." She, too, kept up her winsome facade. "Well, if you must know, he said, 'Shag him silly.'"

"And are you going to take his sage advice?"

"To scrap the divorce or to shag you silly?" She chortled, her nimbus of sexual charisma unmistakable. "I'm not accepting counsel from Lord Wrenworth at this juncture, or from anyone else stupid enough to think that I should remain married to you. Frankly, I would have expected better from him. Freddie considers him a friend."

Poor Freddie, he thought.

"Well," she said, as they prepared to go their separate ways. "Should I expect a visit tonight?"

"Unlikely. I don't wish to upset my stomach. But do be on the lookout for them in the coming days."

She rolled her eyes. "I can't wait."

She had said the same thing to him once before, on the last day of their short-lived happiness. Then she had meant it, had been pink-cheeked with delight and anticipation. As had he.

"I can," he said.

She sighed, a weary flutter of air. "Go to hell, Camden."

Chapter Eight

December 1882

Theodora's letter arrived on the midday post three days after Camden's encounter with Miss Rowland. The sheaf of rose-scented paper notified him of her imminent marriage to a Polish nobleman—imminent only in the past tense. The letter had been composed two days before the date of the wedding, but not posted for another three days.

Camden could not imagine Theodora being married to anyone else. People in general made her nervous; even he did, to some extent, though she'd let him hold her hand and kiss her. She'd have been happiest far removed from the rest of humanity, a musical recluse in a chalet high up the Alps, with no neighbors but the cows at their summer pasture.

He worried about her. But even as he did, he could not stem the tide of excitement that the news engendered. Desire. Fascinated lust. Sensual bedazzlement. Covetousness by any other name was still rapacious. He wanted Miss Rowland. He wanted to laugh with her. He wanted to burn with her. And now he could.

If he married her.

Marriage, however, was a serious matter, the commitment of a lifetime, a decision not to be rushed. He tried to approach the matter rationally, but like idiotic, lust-addled young men since time immemorial—to which club he never imagined he'd belong—all he could think of was Miss Rowland's eagerness on their wedding night.

She'd probably be the one to come into his room, rather than the other way around. She'd allow him to keep all the lights on so he could visually devour her to his heart's content. She'd spread her legs wide, then wrap them tightly about him. And he might even make her look at what he'd do to her, so he could watch her flushed cheeks, her lust-glazed eyes, and listen to her moans and whimpers of pleasure.

God, he would make love to her for days running.

After a night of internal debate, during which much voluptuous fantasizing and very little sensible debate occurred, Camden resolved to put the choice to the Fates. If Miss Rowland was there again by the stream that day, he'd propose to her within the week. If not, he'd take it as a sign that he should hold off until the end of next term to allow time for more solemn reflection.

He spent the entire day at the bank of the brook, pacing up and down, all but climbing the naked trees. But she did not come. Not in the morning, not in the afternoon, not when the sky turned blue-black. And that was when he realized he was far gone: Not only was he immensely unhappy with the Fates, but he'd decided that the Fates could all go drown in a cesspit.

He returned his horse to the stable and requested a brougham be readied for him immediately.

The footman hesitated and looked inquiringly at Gigi. Her plate was still almost full. She pushed it aside. The plate disappeared to be replaced by another, a compote of pears.

"Gigi, you hardly ate anything," said Mrs. Rowland, picking up her fork. "I thought you liked venison."

Gigi picked up her own fork and excavated a cube of pear from the clear syrup. She was being too obvious in her preoccupation. Her mother never worried that she ate too little. Quite the opposite. Mrs. Rowland usually feared that Gigi's appetite was too robust, that her corsets wouldn't lace tightly enough to achieve any decent approximation of the wasp waist.

She stared at her fork and could not accomplish the simple task of putting it in her mouth. Her stomach churned already. She had no confidence it could handle the sugar-drenched piece of fruit.

She set down the fork. "I'm not that hungry tonight."

Merely terrified.

What she'd done was in every way unprincipled, and quite possibly criminal. Worse, she'd not only perpetrated a fraud, she'd made an incompetent mash of it. She'd been too impatient, her methods too crude. Any half-wit could pick up the rank odor of villainy and sniff the trail right to her door.

What would Lord Tremaine do should he find out? And what would he *think* of her?

A footman entered the dining room and spoke a few low words to Hollis, their butler. Hollis then approached Mrs. Rowland. "Ma'am, Lord Tremaine is here. Should I ask him to wait until dinner is finished?"

It was a good thing Gigi had quit all pretense of eating, or she'd have dropped everything in her hand.

Mrs. Rowland rose, radiant with excitement. "Absolutely not. We shall go greet him this instant. Come, Gigi. I've a suspicion that Lord Tremaine didn't come all the way to see *me.*"

Mrs. Rowland was no doubt hearing wedding bells. But scandal and ruin loomed large in Gigi's mind. She would live out the rest of her life like Miss What's-her-name, the mad old spinster in a wedding dress, laying waste to her estate and infecting everyone with her bitterness.

She had no choice but to follow her mother, bleakly, grimly, a foot soldier who shared little of the general's optimism for victory and spoils, who saw only the bloodbath ahead.

He was there, standing in the middle of the drawing room—the epitome of her desires, the instrument of her downfall, the eligible young scion who groomed horses and ran just slightly shady games of probability.

"My lord Tremaine," gushed Mrs. Rowland. "Such a

pleasure to see you, as always. What brings you to our humble abode at this unusual hour?"

"Mrs. Rowland. Miss Rowland." Did he glance at her? Was that a flash of intense longing or chagrin? "I do apologize for intruding on your evening."

"Nonsense," said Mrs. Rowland airily. "You know you are always welcome here, any time. Now do answer my question. My curiosity slays me."

"I'm here for a private word with Miss Rowland," replied Lord Tremaine, with breathtaking directness. "With your permission, of course, Mrs. Rowland."

For the very first time in her life, Gigi felt faint without having first suffered a concussion. Either he'd come to denounce her or he'd come to propose to her. Unthinkable as it might have been a few days ago, she fervently hoped it was the former. He'd castigate her for the scum that she was. She'd grovel hopelessly for forgiveness. Then he'd depart and she'd lock herself in her room and bang her head on the wall until the wall gave.

"Most certainly," acceded Mrs. Rowland, with admirable restraint.

She withdrew from the room, closing the door behind her. Gigi did not dare look at him. She was certain that that, in itself, already betrayed her culpability.

He drew close to her. "Miss Rowland, will you marry me?"

More bloodcurdling words she'd never heard. Her head snapped up. Her eyes met his. "Three days ago you were determined to marry someone else."

"Today I'm determined to marry you."

"What happened in the meantime to change your mind so drastically?"

"I received a letter from Miss von Schweppenburg. She has married into the Princely House of Lobomirski."

No, she has not. Gigi had plucked that name out of a book on European nobility she'd found in her mother's collection. She'd studied Miss von Schweppenburg's note, then composed her deception, carefully incorporating Miss von Schweppenburg's half apologies and powerless wistfulness. Then she'd taken everything to Briarmeadow's gamekeeper, an old man who'd been a forger in his youth and who regarded her with an indulgent, grandfatherly fondness.

"I see," she said weakly. "So you've decided to be practical."

"I suppose you could say part of my decision was motivated by pragmatism," he said quietly, coming so close that she could smell the cold crisp scent of winter that still clung to his jacket. "Though for the life of me, I can't remember any of those reasons."

He tipped her chin up and kissed her.

She'd kissed men before—several—when she got bored at balls or chafed from her mother's stricture. She considered the activity more bizarre than interesting and had sometimes studied the man she kissed with her eyes wide open, calculating the size of his debt.

But from the moment Lord Tremaine's lips touched hers, she was consumed, like a child tasting a lump of sugar for the very first time, overcome by the sweetness of it all. His kiss was as light as meringue, as gentle as the opening notes of the *Moonlight Sonata,* and as nourishing as the first rain of spring after an endless winter drought.

Light-headed and amazed, she drank in the kiss. Until simply being kissed by him wasn't enough anymore. She cupped his face and kissed him back with something far beyond enthusiasm, something closer to desperation, tremulous and wild.

She heard the muffled groan in his larynx, felt the physical change that signaled his arousal. He broke the kiss, pushed her an arm's length away, and stared at her, his breaths heavy and labored.

"My God, if your mother wasn't on the other side of the door..." He blinked, then blinked again. "Was that a yes?"

It was not yet too late. She could still take the nobler path, confess everything, apologize, and keep her self-respect.

And lose him. If he knew the truth, he would despise her. She couldn't face his anger. Or his scorn. Couldn't live without him. Not yet, not yet.

She wrapped her arms about his waist and laid her cheek against his shoulder. "Yes."

The joy she felt at his fierce embrace was riddled with terror. But she'd made her choice. She would have him, for better or worse. She would keep him in the dark, for as long as possible.

And when they were married, she would look upon his sleeping form, marvel at her vast good fortune, and ignore the constant encroachment of fear that tainted her very soul.

* * *

Camden had no idea he had it in him to be so happy. He was not the kind to derive unbridled joy from the pulse of the universe or any such nonsense. He never rolled out of bed wanting to breathe deeply of life itself—a poor man with well-meaning but inept parents to coddle and younger siblings to support had no time for such silly luxuries.

But with her by his side, he couldn't help being exuberant. She possessed magical properties, strong and bracing as a draft of the finest vodka and yet keeping him always at a delightful degree of tipsiness, that elusive point of equilibrium at which all the spheres of heaven came into exquisite alignment and a mere mortal sprouted wings.

During their three-week engagement, he called on her with a frequency that was positively indecent, on most days riding over to Briarmeadow both morning and afternoon and accepting her mother's invitations to remain for tea and dinner without so much as a perfunctory protest that he must not impose too much on his kind hostesses.

He loved talking to Gigi. Her view of the world was as jaundiced and unromantic as his own. They agreed that, at the moment, neither of them amounted to anything, as he was no more responsible for his bloodline than she was for her million-pound inheritance.

And yet for an inveterate cynic, she was as easy to please as a puppy. The inadequate bouquets he scavenged from Twelve Pillars' dilapidated greenhouse incited such euphoric responses that Julius Caesar on his triumphant return to Rome after the conquest of Gaul could not have been more madly thrilled. The rather modest engagement ring he bought her, with funds he'd saved for his passage to America and his first workshop, to be modeled after that of Herr Benz, brought her nearly to tears.

The day before the wedding, he drove to her house and sent for her to meet him in front. No gloomy blue cape this time; she arrived like a column of flame, in a mantle of rich strawberry red, with rosy cheeks and wine-colored lips to match.

He grinned, as he always did now when he met her. He was an ass, to be sure, but a happy ass. "I have something for you," he said.

She laughed giddily when she opened the small wrapped package to reveal a still-warm pork bun. "Now I truly have seen everything. Dare I guess you pillaged every last flower from your greenhouse yesterday?"

She glanced about them in the mischievous way she had, signaling to him that she was about to come forward and kiss him, the public nature of her front lawn be damned. He stopped her, holding her forearms with his hands, so that she couldn't get any closer.

"I have something else for you."

"I know what you have for me," she said saucily. "You wouldn't let me touch it yesterday."

"You can touch it today," he whispered.

"What?!" She was still a virgin, after all. "Out here, where everyone can see us?"

"Oh, yes." He laughed at her expression of shock and mortified interest.

"No!"

"All right, then, I'll take the puppy and go home."

"A puppy?" she squealed, like the nineteen-year-old she was. "A puppy! Where is it? Where is it?"

He lifted the basket out of the carriage, but swung it away from her eager hands just as she reached for it. "I understand you don't wish to touch it in public."

She grabbed the other end of the basket. "Oh, give me, give me! Pleeeease. I'll do anything."

He laughed and relented. She fumbled open the lid of the basket and out poked the brown-and-white head of a corgi puppy, wearing behind its neck a slightly lopsided blue bow made from ribbons Camden had pilfered from Claudia. Gigi squealed again and lifted the puppy. It regarded her with serious, intelligent eyes, not quite as thrilled as she was at their meeting but pleased and well-behaved nevertheless.

"Is it a boy or a girl?" she inquired breathlessly, offering it pieces of the pork bun. "How old is it? Does it have a name?"

Camden cast a glance at the puppy's rather obvious testicles. Perhaps she wasn't as knowledgeable as he'd thought. "He's a boy. Ten weeks old. And I've decided to call him Croesus in honor of you."

"Croesus, my love." She touched her cheek to the puppy's nose. "I shall get you a grand gilded water bowl, Croesus. And we will be the best of friends forever and ever."

At last she looked back at Camden. "But how did you know I've always wanted a puppy?"

"Your mother told me. She said she preferred cats and you pined for a dog."

"When?"

"The day we met. After dinner. You were there. Don't you remember?"

She shook her head. "No, I don't."

"No doubt you were too busy looking at me."

Her hand came up to her mouth. But then a slow smile spread across her face. "You noticed?"

He was tempted to tell her that not even at a memorably farcical soirée in St. Petersburg, during which both the hostess *and* the host attempted to seduce him, had he been ogled that much. "I noticed."

"Oh, dear."

She buried her face against the puppy's neck. She was blushing and, God help him, he had an erection the size of Bedfordshire.

"Thank you," she said, her voice muffled by Croesus's coat. "It's the best present anyone has ever given me."

He was touched and humbled. "It makes me happy to see you happy."

"Until tomorrow, then." She leaned in and kissed him, a sweet, lingering kiss. "I can't wait."

"It will be the longest twenty-four hours of my life," he said, kissing her one last time on the tip of her nose. "An eternity."

The next twenty-four hours turned out to be exactly that: an eternity, a hellish eternity.

Chapter Nine

The music did not register at first. Gigi was not accustomed to hearing music in her own house when she hadn't paid for it. She dropped the report in her hand and listened to the faint but unmistakable sounds of a piano being assaulted.

In his basket next to the bed, Croesus whimpered, snorted, and opened his eyes. Poor thing wasn't able to sleep well at night, perhaps because of all the naps he now took during the day. He shook his neck, rose on his short legs, and began his laborious ascent up the steps made especially for him after he could no longer bound up on her bed with only the aid of the bed stool.

She flung aside the counterpane and scooped him up. "It's that stupid husband of mine," she said to the old pup. "Instead of banging me, he's banging the damned piano. Let's go and tell him to shut up."

Her husband started something dramatic and harsh as she descended the staircase—*bong bong bong bong, bing bing bing bing*—a piece composed by the overly somber

Herr Beethoven, no doubt. With a sigh, Gigi threw open the door of the music room.

He had changed into a silk dressing gown, as sleek and dark as the piano itself. His hair was rumpled, but otherwise he looked serious, intent, a man with a purpose. An excellent man, the consensus had always been: a most dutiful son, a caring brother, a faithful friend—all that and social graces too.

And a streak of subterranean viciousness that had to be experienced to be believed.

"I beg your pardon," she said. "But some of us need to sleep so that we can get up early in the morning."

He stopped playing and looked at her oddly. It took another moment to register that he wasn't looking at *her* but at Croesus.

"Is that Croesus?" He frowned.

"It is."

He left the piano bench and came next to her, studying Croesus, his frown deepening. "What's the matter with him?"

She glanced down. Croesus seemed no different from how he usually was. "Nothing," she said, her voice sharp with defensiveness. She liked to think that she provided Croesus a happy, comfortable life. "He's as well as an old dog can be."

Croesus was ten and a half years of age, his once lustrous coat now dull and gray. His eyes were rheumy. He drooped, wheezed, tired easily, and ate poorly. But when he did have an appetite, he dined on foie gras sprinkled with sautéed mushrooms. And in ill health he was attended by London's best veterinarian.

Camden reached out toward Croesus. "Come here, old bloke."

Croesus regarded him with drowsy eyes. He didn't move. But neither did he protest when Camden simply took him.

"Do you remember me?" he said.

"I highly doubt it."

Camden ignored her snippy answer. "I've two pups in New York." He spoke to Croesus. "Hannah and Bernard, a rambunctious pair. They would be pleased to meet you someday."

She didn't understand why information so mundane and unremarkable as his having dogs should cause her a moment of scorching pain.

"I see you don't remember me." He gave the fur behind Croesus's ear a wistful scratch. "I have missed you."

"I'd like to have him back," Gigi said coldly.

He complied, but not before holding Croesus close and kissing one of the old dog's ears. "Your piano needs to be tuned."

"Nobody plays it."

"A shame." He turned his head and gave the instrument an appreciative glance. "An Érard piano should be played."

"You can take it with you when you go back to New York. A divorce present." She had ordered it as a wedding present for him. But it hadn't arrived until months after he left.

His gaze returned to her. "Thank you, I might. Especially since it already has my initials inscribed."

He was standing close enough that she imagined

she could smell him, the scent of a man after midnight—naked skin under silk dressing gown. "Get to it, will you?" she murmured. "All this sexual skittishness is not very attractive in a man."

"Yes, yes, I'm well aware. But the fact remains, I'm loath to touch you."

"Turn off all the lights. Pretend I'm someone else."

"That would be difficult. You tend to be vocal."

She colored. She couldn't help it. "I'll sew my lips shut."

He shook his head slowly. "It's no use. You breathe and I'll know it's you."

Ten years ago she'd have taken it for a declaration of love. Her heart still gave a throb, a lonely echo.

He bowed. "One more piece and I'm off to bed."

As she left, he began playing something as soft and haunting as the last roses of summer. She recognized it in two bars: *Liebesträume*. He and Mrs. Rowland had played it together that first night of their acquaintance. Even Gigi, incompetent musician that she was, could pick out that melody on the piano with one hand.

Dream of Love. All that she ever had with him.

Mrs. Rowland's campaign to woo the duke had hit a snag.

For a day or so, things went terribly well. The case of Châteu Lafite went promptly to Ludlow Court. A gracious thank-you note came back just as promptly, accompanied by a basket of apricot and peach preserves from Ludlow Court's own orchards.

Then nothing. Victoria sent an invitation to the duke for her next charity gala. He gave a generous cheque, but declined to attend the event. Two days later, she plucked up the audacity to call upon Ludlow Court in person, only to be told that the duke was not at home.

It'd been five years since she resettled in Devon in her childhood house, which she'd purchased from her nephew. Five years during which to observe the duke's comings and goings. She knew perfectly well that he never went anywhere else except for his daily walk.

Which left her no choice but to intercept him during his walk again.

She pretended to inspect the roses in the front garden, a pair of snipping scissors in hand, never mind that no self-respecting gardener ever did her cuttings in the middle of the afternoon. Her heart thumped as he came around the bend in the path at his usual hour. But by the time she'd maneuvered herself next to the low gate by the path, she barely got a "good afternoon" out of him before he sailed on past.

The next day she waited near the front of the garden, to no better results. The duke refused to be drawn into chitchat. Her comment on the weather only garnered the same "good afternoon" as the day before. For three days after that it rained. He walked in mackintosh and galoshes. But she could not possibly work in the garden—or even pretend to—in a downpour.

She gritted her teeth and decided to make an even greater nuisance of herself. She would walk *with* him. As God was her witness, she would bag, truss, and deliver this duke to Gigi at whatever cost to her own dignity.

Clad in a white walking dress and sensible walking boots, she waited in the front parlor of the cottage. When he appeared around the bend in the distance, she pounced, her tassel-fringed parasol in tow.

"I've decided to take up some exercise myself, Your Grace." She smiled as she closed the garden gate behind her. "Do you mind if I walk with you?"

He raised a pair of pince-nez from around his neck and looked down at her through the lenses. Goodness gracious but the man was ducal in every little gesture. He was not unusually tall, about five foot ten, but one chill look from him and the Colossus of Rhodes would feel like a midget.

He didn't give express permission. He merely dropped the pince-nez and nodded, murmuring, "Madam." And immediately resumed his walk, leaving Victoria to scamper in his wake, hurrying to catch up.

She had known, of course, that he walked fast. But it didn't dawn upon her until she'd tried to catch up with him for ten minutes just how fast he walked. For a rare moment she wished she had Gigi's tremendous height instead of her own more demure five feet two inches.

Chucking aside all ladylike restraints, she broke into a half run, cursing the narrow confines of her skirts, and finally ended up at his side. She had prepared various openings, bits and pieces of local trivia. But by the time she finished enumerating interesting packets of historical details concerning the house next down the lane, she'd be five feet behind him again. And having been very ladylike all her life, she wasn't sure she could manage another run without expiring of apoplexy.

So she got to the point. "Would you care for dinner at my house two weeks from Wednesday, Your Grace? My daughter will be visiting that week. I'm sure she'd be delighted to meet you."

She'd have to go up to London and drag Gigi down. But that she'd worry about later.

"I am a very fussy eater, Mrs. Rowland, and usually do not enjoy meals prepared by anyone but my own cook."

Drat it. Why must he be so difficult? What did a woman have to do to get him into her house? Dance naked in front of him? Then no doubt he'd complain of vertigo.

"I'm sure we could—"

"But I might consider accepting your invitation if you would grant me a favor in return."

If it weren't so darned exhausting to keep up with him, she'd have halted in her tracks, stunned. "I would be honored. What might I do for you, Your Grace?"

"I am an admirer of the peace and quiet of the country life, as you well know," he said. Did she detect a trace of sarcasm in his voice? "But even the most ardent admirer of the country life sometimes misses the pleasures of the town."

"Indeed."

"I haven't gambled for the past fifteen years."

This duke, a gambler? But he was a recluse, a Homeric scholar with his nose buried in old parchment. "I see," she said, though she didn't.

"I hear the siren call of a green baize table. But I do not wish to go to London to satisfy myself. Will you be so gracious as to play a few hands with me?"

This time she did come to a dead stop. "Me? Gamble?"

She had never even bet a shilling. Gambling, in her opinion, was about the daftest thing a woman could do, other than divorcing a man who would one day be a duke.

"Of course, I would understand if you object to—"

"Not at all," she heard herself say. "I have no objections whatsoever to a bit of harmless betting."

"I like it more interesting than that," he said. "One thousand pounds a hand."

"And I admire men who play for high stakes," she squeaked.

What was wrong with her? When she accepted giving up her dignity, she hadn't planned on surrendering every last ounce of her good sense as well. And lying outright, complimenting him on the most foolish, most self-destructive trait a man could possess! There came a time in every good Protestant's life when she yearned for a simple, sin-absolving trip to the papists' confession booth.

"Very well, then." The Duke of Perrin nodded his approval. "Shall we set a date and a time?"

Chapter Ten

"My dear cousin, the Grand Duke Aleksey, is getting married today," said the Countess von Loffler-Lisch—more affectionately known as Aunt Ploni, short for Appolonia. She was a second cousin of Camden's mother and had come all the way from Nice to attend his wedding. "I hear the bride is some gold-digging nobody."

He would be called that very same if he didn't stand in direct line of succession to a ducal title, Camden thought wryly. Instead, Gigi would bear the brunt of the snickering their hasty marriage was certain to engender, for her feats of social mountaineering.

"Your noble cousin's wedding would have been the grander affair," said Camden.

"Very likely." The elderly countess nodded, her hair a rare shade of pure silver and elaborately coiffed. "*Zut!* I can't recall the bride's name. Elenora von Schellersheim? Von Scheffer-Boyadel? Or is her name not even Elenora?"

Camden smiled. Aunt Ploni was known for her

prodigious memory. It must gall her to no end not re-membering something right at the tip of her tongue.

He sat down next to her and poured more curaçao into her digestif glass. "Where is the bride from?"

"Somewhere on the border with Poland, I think."

"We know some people from there," he said. Theodora, for one.

The countess frowned and tried to concentrate amid the lively conversation flowing in the great draw-ing room at Twelve Pillars. Thirty of Camden's relatives had arrived from the Continent to attend the wedding, despite the short notice. And his mother was ever so pleased to finally be able to receive people in a mansion, however neglected, of her own.

"Von Schweinfurt?" Aunt Ploni refused to give up. "I do hate growing old. I never forgot a name when I was younger. Let's see. Von Schwanwisch?"

"Von Schnurbein? Von Schottenstein?" Camden teased her. He was in a buoyant mood. Tomorrow this time he would be getting married to the most remark-able girl he'd ever met. And tomorrow night—

"Von Schweppenburg!" the countess exclaimed. "There, that's it! Haven't quite lost all my marbles af-ter all."

"Von Schweppenburg?" He'd accidentally electro-cuted himself once during an experiment at the Polytechnique. He felt exactly the same shock in his fingertips now. "You mean Count Georg von Schweppenburg's widow?"

"Dear me, not quite that bad. His daughter.

Theodora, that's her name, not Elenora, after all. Poor Alesha is quite smitten."

Something droned in the back of his head, an incipient alarm that he tried to dismiss. Titles that had their origins during the Holy Roman Empire went on in perpetuity to all male issue. There could very well be another late Count Georg, from a lateral branch of the von Schweppenburg family, who had a marriageable daughter named Theodora.

But what were the chances? No, they were speaking of *his* Theodora here, the one whose happiness he had once hoped to secure. But how? How could she marry two men in one month? The simple answer was that she couldn't. Either the countess was wrong or Theodora herself was wrong. A laughable choice, really. Of course Theodora would know the name of the man she was going to marry. The countess had to be mistaken.

"I met her years ago, when we were in Peters," he said carefully. "I thought she married some Polish prince."

The countess snorted. "Now, wouldn't that be interesting, a real live bigamist? Unfortunately, I've no hope for it. According to Alesha, his intended is as pure as the arctic ice field, with a mother who watches her every move. You must be mistaken, my boy."

The clamor in his head escalated. He poured a goblet full of the digestif and downed it in one long gulp. The cognac at the base of the liqueur burned in his throat, but the sensation barely registered.

"It's only two o'clock in the afternoon. A bit early to be doing your last bout of bachelor drinking, eh?" cackled Aunt Ploni. "Not getting cold feet, are you?"

He wouldn't know if his feet were cold. He couldn't feel any of his limbs. The only thing he felt was confusion and a rising sense of peril, as if the solid ground beneath him had suddenly splintered, cracking dark webs of fissure and fracture as far as he could see.

He rose and bowed to the countess. "Hardly. But I do beg your pardon, noble cousin. There is a small matter that requires my attention. I hope to see you again at dinner."

Camden couldn't think any better away from the drawing room. He wandered the silent, drafty corridors as bits and pieces of what Aunt Ploni had said streaked about in his head like panicky hens facing a weasel invasion.

He didn't exactly understand why, but he was scared witless. What frightened him most was that he knew, deep in his guts, that Aunt Ploni had not been mistaken.

At a turn in the hallway, near the front of the house, he bumped right into a young footman carrying a tray of letters. "Beg your pardon, milord!" the footman apologized immediately, and got down on all fours to retrieve the scattered missives.

As the footman gathered up the letters, Camden saw two addressed to him. He recognized the handwriting of his friends. The new university term had already started; they must be wondering why he hadn't returned yet. He had not informed his classmates of his upcoming marriage—he and Gigi had decided to throw a surprise reception in Paris, in the spacious apartment her agent had located for them on Montagne Sainte Geneviève in the Quartier Latin, a stone's throw from his classes. A few essential items of furnishing had already been set up at the apartment, where a cook and a maid had also taken up residence in preparation for their arrival.

He held out his hand for the tray. "I'll take them, Elwood."

Elwood looked baffled. "But, sir, Mr. Beckett said all letters must go to him first, so he could sort them out."

"Since when?"

"Since right about Christmas last, sir. Mr. Beckett said His Grace didn't like too many letters begging him for charity."

What? Camden almost said the word aloud. His father had never met a beggar for whom he didn't have a coin to spare. It was his very softheartedness that had in part made them paupers.

An appalling suspicion was beginning to coalesce in Camden's mind. He wanted to bat it away with something heavy and powerful—a club, a mace—to disperse the filaments of deductions and inferences that threatened to choke his perfect contentment. He wanted to forget what he had heard about the majordomo just now, ignore the clamor in his head that had risen to a screaming siren, and pretend that everything was exactly as it should be.

Tomorrow he was getting married. He couldn't wait to sleep with that girl. He couldn't wait to wake up next to her every day, bask in her adoration, and delight in her verve.

"Very well, take these to Beckett," he said.

"Yes, sir."

Camden watched the footman march down the hall-way. *Let him go. Let him go. Don't ask questions. Don't think. Don't probe.*

"Wait," he commanded.

Elwood turned around obediently. "Yes, sir?"

"Tell Beckett I would like to see him in my apartment in fifteen minutes."

Chapter Eleven

A gentleman's club had seemed the perfect remedy after a tiring, weeklong business trip to the Continent, during which he'd thought very little of his business and too much of his wife. But Camden was beginning to regret his freshly minted membership. He had never set foot inside an English gentleman's club before, but he had harbored the distinct impression that it would be a quiet, calm place, filled with men escaping the strictures of wives and hearths, drinking scotch, holding desultory political debates, and snoring softly into their copies of the *Times*.

Certainly the interior of the club, which looked as if it had not been touched in half a century—fading burgundy drapes, wallpaper splotchily darkened by gaslights, and furnishing that in another decade or so would be called genteelly shabby—had seemed conducive to somnolence, giving him the false hope that he'd be able to while away the afternoon, brooding in peace. And he had done so for a few minutes, until a crowd begging for introductions surrounded him.

The conversation had quickly turned to Camden's various holdings. He hadn't quite believed Mrs. Rowland when she declared in one of her letters that Society had changed and that people could not shut up about money these days. Now he did.

"How much would such a yacht cost?" asked one eager young man.

"Is there a sizable profit to be realized?" asked another.

Perhaps the agricultural depression that had cut many a large estate's income by half had something to do with it. The aristocracy was in a pinch. The manor, the carriages, and the servants all bled money, which was getting scarcer by the day. Unemployment, for centuries the gentlemanly standard—so that one could devote one's time to serving as parliamentarian and magistrate—was becoming more and more of an untenable position. But as of yet, few gentlemen had the audacity to work. So they talked, to scratch the itch of collective anxiety.

"Such a yacht costs enough that only a handful of America's richest men can afford one," Camden said. "But, alas, not so much that those who supply them can claim instant riches."

If he were to solely rely on the firm he owned that designed and built yachts, he'd be a well-off man but nowhere near wealthy enough to hobnob with Manhattan's elite. It was his other maritime ventures, the freight-shipping line and the shipyard that built commercial vessels, that comprised what Americans called the "meat-and-potato" portion of his portfolio.

"How does one come into possession of such a firm?" asked yet another man from the group of interlocutors, this one not as young as the others—and, judging by his silhouette, sporting a corset beneath his waistcoat.

Camden glanced toward the grandfather clock that stood between two bookshelves against the far wall. Whatever the time was, he was going to say that he was expected elsewhere in half an hour. The time was quarter past three, and beside the clock stood Lord Wrenworth, observing the mob about Camden with amusement.

"How?" Camden looked back at the corseted man. "Good luck, good timing, and a wife who is worth her weight in gold, my dear fellow."

His answer was received with a silence halfway between shock and awe. He took the opportunity to stand up. "Excuse me, gentlemen. I'd like to have a word with Lord Wrenworth."

My daughter sends me postcards from the Lake District. I hear Lord Wrenworth is also there.

My daughter is going to Scotland with a large party of friends, Lord Wrenworth included, for a sennight.

My daughter, when I last saw her at a dinner, sported a fetching pair of diamond bracelets that I'd never seen before. She was unusually coy about their provenance.

Mrs. Rowland had been overly lavish in her praise of Lord Wrenworth—*a man all men want to be and all women want to bewitch*—but not by much. The man seemed effortlessly graceful, effortlessly fashionable, and effortlessly calm and collected.

"Quite a crowd you were drawing, my lord Tremaine," Lord Wrenworth said with a smile, as he and Camden shook hands. "You are an object of great curiosity around these parts."

"Ah, yes, the latest addition to the circus, et cetera," said Camden. "You, sir, are fortunate to be so well situated that you need not soil your mind with thoughts of commerce."

Lord Wrenworth laughed. "As to that, my lord, you are very much mistaken. Rich peers need money every bit as much as poor peers—we have far greater expenditures. But I daresay your material success fuels only part of the collective curiosity."

"Let me guess, there's that little matter of the divorce."

"Short of a good, old-fashioned murder, a divorce with charges of adultery leveled is the best anyone can hope for when the mood calls for some entertaining gossip."

"Indeed. What have you heard?"

Lord Wrenworth raised an eyebrow but proceeded to answer Camden's question. "I'm blessed with a battalion of sisters-in-law. One, with impeccable sources, declares that you are willing to submit to an annulment should Lady Tremaine hand over half of her worth and promise to travel to her honeymoon destination on your flagship luxury liner."

"Interesting. I do not deal in passenger transit."

"You must be mistaken," said Lord Wrenworth.

"Though, to be sure, another one of Lady Wrenworth's sisters, with sources equally infallible, insists that you are a hairbreadth away from a grand reconciliation."

Camden nodded. "And you are in favor of the old status quo. Lady Tremaine is quite peeved with you, I might as well let you know. She thought you'd be a better friend to Lord Frederick."

"Then that would make me less of a friend to her," said Lord Wrenworth, no longer glib. "Lord Frederick, though he is a man of unimpeachable goodness— Speak of the devil. The rumormongers will have new tales to tell tonight."

He pointed his chin toward the door. Camden turned to see a young man coming toward them. Though he stooped slightly, he was still tall, a hair under six foot. He had a round face, a firm jaw, and clear, uncomplicated eyes. Elsewhere in the room, men stopped what they were doing and stared openly at his progress, glancing from Camden to him and back, but he remained oblivious to the attraction he had become.

The young man offered his hand to Lord Wrenworth. "Lord Wren, pleased to see you." He had a melodious, surprisingly *basso profundo* voice. "Was just thinking of sending a note around. Lady Wren asked me a couple of months ago if I would paint a portrait of her. Well, I told her that I wasn't much good at portraits. But these days—well, you know what's going on—I seem to have lots of time on my hands. If she is still interested—"

"I'm sure she would be delighted, Freddie," Lord Wrenworth said smoothly. He turned to Camden.

"Lord Tremaine, may I present Lord Frederick Stuart? Freddie, Lord Tremaine."

Camden extended his hand. "A pleasure, sir."

Lord Frederick blinked. He stared at Camden for a second, as if expecting something dire. Then he swallowed and grasped Camden's hand with his own, which was large and slightly plump. "Right ho. Pleased, I'm sure, milord."

For some reason, despite everything Mrs. Rowland had written, Camden had expected to see a prime specimen of a man. Lord Frederick was not that man. Next to Lord Wrenworth, he seemed all too ordinary, his looks pleasant but unremarkable, his attire a year or two behind the forefront of fashion, his demeanor unsophisticated.

"You are an artist, Lord Frederick?"

"No, no, I only dabble."

"Nonsense," said Lord Wrenworth. "Lord Frederick is tremendously accomplished for his age."

His age—yet something else Camden hadn't expected. Lord Frederick could not have lived through more than twenty-four winters, a mere babe, barely old enough to grow hairs on his chin.

"Lord Wrenworth is much too kind," Lord Frederick mumbled. Camden could see he was beginning to sweat, despite the cool interior of the club.

"I beg to differ," said Wrenworth. "I have one of Freddie's pieces at home. Lady Wrenworth quite admires it. In fact, I believe Lady—"

Suddenly Lord Frederick looked quite panic-stricken. "Wren!"

Lord Wrenworth was taken aback. "Yes, Freddie?"

Lord Frederick could not come up with a slick answer. "I...uh...I forgot."

"What were you about to say, my lord Wrenworth?" Camden asked.

"Only that I believe my mother-in-law begged to have it," said Lord Wrenworth. "But Lady Wrenworth refused to part with it."

"Oh," said Lord Frederick, turning a shade of carmine to rival the drapes.

The two older men exchanged a look. Lord Wrenworth shrugged subtly, as if he had no idea as to the reason behind Lord Frederick's outburst. But Camden had already guessed. "Is Lady Tremaine, like Lady Wrenworth, an admirer of your work, Lord Frederick?"

Lord Frederick looked to Lord Wrenworth for recourse, but the latter chose not to involve himself, leaving Lord Frederick to meet Camden's direct question by himself. "Uh, Lady Tremaine has always been most kind to...my efforts. She is a great collector of art."

Not something Camden would have said about his wife. But he supposed it was possible that, in a society enamored of the classical styles and subjects of Sir Frederick Leighton and Lawrence Alma-Tadema, she could very well host one of the largest collections of Impressionist paintings. "You approve of the latest trends in art, I take it?"

"I do, sir, indeed." Lord Frederick relaxed slightly.

"Then you must come see me the next time you

happen to be in New York City. My collection is far superior to Lady Tremaine's, at least in quantity."

The poor boy clearly struggled, wondering whether he was being played for a fool, but he chose to answer Camden's invitation as if it had been issued in good faith. "I shall be honored, sir."

In that moment Camden saw what Gigi must have seen in the boy: his goodness, his sincerity, his willingness to think the best of everyone he met, a willingness that arose less from naïveté than from an inborn sweetness.

Lord Frederick hesitated. "Would you be returning to America very soon or would you be with us for a while?"

And courage too, to ask that question outright of him. "I expect I should remain in London until the matter of my divorce is settled."

Lord Frederick's blush now exceeded Hungarian paprika in depth of color and vividness. Lord Wrenworth took his watch out and glanced at it. "Dear me, I should have met Lady Wrenworth at the bookshop five minutes ago. You must excuse me, gentlemen. Hell hath no fury like a woman made to wait."

To Lord Frederick's credit, he didn't run, though the desire to do so was writ plain on his face. Camden gazed around the large common room. Newspapers suddenly rustled, conversations recommenced, cigars that had been dropping ashes on the scarlet-and-blue carpet rose once again to mustached lips.

Satisfied that the rampant, untoward curiosity in

the room had been temporarily curbed, Camden returned his attention to Lord Frederick. "I understand that you wish to marry my wife."

The color drained from Lord Frederick's face, but he stood his ground. "I do."

"Why?"

"I love her."

Camden had no choice but to believe him. Lord Frederick's answer brimmed with the kind of clarity born of the deepest conviction. He ignored the stab of pain in his chest. "Other than that?"

"I beg your pardon?"

"Love is an unreliable emotion. What is it about Lady Tremaine that makes you think you won't regret marrying her?"

Lord Frederick swallowed. "She is kind, wise, and courageous. She understands the world but doesn't let it corrupt her. She is magnificent. She is like...like..." He was lost for words.

"Like the sun in the sky?" Camden prompted, sighing inwardly.

"Yes, exactly," said Lord Frederick. "How...how did you guess, sir?"

Because I once thought the same. And sometimes still think it.

"Luck," answered Camden. "Tell me, young man, have you ever considered that it might not be easy being married to a woman like that?"

Lord Frederick looked perplexed, like a child being told that there *was* such a thing as too much ice cream, when he had only ever been allowed a few spoonfuls at a time. "How so?"

Camden shook his head. What could he say? "Do not mind the rambling of an old man." He offered his hand again. "I wish you the best of luck."

"Thank you, sir." Lord Frederick sounded both relieved and grateful. "Thank you. I wish you the same."

May the better man prevail.

The reply rose nearly to the tip of Camden's tongue before he realized what he was about to say and swallowed it whole. He couldn't possibly have meant anything close to that. He couldn't possibly even have thought it. He had no use for her. He did not want her back. It was but the flotsam of his psyche, washed ashore in a sudden surge of masculine possessiveness.

He nodded at Lord Frederick and a few other men, retrieved his hat and walking stick, and exited the club into the midst of a fine afternoon. It was all wrong. The sky should be ominous, the wind cold, the rain fierce. He would have welcomed that, welcomed the drenching discomfort and isolation of an icy downpour.

Instead, he must endure the mercilessly beautiful sunshine of an early summer day and listen to birds chirp and children laugh as all his carefully constructed rationales threatened to crumble about him.

She was wrong. It wasn't about Theodora. It had never been about Theodora. It was always about *her*.

Gigi was giving Victoria trouble.

"Duke of Perrin." She frowned. "How do you know him?"

This was not the reaction Victoria had expected

from Gigi. She had mentioned the duke only most incidentally, while trying to persuade Gigi to take some time away from London. "He happens to be my neighbor. We met on one of his daily walks."

"I'm surprised you allowed him to introduce himself to you." A maid in a white shirt, black skirts, and a long bib apron came by and filled their glasses with mineral water. Victoria had arranged for them to meet at a ladies' tea shop. She didn't trust Gigi's servants not to gossip. "I thought you usually stayed well away from cads and roués."

"Cads and roués!" Victoria cried. "What does that have to do with His Grace? He is very well respected, I will have you know."

"He had a near-fatal hunting accident some fifteen years ago. After that he retired from society. And I will have *you* know that until then he was the veriest lecher, gambler, and all-around reprobate."

Victoria dabbed at her upper lip with her napkin to hide her wide-open mouth. The duke had been her neighbor in her youth. And he was her neighbor now. But she had to admit that she had no idea what he had done with himself during the twenty-odd years in the middle.

"Well, he can't be any worse than Carrington, can he?"

"Carrington?" Gigi stared at her. "Why are you comparing him to Carrington? Are you thinking of marrying him?"

"No, of course not!" Victoria denied hotly. The next

instant she wished she hadn't, because Gigi's eyes narrowed with suspicion.

"Then what are you doing, inviting him to dinner?" Her voice turned chillier with each word. "Tell me you aren't planning some lunacy to make me into the next Duchess of Perrin."

Victoria sighed. "It can't hurt, can it?"

"Mother, I believe I have told you already that I am going to marry Lord Frederick Stuart once I'm divorced from Tremaine." Gigi spoke slowly, as if to a very dull child.

"But you won't be divorced for a while yet," Victoria pointed out reasonably. "Your feelings for Lord Frederick might very well have changed by then."

"Are you calling me fickle?"

"No, of course not." Oh, dear, however did one explain to a girl that her intended had less brains than a chipmunk? "I'm only saying that, well, I don't think Lord Frederick is the best man for you."

"He is a good, gentle, and kind man of absolutely no vices. He loves me very much. What other man can be better for me?"

Crumbs. The girl was daring her. "But you must consider this carefully. You are a clever woman. Can you really respect a man who does not possess the same perspicuity?"

"Why don't you just come out and say you think he is dense?"

Oh, stupid girl. "All right. I think he is dense, denser than Nesselrode pudding. And I can't stand the thought of you being married to him. He is not good enough to carry your shoes."

Gigi stood up calmly. "It is good to see you, Mother. I wish you a pleasant stay in London. But I regret I cannot come to Devon next week, the week after, or the week after that. Good day."

Victoria resisted the urge to put her face into her hands. She was bewildered. She had been so careful not to mention Camden or to criticize Gigi on the petition for divorce. And now she couldn't state the obvious concerning Lord Frederick either?

Gigi arrived home fuming. What was wrong with her mother? A millennium had passed since Gigi had come to see the utter meaninglessness of a title. But still Mrs. Rowland cleaved to the illusion that a strawberry-leaf coronet cured all ills.

She went in search of Croesus. Nothing and no one soothed her the way Croesus did, with his patient understanding and constant affection. But Croesus was neither in her bedchamber nor in the kitchen, where he occasionally went when his appetite returned.

Suddenly she felt a shiver of fear. "Where is Croesus?" she asked Goodman. "Is he—"

"No, madam. He is well. I believe he is with Lord Tremaine in the conservatory."

So Camden had come back from wherever he had been the past week. "Very good. I'll go rescue him."

The conservatory stretched nearly the entire width of the house. From the outside, it was an oasis of verdancy, even on the dreariest days of winter—the vines and fern fronds weaving a green cascade through the clear glass walls. From the inside, the structure offered an unimpeded view of the street beneath and the park beyond.

Camden sat sprawled on a wicker chair at the far end of the conservatory, his arms stretched over the back of the chair, his stockinged feet propped up on a wicker ottoman before him. Croesus lay snoozing next to him.

Camden had his profile to her, that strong, flawless profile that had so reminded her of a statue of Apollo Belvedere. He glanced away from the open windows at the sound of her approach, but he did not rise. "My lady Tremaine," he said with mock courtesy.

She ignored him, scooped up Croesus—who wriggled and snorted, then settled into the crook of her elbow and went on with his nap—and turned to leave.

"I was introduced to Lord Frederick earlier this afternoon, at the club," said her husband. "It was an edifying encounter."

She whipped around. "Let me guess. You found him to possess all the intelligence of a boiled egg."

Let him dare to agree with her. She was quite in the mood for slapping someone. Him.

"I did not find him either eloquent or worldly. But that was not the thrust of my remark."

"What was the thrust of your remark, then?" she asked, suspicious.

"That he would make some woman an excellent husband. He is sincere, steadfast, and loyal."

She was stunned. "Thank you."

His gaze returned to the outside world. A pleasant breeze invaded the conservatory, ruffling his thick, straight hair. Carriages on exodus from the park crammed the street below. The air echoed with coachmen's calls, cautioning their horses and one another to pay heed to the logjam.

Apparently, their little exchange was over. But Camden's remarkable compliment to Freddie had bred an opportunity that she could not let pass. "Would you do the honorable deed and release me from this marriage? I love Freddie, and he loves me. Let us marry while we are still young enough to forge a life together."

In his perfect stillness she sensed a sudden stiffening.

"Please," she said slowly. "I beg you. Release me."

His gaze remained fixed on the daily tide of phaetons and barouches, of England's vanity and pride on parade. "I didn't say he would make *you* a good husband."

"And what would *you* know about making anyone a good husband?" She regretted the words as soon as they left her lips. But there was no taking them back now.

"Absolutely nothing," he admitted without hesitation. "But at least I saw a few of your faults. I thought you interesting and appealing in spite of them, or perhaps because of them. Lord Frederick worships the ground you walk on because you have the kind of strength, resilience, and nerve he can only dream of. When he looks at you he sees only the halo he has erected about you."

"What's wrong with being perfect in the eyes of my beloved?"

His eyes locked with hers. "I look at him and I see a man who thinks we are going to be as chaste as God and Mary in this house. Does he know you are protecting him from the truth? Does he know that a few big lies in the service of love are nothing to you? That your strength extends to remorseless ruthlessness?"

She'd have spat on the floor if she hadn't been raised by Victoria Rowland. "I look at you and I see a man who is still stuck in 1883. Does he know that ten years have passed? Does he know that I have moved on, that he is the relentless, ruthless one now? And does he really think I plan to tell the man I love that I'm to be impregnated by another, against my wish?"

Someone laughed in the distance, a shrill, feminine giggle. Croesus whimpered and shifted in her arms. She was crushing him with the stiffness of her grip. She let out a shaky breath and forced her muscles to relax.

He pressed two fingertips to his right temple. "You make it sound so ugly, my dear. Don't you think I deserve to get something out of this marriage before you traipse into your happily-ever-after?"

"I don't know," she said. "And I don't care. All I know is that Freddie is my last chance for happiness in this life. I will marry him if I have to turn into Lady Macbeth and destroy all who stand in my path."

His eyes narrowed. They were the dark green of a nightmare forest. "Warming up to your old tricks?"

"How can I fail to be unscrupulous when you keep reminding me that I am?" Her heart was a swamp of bitterness, at him, at herself. "We will begin our one year tonight. Not later. Not whenever you finally feel like it. Tonight. And I don't give a ha'penny if you have to spend the rest of the night puking."

He merely smiled.

Chapter Twelve

Beckett, Twelve Pillars' majordomo, was a man in his early fifties, tall, thin, and balding. Camden found him highly efficient, despite his occasional unctuousness—presumably Carrington had liked his servants obsequious.

"You wish to see me, Lord Tremaine?" asked Beckett.

Without speaking, Camden motioned the majordomo to sit. He himself remained standing. The older man settled uneasily into the indicated chair.

Camden stared at him, because he wasn't yet sure where to begin and because he wished to intimidate. After twenty seconds Beckett had trouble meeting his eyes. After three minutes, he was fidgeting and surreptitiously wiping away at his forehead and upper lip.

"You do know, Beckett, that abusing your employer's trust is a crime punishable by law, don't you?"

Beckett's head snapped up. For a moment, his expression was one of sheer panic. But he hadn't risen to be the head of staff in a ducal household without having learned a thing or two about self-control. In the next second, he replied in a normal voice, "Of course, my lord. I am more than aware. Loyalty is my creed."

But his fear-stricken look had already given too much away. He was guilty. But of what?

"I admire your composure, Beckett. It must not be easy to appear calm when you are quaking in your shoes."

"I...I'm afraid I don't know what you are talking about, sir."

"I think you do, Beckett. And I think you are filled with dismay, horror, and, I hope, some shame at being found out. If I were you, I wouldn't carry this protestation of innocence any further. If you would not admit your errors to me in private, I shall be forced to go to His Grace and expose your lies, then he would have no choice but to call in the constables."

Beckett was not about to give up easily. "Sir, if I've done something that has displeased you, please let me know what it is."

Therein lay the difficulty of the matter. Camden had nothing concrete against Beckett, only the knowledge that Beckett had disrupted the usual pattern of mail delivery within the house and that Camden had a letter from Theodora that he was beginning to believe wasn't from Theodora at all, God help him.

He walked to the mantel and pretended to study the framed seascape above it. If there was any link between Beckett and Theodora's letter, it was only an indirect one. He was acting at someone else's behest, a paid agent.

Camden turned around and bluffed. "I know why you have all the mail delivered to you first. You see, Beckett, I have bad news for you. Your puppeteer has no more use for you and doesn't care to pay the remainder of your fee. So he has decided to throw you to the wolves."

"No!" Beckett bolted out of the chair. "The bastard!"

His ragged breathing suffused the stillness of the room. Then, realizing he had completely given himself away, he sank down into the chair and lowered his face into his palms.

"Forgive me, my lord. But I've not done anything. Nothing, I swear. I was told only to watch out for any letters that came for you from abroad. Those I was to hand to the man. But he never took one of them either. He just looked at them and gave them back to me."

Any letter that came for *him* from *abroad*. Camden felt something implode in his chest, as if his lungs had collapsed. "Are you sure you've done nothing?"

"There..." Beckett wiped his face with his handkerchief. "There was this one time, in the beginning, when the man gave me back the letters and I was sure one of them hadn't been there earlier."

One letter. That was all it took. One letter.

"Where and when do you meet this man?"

"Outside the gate, on Tuesday and Friday afternoons."

"And what if you can't meet him in person, for some reason?"

"Then I'm to wrap the letters carefully and place the

package under a rock by the gooseberry bush to the left of the gate. He comes at three."

Today was Friday. The time was twenty-five minutes before three.

"Too bad," Camden said. "I imagine he will not come anymore. Or I could have him thrown in jail also."

Beckett paled. "But, my lord, you said...you said—"

"I know what I said. I expect your resignation to be handed in to His Grace tomorrow after dinner."

"Yes, sir. Thank you, sir." Beckett all but kissed Camden's feet.

"Go."

As Beckett made his unsteady way to the door, Camden remembered one last thing. "How much were you paid up front?"

Beckett hesitated. "Two thousand pounds. I have a natural son, my lord. He is in trouble. I used the money to pay off his debts. I will restitute it to you as soon as I may."

Camden pressed his fingers hard against his temple. "I don't want it. And I don't wish to see you ever again. Leave."

Two thousand up front, two thousand later. Who had this kind of money to throw away? And why would anyone want to do it? All the evidence pointed to only one direction. But he couldn't bear to acknowledge it. Perhaps, he prayed, perhaps he was wrong. Perhaps the fear that knotted his guts wasn't a sign of inevitability but only a result of his overactive imagination.

Perhaps there was still hope.

* * *

Two and a half hours later, there was no longer any possibility of denial.

Camden wrapped the two letters from his friends, hid them as Beckett had done, and waited. A man did come, a raffish-looking man in his sixties, in a dogcart pulled by an ancient nag. He looked around carefully, then went for the gooseberry bush. As Beckett had described, he quickly glanced over the letters, then put them back where he'd found them.

The man maneuvered the dogcart around and started back the way he'd come. Camden followed at a distance, on foot, the pain in his chest growing more vicious with each passing mile, all the way to the bitter end as the man and his cart disappeared between the gates of Briarmeadow, the chimneys of his fiancée's house just visible in the fading light above the tops of the naked poplars.

Something shriveled and died in him. He began to walk, then run, away from Briarmeadow, away from her. Gigi, lovely, treacherous Gigi. Was it only this morning that he had come this way, as eager to please and impress her as any stupid puppy that ever lived?

He didn't know how far or how long he sprinted, or at what point he finally crumpled to the ground, his eyes dry, his mind numb except for a splitting headache, the anvils of Lucifer beating every last shred of illusion out of him.

She had done it. For some reason she had decided that she must have him, so she'd had the letter forged. Of course it was her; she was by far the most devious person he had ever come across. And he, horny fool that he was, had played along ever so willingly. How immeasurable her satisfaction must have been to see him this morning, knowing that her victory was complete and that he'd melt in her hand as readily as a piece of suet.

Anger—burning, icy, dark as the pits of hell—rose slowly in him, until degree by degree it had taken over every cell of his body. He clung to that anger, for it dispelled pain and kept it at bay.

Vengeance, he would have vengeance. She was willing to shell out four thousand pounds for him, was she? Then the lady mustn't be disappointed. She would see that he was every bit her equal in duplicity and heartlessness.

He pried himself off the ground and went on running, not stopping again until he was in view of Twelve Pillars. A stray thought wrestled free from his tight control as he marched toward the house. It pined over how close to paradise he'd come, how joyful and carefree he had been only hours ago. It wanted time to turn back and Aunt Ploni to never have come. It wanted to beat the walls and wail. *Gigi, you stupid, stupid girl! Why couldn't you have waited? Theodora got married today. Today! I would have been—*

Shut up! Shut up! I will shoot you myself if you ever whine for that girl again.

Vengeance, remember, only vengeance.

Chapter Thirteen

Langford was restless.

For the past fifteen years, his evenings had consisted of dinner, a cigar, the day's copy of the *Times,* and one last hour of scholarly reading. And for about thirteen of those fifteen years, twice a week, his current London mistress would arrive just as he laid aside Plato's *Symposium* or Aeschylus's *Myrmidons.* The first year after his return to Devonshire he had tried, without consistent success, to set up a more local arrangement. For the past twelve months or so, he had been celibate.

He had never been an advocate for celibacy, nor was he one now. He had, perhaps, simply become too much of a village bumpkin to make the rounds of the London flesh market. Or perhaps he had no more need for the old carnal calisthenics, having grown prematurely asexual via the combination of solitude and scholarly pursuits.

And he hadn't missed it terribly, until tonight. He

would not mind knowing that a woman was stepping off the 9:23 train at the town of Totnes at that moment, about to be conveyed four miles southeast to Ludlow Court.

The tranquillity of his library had become somnolent and tedious. His evening routine, with its careful variety of cigars, *Punch,* and an occasional novel, was as sterile as the capons his cook served on Thursdays. Even having his dessert first tonight had done nothing to alleviate the oppressive sameness, except making him feel acutely ridiculous.

The problem was not lethargy, which afflicted him from time to time. Rather, he suffered from a surfeit of energy. He was pacing like a windup Christmas toy soldier under the generalship of a three-year-old boy.

A knock came at the library door. His butler, Reeves, entered, bearing the evening post. Langford scanned the three envelopes. Two were correspondence from other scholars, one German, one Greek. The last was a letter from his cousin Caroline, otherwise known as Lady Avery, a woman with a religious passion for the sins of others and a philanthropist's delight in sharing her encyclopedic knowledge of Society's every last tempest in a teapot.

He dismissed Reeves and opened Caro's letter, glad for some nonsensical distraction. Caro and her sister Grace, Lady Somersby, used to call on him first thing in the morning, to find out from the servants which lady's abode he had visited the night before or if any cyprians—the precise number, please—had been brought into his own house. He had personally supervised the "accidental" dumping of buckets of cold water as they stood before his door one morning, ringing. But their fearsome dedication to their craft was such that they'd returned the next day with umbrellas.

Perhaps as a tribute to all the delicious, scandalous tidbits he'd provided, which had elevated them to the top of the rumormongering pyramid, Caro wrote him every month about the latest *on-dits*. At the beginning of his self-imposed exile, he had tossed the letters unopened into the fire. But as the years went by, her clockwork persistence wore down his resistance. He was ashamed to admit to it, but he had become addicted to the monthly dose of adultery, vanity, and lunacy.

This month's installment had Lady Southwell giving birth to yet another child who looked nothing like Lord Southwell but bore every resemblance to the Honorable Mr. Rumford; Sir Roland George setting up two mistresses in the same house; and Lord Whitney Wyld reputedly being caught with his brother's fiancée in a cupboard.

But Caro saved the best for last—an honest-to-goodness divorce, involving not just anyone but one of the country's richest heiresses and a duke's heir, said to be worth a mint himself. Caro wrote giddily and at length of the marchioness's determination to marry her young admirer, the marquess's cryptic intentions, and the wild conjectures circulating about town concerning the outcome of the case. They had put on a most amicable front before others, but behind closed doors what was taking place? Were they poisoning each other's coffee? Each spreading false rumors about the other? Or, unlikely but not impossible, sharing a giggle together at the expense of that dunce Lord Frederick Stuart?

The Railroad Heiress, Caro had called the Marchioness of Tremaine. The Railroad Heiress who almost married a duke, then managed to marry her dead fiancé's cousin within an indecently short period, but never got to wear a coronet of strawberry leaves.

He frowned and suddenly realized where he had seen Mrs. Rowland before. Right there, on that same country lane, before that same cottage.

It must have been a good thirty years ago. He had been home on holiday from Eton, bored out of his mind, itching to do something wild and stupid but not quite wanting the news of it to get back to his parents.

His father had been bedridden for several years and would die in a few weeks. But Langford hadn't known that at the time. He resented his sire's interminable, and seemingly pointless, illness. At school he could slur against the pall that hung permanently over Ludlow Court by making savage jokes involving his useless father's bodily output and the middle-aged, round-faced nursemaid who handled the effluvia with what he considered obscene good cheer. At home he had no such recourse. He could only try to distance himself from the house as much and as often as possible.

So he undertook long daily walks. And it was on one of those walks that he saw her, emerging from the cottage to a waiting barouche in the lane.

She had been jaw-droppingly beautiful. Having lost his virginity a few months before, he considered himself sophisticated. But he gawked. Not only were her features lovely, her figure was divine. She moved with the grace of a nymph and the fluidity of a Nereid.

A man he thought to be her father climbed into the open carriage after her. But then a second man, gray-haired and stooped, approached the carriage. She leaned out and kissed him on the cheek. "Good-bye, Father."

She was on his mind quite a bit in the following days. He found out that she was indeed married to someone twice her age, a man who manufactured rails and industrial machinery. A shame, he thought, though why it was a shame he never explored. He certainly had no intention of marrying her, though he would have loved to seduce her.

Then his father died, and guilt consumed him. She faded from memory. He embarked on the life of a rogue until he returned to Devon. How long had she been back? They had lived as neighbors for years without the least neighborly interaction.

Until now. Until she'd barged into his path with all the subtlety of an avalanche. He had wondered that he let himself be drawn into her schemes with so little resistance. Perhaps some part of him had recognized her before his conscious mind did. Perhaps the Fates were up to their old tricks. Or perhaps he was simply a man deprived of feminine contacts and she was still the most beautiful woman he'd ever seen.

* * *

Victoria was learning far more than she wanted about the Duke of Perrin.

She had a cordial but frustrating dinner with Camden at her London hotel. The boy was slippery as an eel and gave her elegant answers that upon further reflection contained exactly nothing of substance.

After Camden left, she took herself to the theater, where she was most enthusiastically accosted by Lady Avery and her sister, Lady Somersby, two women with whom she had the most incidental acquaintance. They were, of course, after news of Gigi.

Victoria obliged. She told them that Gigi was having second thoughts. Who wouldn't? Just look at Lord Tremaine. Lady Avery and Lady Somersby concurred, the latter waving her handkerchief emphatically. Lord Tremaine was divine, simply divine. She also told them that Camden was working subtly to regain Gigi. No, not that he'd confess any such thing to her, but he did dine with her this evening—so genial of him—and she saw no hurry on his part to proceed with the divorce. In fact, the two of them were coming to visit her very soon at her cottage.

Well, she wasn't obliged to tell them any truth, was she?

So delighted were Ladies Avery and Somersby with the "intelligence" she provided that they invited her to sit in their box. Still peeved with Gigi, Victoria agreed.

"We see far too little of you in town," Lady Somersby lamented halfway through the second act of *Rigoletto*.

"I suppose it's because Devon is infinitely more beautiful."

"Our cousin lives in Devon!" exclaimed Lady Avery.

"That's right," agreed Lady Somersby. "Where is he exactly?"

"Between Totnes and a little village called Stoke Gabriel," Lady Avery said. "You must have heard of him, Mrs. Rowland. Our cousin is the Duke of Perrin."

For once, Victoria wasn't certain what to say. "Ah, yes, I might have heard of him."

"How could you not?" Lady Somersby giggled. "Gracious me, I do miss that dear boy. Kept us busy, didn't he, in his day."

"Do you remember the time he won ten thousand pounds in one night, and lost twelve thousand the next, and then won another nine thousand the third night?"

"Oh, yes. But he still came out seven thousand pounds ahead. So he bought himself a new set of matched bays and leased all of Madame Mignonne's girls for a sennight."

"What about that brawl over him, between that American woman and Lady Harriet Blakeley? They slapped each other like two fishwives. And then the two of them found out he was also having a liaison with Lady Fancot!"

"Surely . . ." Victoria mumbled. "Surely these rumors are much exaggerated."

Lady Somersby and Lady Avery exchanged a look, as if Victoria had suggested that the Prince of Wales was a lily-white virgin. "My dear Mrs. Rowland," Lady Somersby said, every syllable drawn out for emphasis. "*These* are not rumors. These events happened as we pronounced, their truths as indubitable as those of the Scripture. If we wished to traffic in rumors, we'd have told you about what we have heard concerning his affair with Lady Fancot."

Lady Avery nodded gleefully. "Ropes, whips, chains, and items whose descriptions are quite beyond us, except that they are of foreign manufacture and iniquitous nature."

Victoria felt slightly ill. To be sure, Gigi was no shrinking violet. But ropes, whips, chains, and those... other things!

Then she remembered to her horror that she still owed the Duke of Perrin an evening of gambling, just the two of them, across a card table. Had he some ulterior motive other than a yen for the dubious excitement of betting? Did he mean to truss her up with her own curtain sashes and... and what?

She whimpered.

"Exactly," Lady Avery said with no little satisfaction. "And we won't even mention the time he set Lady Wimpey's bed on fire."

Chapter Fourteen

Gigi jerked awake in the small hours of the morning, gasping and covered in cold perspiration. In her dream, she had been running in her nightgown, chasing after something in the dark, screaming, "Come back! Come back to me!"

Was it an ill omen, this dream? Or was it her conscience, festering in the dungeon of the past three weeks, finally breaking out of captivity and, spitting mad, coming to settle the score with her?

She touched the engagement ring Camden had given her. It was reassuringly snug on her finger, the gold band as warm as her own skin, the facets of the sapphire cool as silk. At the foot of her bed, Croesus snorted in his padded wicker tray. She scooted until her head was level with his. He smelled clean and warm. She took hold of one of his paws and felt some of the fear drain out of her.

She let herself breathe again. All was well. And who

needed a conscience when she had happiness by the bushel?

Right?

Hell did not begin to describe it.

Camden stood at the center of a maelstrom of joy and goodwill, drowning. The ceremony. The unending congratulations. The wedding breakfast. The flash and bang of the photographer recording the occasion for all posterity. So much laughter. So much cheer. So much genuine pleasure all around. He felt a complete fraud, a bigger fraud than she, if that was possible.

Several times his will nearly broke. People were happy for him. For them. Mrs. Rowland had tears in her eyes. So did Claudia. Surrounded by a sea of tulle and organza, with Briarmeadow decked to the rafters in daffodils and tulips, as fragrant as the first day of spring, they thought it a fairy tale still, the one marriage of convenience out of thousands so fortunate as to become a blissful, devoted union. The weight of his deception choked him.

It was she, in the end, who salvaged his iniquitous intentions, she with her radiance that struck him a physical blow every time he looked upon her. Every ebullient, cocksure smile from her was a little death for him, every mirthful giggle a stab in the heart.

Even so, he almost couldn't.

After the reception, they traveled fifteen miles to another Rowland house nearer to Bedford for their wedding night. The two of them, alone—if one didn't count

Croesus—in the oppressive confines of the brougham. Giddy and loquacious from the champagne, his new wife strategized the surprise reception that they would throw for his friends.

The apartment her agent had found for them in the Quartier Latin, overlooking Rue Mouffetard, had ten rooms. How many people did he think could fit into such an apartment? Would her governess-taught French suffice for the evening's conversation? And if they served foie gras and caviar, perhaps his friends might not notice that they had hardly any furniture?

Her childish enthusiasm for the life that they would never share clawed at him with a ferocity he did not want to understand. An incandescent light illuminated her eyes, a light of hope and fervor. It made her intoxicating, enchanting, beautiful, despite *everything* he knew, despite the effrontery and selfishness that were the warp and woof of her corrupt femininity.

He wanted to violate her then, to assert his power over her in the crudest, foulest manner, to crush her and snuff that lovely light. It would have been malevolent, but honest, to a degree.

He held back because of his own reciprocal corruptness. It would have been too easy for her. Shattering, yes, but shattering all at once. He did not want that. He did not want her to recognize the beast in him. He wanted her to panic, to despair, but to still want him, still think him the most perfect man that ever lived.

That was how he would go on tormenting her, after his physical departure from her life. A baroque plan, byzantine even, a plan that both pleased and shamed him.

He awaited only the night, this one grotesque, terrible night.

Camden was drinking cognac directly from a decanter when the connecting door between the bedchambers opened. He turned around and took another swig, barely feeling the fire sliding down his throat.

She was swathed in a blaze of virginal white. But her hair, a great glossy mass of it, tumbled free and unbound, like a cascade of the river Styx. The tips of her toes, round and pretty, peeked out from the hem of the white robe. He suddenly felt drunk.

"You didn't come," she said softly, plaintively.

He glanced at the clock on the mantel. It had been only a few minutes since her maid had left. "I made a bet with myself that you'd come for me first."

"You made me nervous," she said, twirling one end of the silk sash that held her robe together. "I thought..." Her voice trailed off.

"What did you think?"

"I was afraid you might be having second thoughts."

A ray of hope pierced him. If she confessed now, if she was drowning in remorse, rightfully fearful but still courageous enough to admit what she had done and take responsibility, he would forgive her. Not in an instant, but he would. And in return, he would come clean about his own fiendish plot.

"Why would you think that?" he said.

Do the right thing, Gigi. Do the right thing.

She hesitated. For a fleeting instant, she looked conflicted and frightened. But in the next moment, she was again in control of herself, a young Cleopatra out for her own best advantage. Her eyes traveled down his person and slowly back up again. "Wedding-night jitters, I suppose. Nothing more."

Instead of honesty, she had fallen back on that old cliché: feminine wiles. She thought him so stupid that he'd go on in an erotic daze and never notice that he sported an ass's head.

Rage, great and raw, exploded in him. He tossed aside the decanter. In a heartbeat, he'd already covered half the distance between them. He was going to dangle her lying, scheming rump out the window until she screamed, begged, and sobbed the truth at last.

She opened her robe and let it fall. Beneath the robe she wore a chemise as transparent as a water goblet, a layer of gossamer that hid nothing.

He stopped and stared, his body reacting instantly. She was a pornographer's dream: high, firm breasts, rosy nipples pointed at a man's eyes, miles of legs, and hips that flared decadently, magnificently, hips meant for a man's hard grasp as he drove himself full hilt into her.

You bitch, he thought, in a dozen languages. *You prick.* That was for himself. The die was cast at last, the choice finally made. The high roads would be deserted and untrod. He had embarked on the path to purgatory.

Fire blazed in the grate, but the English winter crept damp and insidious along walls and floors. He closed the distance between them. "Come to bed," he said, taking her by the wrist. "You must be cold."

Beneath the pad of his index finger, her pulse raced madly—her mind was cold and calculating, but her blood certainly ran hot. She followed him obediently and let him usher her up the stool and under the bedspread.

She sat straight against a mound of pillows, the bedspread reaching only slightly past her abdomen. Her gaze flitted to him, then darted to a corner of the room. Her fingers clutched the covers.

What was she afraid of now? Solomon himself could not discern Camden's ultimate goals, so eclipsed were they by the inferno of lust that threatened to flame out of control.

Understanding dawned with all the gentleness of an artillery-shell impact. She was nervous because she was a virgin, and this would be her first time with a man. He almost laughed. How normal. How charming. How frigging sweet.

God help him.

He undressed slowly, shedding honor and rectitude alongside waistcoat and shirt. Her curiosity must have prevailed over her uncharacteristic shyness, for she watched him as if he were the very miracle for which she'd spent a lifetime on her knees, devoutly praying.

Don't look at me like that! he wanted to bellow. *I am as unprincipled, disingenuous, and blackhearted as you. More, if anything. God, don't look at me like that.* But she did, her eyes shining with the kind of trust and devotion that hadn't been seen since the Age of Chivalry.

He climbed onto the treacherously soft bed on the side away from her and sat as she did, upright, a wall of pillows behind his back, the bedspread drawn over his trousers. For once, he wished he'd debauched his way through St. Petersburg, Berlin, and Paris. His body burned with hellfire, but his mind was an abysmal blank. How did one make love, exactly, to a girl one despised with greater intensity than all the love in the world put together?

She cleared her throat. "Would you...uh...be needing a nightshirt?"

He chuckled despite himself, and the answer came to him. The only way to do it was to make love to her as if the past thirty hours had never taken place, as if his heart still overflowed with optimism and tenderness.

He slid a strand of her hair between his unsteady fingers. It was as cool as well water. He lifted it and pressed it to his lips, inhaling its sweet cleanness, as fragrant as a blade of young leaf. "No, thank you," he said. "I don't think I'll need a nightshirt tonight."

She cleared her throat again, more softly. "Well, then, should we say our prayers and go to sleep?"

He laughed. Frightening how easy it was to slip back into the earlier hours of the day before, to be amused and delighted with her every utterance. He gathered her to him, kissed her, and tasted the lingering astringency of her tooth powder, flavored with sweet birch oil.

Her mouth was all warm eagerness. Her hair cascaded over his arm and chest, jolting him with its featherlight caresses. And her scent. He was driven to distraction by the fiendish freshness of her skin, as wholesome as new milk that still faintly steamed.

He would never have her again. Never. The realization bludgeoned him. The unfairness of it. He wanted to smash the bed, the windowpanes, the fireplace. He wanted to shake her until her thick skull rattled. *What have you done to me? What have you done to us?*

Instead, he became slower, more gentle, more tender. He kissed every square inch of her face and undressed and worshipped every undulation of her body. The satiny texture of her nipples was the sweetest thing he'd ever tasted, the moans of her pleasure the most melodious sounds to ever vibrate the air of this earth.

And how she responded to him. She was a schoolboy's wet dream come to life, fervent, willing, all but trembling with desire. Her hands roved avid and avaricious, searing him with their unchaste touches. Her mouth followed her hands, nibbling, licking, loving every nook and cranny of his body.

When he at last entered her, she branded him with her scorching heat. His invasion hurt her. He apologized incoherently, barely comprehending his hypocrisy—he was despondent at causing her physical pain, yet he looked forward with savagery to breaking her spirit.

To slide completely into her, to penetrate those silken, strong walls of her sheath, with her gasps and whimpers and little breaths of "yes" and "more" scalding his ears, was to lose a bit of his mind each time. He whispered sweet nothings into her ear, words both reverent and wicked, and ate up her moans of arousal. He touched her where he filled her, reveled in her melted-butter sleekness, and loved the frenzy it drove her into.

If only the pain in his heart didn't multiply a little with each thrust, each caress, each endearment. But pleasure swelled and roiled through him despite his desolation. Her rich voluptuousness possessed him. Conquered and defeated him. When she wrapped her long legs entirely about him, he lost his last shred of control.

The sensations walloped him, keener, wilder, more powerfully delicious than any he'd known or even imagined. He gave in, surrendered, only vaguely aware of his grunts and imprecations, of the heavy motions of his body as he ground into her, emptied into her.

"Oh, God, Gigi," he mumbled. "Gigi."

There, he'd done it. The most despicable act of his life. Now she would go to sleep, leaving him to stare at the ceiling for the rest of the night. He would rise before dawn, dismiss the servants for the day, and deal with her as necessary in the cold light of morning.

But she didn't go to sleep. She clung to him, rained kisses upon his shoulder and arm, giggled, and said, "Do it again."

And he was rock hard again, just like that.

As he turned to her, in stupefied desire, in craving that corroded him from the inside out, he saw the enormity of his mistake. He hadn't embarked on the path to purgatory. He had knocked on the gates of hell.

Chapter Fifteen

Gigi prepared the Dutch cap with a French ointment. She had obtained both the day after her husband's return, at the shop of a very discreet chemist not far from Piccadilly Circus. The ointment promised to greatly reduce the potency of a man's ejaculate, and the cap should block what could not be weakened.

With the Dutch cap lodged in place, she donned the blue chemise she had pulled out from the bottom of a chest. *"Très special,"* the Parisienne who'd sold it to her had said, and winked at her. It was special because most chemises did not have a décolletage that formed a saddle beneath the breasts, pushing them up high and bare for a man's delectation.

The silk smelled of the sachets of dried lavender that had been packed with it. She had bought it eons ago, before she gave up on Camden. She no longer remembered why she hadn't gotten rid of it.

The chemise, alas, did not feel seductive, only grimly ridiculous. But she had to put some effort into it, had to do *something*. She pulled on a robe and left her dressing room, praying that whatever valor she mustered would be enough to see her through the humiliation of the night.

Croesus was there, sleeping in his basket next to her bed. She crouched down and touched his head, running her fingers through his soft fur. The connecting door between her bedroom and Camden's opened. Camden stepped in.

Except for his shoes, he was fully dressed, as if he had just returned from a night on the town. Her heart lurched. She supposed it was because he was as beautiful as an avenging angel. Because he had been her first love. And—added her cynical voice—because she couldn't have him.

She slowly straightened, tightening the belt on her robe as she rose. "My lord Tremaine, what brings you to my lair of vices?"

"I had dinner with your mother." He set down a book on her vanity table. "She wants you to have this book."

She barely glanced at the book. "Surely that could wait 'til tomorrow."

The corners of his lips lifted, reminding her of the way he used to smile at her, in those antediluvian days. She had ribbed him for smiling too much, for not being thin-lipped and icy-miened enough for all his aristocratic lineage. "I suppose it could have waited," he said. "But as I was coming this way anyway..."

Given all his avowals of aversion and antipathy, she

could scarcely believe what she was hearing. "I thought you couldn't stand bedding me."

"I asked myself, who am I to stand in the way of your effulgent future happiness?"

She should be relieved. She should be leaping and cartwheeling, she who had been pushing him from day one. Yet a mixture of chagrin and panic suddenly assaulted her. She could not take it. She could not bear for him to touch her tonight. She had to fight not to step back and put greater distance between them.

"I'm surprised you haven't broken out in boils at the mere prospect of it."

"I have a slop bucket ready in my room," he said. "You will excuse me if I rush back afterward. Now, shall we?"

Belatedly, she remembered her *"très spécial"* chemise. She didn't want him to see it. "The light switch is behind you."

He shook his head. "I don't want to accidentally step on Croesus. Or grope for the door on my way out, in"—he looked at the clock—"three minutes."

Three minutes. Had they come to this? Unbidden, the memories of her wedding night returned. He had stoked the fires of her desire with such exquisite patience, such finely attuned caresses, that she had literally trembled with the force of her need.

He was suddenly before her, separated from her by nothing but a sliver of air. His hand went to the belt of her robe.

"No!" She gripped his wrist. "There is no need."

His gaze made her feel about as desirable as a barnyard sow. "It's nothing personal. A view of breasts and buttocks moves the process along."

"Let me go to my dressing room for a minute, and then—"

He tugged at the belt. It came loose, and the front of her robe fell open, exposing the injudicious chemise.

If she were truly the woman of infinite cheekiness he believed her to be, she'd thrust out her chest and stare him straight in the eye. But all she could think of were the chilly spring nights in Paris, during those months when she had repeatedly thrown herself at him, wearing equally salacious bits of lace and satin. What had he said the last time he dragged her out of his garret and threw her coat at her? *You look like a tenpenny whore.*

And still she had gone back, only to see him admit a woman beautiful enough to shame the stars. She had stood on the stair landing below his door, stunned, as if he had grabbed her head and slammed it into a wall.

Slowly, almost gently, he drew her robe closed. But his eyes were ungentle. "Did you really expect it to change my mind?"

She shrugged, a bit of her defiance returning. "No. But I would do anything to marry Freddie."

Abruptly, he reached forward and lifted her. She gasped, but he had already set her down again, with her back against a bedpost. He leaned into her, every inch of his body pressed into hers. With a blaze of heat like rivulets of molten ore, she realized that he was full hard against her.

He lowered his head toward hers, as if he were inhaling her. Her heart pounded painfully. When his breath caressed the helix of her ear, she nearly jumped. But he only said, "Poor Lord Frederick. What did he do to deserve you?"

She felt his fingers work the fastening of his trousers. Without once touching her skin, he separated her robe below the belt and lifted the hem of her chemise. Which made it all the more shocking as his erection came into contact with her bare abdomen. He was burning hot.

She closed her eyes and turned her face away from him. But she could not block the sensations he provoked. He entered her with an ease that shamed her, long, slow thrusts that had her clenching at her robe, the wretchedness in her heart cutting deeper with each flare of pleasure.

The slight catch in his breath, the sudden pressure of his hands on her hips, and the abrupt stillness of his lower body signaled his release. He withdrew. Fifteen seconds later he was already walking away from her. She opened her eyes to see him stooping over Croesus's sleeping form. He touched one of the old dog's ears, then moved on, opening and closing the door behind him with barely a sound.

She looked at the clock. Exactly three minutes had passed.

This was what they had come to.

Chapter Sixteen

Gigi awoke to a room awash in pallid light. The clock read half past nine. She bolted straight up— and had to hurriedly gather an armful of bedspread to cover her nakedness. Good heavens! They were supposed to depart for Bedford at nine o'clock, to begin their journey to Paris.

She scrambled out of bed, shrugged into the robe that still lay in a heap on the Kashmiri rug, ran into the mistress's bedroom, and pulled the cord for hot water. Her traveling gown had already been set out the night before. She pulled on drawers, a merino-wool combination, an underchemise, a chemise, and stepped into her pantalettes, two layers of woolen petticoats, and a dress petticoat with an embroidered, scalloped hem.

The next item was her corset. She stopped. Granted, she'd dressed with exceptional speed. But still her maid should have arrived already, hot water in tow. Perhaps she'd made a wrong turn in an unfamiliar house.

She tackled the corset, straining her arms to pull the

laces tight through each set of steel-reinforced eyelets, twisting her neck to check her progress in the mirror.

The door opened.

"Hurry, Edie!" she cried. "I needed to be dressed two hours ago."

It wasn't Edie. It was Camden, all ready to go, looking as if he'd just descended from Mt. Olympus, cool, serene, and perfect. Whereas she was in a disgraceful state of dishabille, her hair a wild disarray.

But he'd already seen her in much less, hadn't he? She'd been a complete wanton, curious and rapacious, and he...well, he hadn't seemed to mind at all. They'd made delicious love well into the small hours of the morning.

"Hullo, Camden," she said, feeling unusually shy. Her cheeks were hot, her throat and belly too.

"Hullo, Gigi," he replied. He had lost all traces of his accent during the past month. Now he sounded as if he had been born and raised in the queen's household.

She struggled a little over what to say, gave up, and smiled at him instead. "Sorry. I will be ready in a minute. Then we can leave."

He studied her, his face serious, his eyes opaque. "Can you manage that by yourself?"

Without waiting for a reply, he came to her aid, turning her around and applying himself to the intricacies of her corset. She sucked in a breath, held it, and admired his progress in the mirror. He had such a light yet sure touch, his hands as dexterous as those of Apollo himself. She loved admiring him, a divine sensation, all joy and breathless pride.

"Done," he said.

She spun around, but he turned away just as she was about to reach for him. She hesitated. Perhaps he did not see her outstretched hand. She grabbed a hairbrush instead. "I don't know why my maid isn't here yet. I've only the most rudimentary idea how to manage my hair."

He stood gazing out a window that overlooked the park behind the house. "No hurry, take your time. I gave the staff the day off. We are not leaving."

"But you are already late for your classes." She dragged the brush through her tangled hair. "The train doesn't depart Bedford 'til half past one. We still have plenty of time."

His lips curved into something that resembled a smile but wasn't. "Perhaps I didn't make myself clear. I didn't say *I* was not leaving."

Many years ago, at a family gathering, one of her cousins had pulled the chair out from under her as she was sitting down. Though the fall had been less than two feet, the collision had jolted every organ inside her body.

She felt like that now, a moment of physical jarring and utter disorientation. "I beg your pardon?"

"I thought I'd come and say good-bye before I left," he said, as if he wasn't proposing to do something as absurd as leaving her the day after their wedding, *the morning after the most memorable wedding night in history.*

"What?" she cried stupidly, too stunned to think.

He glanced at her. His eyes glittered with something she couldn't read, something frightening. "I thought it was always the plan, that we go separate ways after we consummated our marriage, until it was time for heirs."

An utterly asinine response formed in her head. *Don't you know anything about contracts?* she wanted to ask him. *You turned down my offer, therefore that offer no longer stands. This marriage is contracted on an entirely different set of premises.*

"What—what about our reception?" She hated how baffled and despondent she sounded. But she could not grasp how he could have been that devoted, tender lover only hours ago and now speak as if he had never meant for it to be more than a marriage of convenience. Why, then, had he come to see her every day of their engagement? Why had he made plans with her for the future? What about the engagement ring that sparkled upon her finger? What about Croesus?

"There will be no reception," he said.

"But we've already decided on the menu, and the wines . . ." She took a deep breath. *Stop. Stop all that blabbering.*

A new emotion invaded her, a fast-spreading, horrified anger. She'd been played for a dupe. He had never been interested in anything but her money. All the sweet, joyful hours they had shared was but his way of insuring that she did not change her mind on him. She slammed down the brush.

"This is very new to me. I have been under the impression that we were going to live together after our wedding. My mother and I have authorized a good deal of financial outlay to secure us an apartment and a staff in Paris, to ship over my furniture, to"—suddenly she could not bring herself to mention the Érard piano that she had ordered for him—"I'm sure you get the idea. Important decisions have been made on the assumption that I could trust you, that you have acted *in good faith.*"

Calmly, he listened to her tirade, her lecture. Then he turned around and picked up a porcelain figurine of a giggling girl from the vanity table. For one terrifying moment, his eyes burned, and she was sure he was going to throw the thing at her. But he set it down, without a sound. "Have *you* acted in good faith?"

She opened her mouth, but her reply withered before his stare. She had no idea he could look at anyone, much less at her, like that. It was the gaze of Achilles the man-killer just before he slaughtered Hector, a gaze that held nothing but blood rage.

It scared her all the more that he seemed otherwise as collected and civil as he had ever been.

"I . . . I don't know what you are talking about."

"Don't you? I find it surprising. How do you forget your own schemes?"

The deafening cacophony in her head was the crashing of her happiness, that grand, shiny edifice that she had built upon a foundation of quicksand. She swallowed, trying to stay above the bog of despair.

"I'm curious about one thing. Where did you find a forger? Did you have to wade into a den of confidence artists? Or are they to be had everywhere in Bedfordshire?"

"My gamekeeper at Briarmeadow was a forger in his youth," she answered numbly, not realizing until it was too late that she had negated his last doubts, if he had any.

"I see. Quite clever of you."

"How...how long have you known?" she asked, as composedly as she could.

"Since yesterday afternoon."

She reeled. *When you make a pact with the devil,* her father had often told her, *the devil is the only one who comes out ahead.* Would that she'd listened.

He smiled coldly. "Excellent. I'm glad we cleared any and all misunderstandings about our respective good faith on this matter," he said. "I'm sure you understand now why I will be leaving without you."

Intellectually, perhaps. But viscerally, all she knew was that she loved him and he loved her.

"I know you are angry with me now," she said, her voice as tentative as a mouse tiptoeing around a cat. "Would it be all right if I joined you in Paris in two weeks, when you—"

"No."

The finality of his response chilled her. But she would not give up so easily. "You are right, of course. Two weeks does not amount to much time. Would two—"

"No."

"But we are married!" she cried in frustration. "We can't carry on like this."

"I beg to differ. We certainly can. Separate lives mean separate lives."

She hated pleading. She made sure she always dealt from a position of strength, even with her own mother. But what else could she do now? "Please don't. Please don't decide all of our future this moment. Please! Is there anything I can do to change your mind?"

The contempt in his eyes made her feel like something that had just oozed out of a badly mildewed wall. "You can start by offering me an apology, which both decency and good manners require here."

She could have slapped herself. Of course he'd want her to grovel for forgiveness. Her pride, large and thorny, was difficult to swallow, but she forced it. For him. Because she loved him and she could not lose him. "I'm sorry. I really am terribly, terribly sorry."

He was silent for a moment. "Are you? Are you really? Or are you only sorry that you are caught?"

What was the difference? If she hadn't been caught, would an apology even be needed? "For what I did," she said, because that was probably the answer he wanted to hear.

"Stop lying to me." He said each word separately— *Stop. Lying. To. Me.*—as if he ground his teeth as he spoke.

"But I really am sorry." Her voice trembled and she was powerless over it. "I am. Please believe me."

"You are not. You are sorry that I won't continue to be your dupe, that I won't take you at your word, and that you will be left behind with none of that perfect married life that you thought you were getting."

Her anger abruptly rose to the fore again. Why had he asked for an apology when he had no intention of accepting any? Why had he forced her to abase herself for nothing at all? "Perhaps I wouldn't have had to do any of this if you hadn't been as dense as a peat bog. I've met Miss von Schweppenburg. I don't know what you see in her, but she would have made you about as happy as a drowned cat. And she never would have married you anyway. She is her mother's puppet. She has less spine than a bowl of trifle and—"

"That's enough," he said, his voice dangerously smooth. "Now, was that so hard, a bit of honesty?"

She suddenly felt wildly stupid, ranting on about Miss von Schweppenburg, of all people.

"I wish you well," he said. "But I would prefer not to see you again, not in two months, two years, or two decades."

It finally occurred to her that he was dead serious. That what she had done was something hideous, beyond the pale. Unforgivable.

She raced ahead of him and blocked the door with her body. "Please, please, please listen to me. I cannot bear the thought of living without you."

"Bear it," he said grimly. "You'll live. Now kindly move out of my way."

"But you don't understand. I love you."

"Love?" he sneered. "So it's love now, is it? You mean to tell me that love drove you crazed with longing, thereby smashing your moral compass and whipping you down the primrose path?"

She flinched. He had taken the words she meant to say and slapped her with them.

Slowly, he advanced toward her. For the first time in her life, she shrank before another human being. But she refused to move aside, refused to let him simply sail on out of her life. Bracing his arms on either side of her, he brought his face very close to hers and fixed her with a brutal stare. "I wish you hadn't mentioned love, Lady Tremaine." His voice was low, and cold as ashes. "Right now I am this close to throwing you against the wall. Again, and again, and again."

She whimpered.

"It so happens that I know a thing or two about not-quite-requited love, my dear. It so happens that I have lived in that state for a while. I have not seduced Theodora so that she must marry me. I have not misrepresented my fortune. I have not forged some letter that declared my cousin's sudden death, clearing a path to the ducal title for myself. And when she writes me and tells me of her mother berating her because she is ineffectual with potential suitors, do you think I write back informing her that she must regale them with her fear of childbirth and her dislike for running a household?

"No, I tell her if she cannot look them in the eyes, she can look at the ridges of their noses and chances are they won't know the difference. I tell her that smiling with her head lowered is almost as good as smiling with her face raised to someone, perhaps even more alluring. And do you know why I give advice that is contrary to my own interests in the matter?"

She shook her head miserably, wishing time to go back, wishing all her crimes undone. She didn't want to hear about Theodora, didn't want to be reminded that he remained above reproach while she had stooped to swindling.

But he went on inexorably. "Because she trusts me and I do *not* abuse her trust to further my chances with her. Because *being in love does not give you any excuse to be less than honorable*, Lady Tremaine."

He pulled back from her abruptly, his breathing uneven. "You may think you are in love, Gigi, but I doubt very much that you know what love is. Because it has been all about you, what *you* want, what *you* need, what *you* can and cannot do without."

He moved further away. Too late did Gigi remember that the bedchamber had two doors.

He opened the second door and left without another word.

And she could only watch as he disappeared from her view, from her life.

Chapter Seventeen

He had not done too badly, considering the ungodly chemise she had sported. The jolt of lust had been explosive, the jolt of anger almost nonexistent.

I must be getting mellow with age, Camden mused. How he used to fly into a righteous rage when she'd barge her way into his cramped apartment in Paris, then fling aside her long mantle to reveal bits of provocative nothing that would have made the Marquis de Sade drop his whip in stupefaction.

The insult. That she believed he'd let his penis control his mind, that if she could get him to bed, all would be forgiven. He had bleakly delighted in hauling her bodily out to the stair landing and slamming his door in her face. But such vicious enjoyment never lasted long. Over his own pounding heartbeat and harsh breathing, he'd strain to hear every lonely, echoing footstep of her descent.

He'd already be standing by the window in his dark, minuscule *salle de séjour* as she exited into the street.

She'd look up, her face all adolescent anger and bewildered pain, her person stooped and small in the light of the streetlamp. Something inside him broke, without fail, each time.

The night he'd hired Mlle. Flandin had been the worst. What had he said to Gigi just before he closed the door on her? *Don't be so cheaply available if you want me. Go home. If I want you, I know where you are.*

He must have waited at the window for an hour, his anger deteriorating into a corrosive anxiety. Yet his pride forbade that he should give in, walk out of his apartment, and make sure she hadn't fallen down a flight of steps. Eventually she'd emerged on the sidewalk, head down, shoulders hunched, like a battered camp follower. She did not look up at his window as she walked away, she and her lengthening shadow.

Three days later he heard that she had packed up and returned to England. How easily she gave up. He got drunk for the first time in his life, a hideous experience that he would not repeat for another two years, until the day he learned that she had miscarried weeks following their wedding.

He checked his watch again. Fourteen hours and fifty-five minutes before he could have her again.

Someone addressed him by his title. He glanced about the park and saw a woman waving at him from atop a handsome victoria that she drove herself. She wore a dove-gray morning gown and a matching hat atop her dark chestnut hair. Lady Wrenworth. He raised his hand and returned the salute.

They shook hands as he maneuvered his horse into a trot alongside her carriage.

"You are up early, my lord Tremaine," said Lady Wrenworth.

"I prefer the park with the morning mist still in the branches. Is Lord Wrenworth well?"

"He has been quite well since you last saw him yesterday afternoon." Flecks of slyness flavored her reply. It seemed that Lord Wrenworth had married no empty-headed beauty. He supposed she was the best Wrenworth could do after Gigi. "And my lady Tremaine?"

"As unfashionably hale as ever, from what I observed last night." He let a moment pass, during which Lady Wrenworth's eyes widened, before adding, "At dinner."

"And did you take the opportunity to observe the stars too last night? They were out en masse."

It took him a second to remember his glib assertion that he was indeed an amateur astronomer on the night he and the Wrenworths had first been introduced. "I'm afraid I'm more of an armchair enthusiast."

"Most of Society to this day hasn't the slightest clue about Lord Wrenworth's precise fields of study. And I'm ashamed to confess that I myself had no idea of his scientific pursuits until well after we were married. How did you become familiar with his publications, my lord, if you don't mind my curiosity?"

How? *My daughter has not been quite herself since her unfortunate miscarriage in March two years ago. But her recent friendship with Lord Wrenworth has had quite a salubrious effect on her.*

"I read scientific and technological papers as a matter of course, both to gratify my interest and to keep up with the latest advances." Quite honest so far. "One simply cannot mistake Lord Wrenworth's brilliance."

The second part wasn't a lie either. Lord Wrenworth was, without a doubt, brilliant. But he was but one bright star in a galaxy of luminaries, in an age when advances in human understanding and machine prowess came fast and furious. Camden would not have singled him out had he not been Gigi's first paramour.

"Thank you." Lady Wrenworth glowed. "I quite share that opinion."

She drove off with a friendly wave.

Fourteen hours and forty-three minutes. Would this day never pass?

"I beg your pardon, Lady Tremaine."

Gigi paused in her search for Freddie amid the throng at the Carlisles'. "Miss Carlisle."

"Freddie asked me to tell you that he is in the garden," said Miss Carlisle. "Behind the rose trellis."

Gigi almost laughed. Only Freddie would think it necessary to mention—to a woman who secretly loved him, no less—that he'd be "behind the rose trellis," a spot of seclusion highly conducive to behavior not countenanced inside the ballroom. "Thank you, though perhaps he shouldn't have troubled you."

"It's no trouble," Miss Carlisle said softly.

Miss Carlisle was more handsome than pretty, but she had bright eyes and a sharp, quick wit. At twenty-three, she was in her fourth season and widely believed by many to have no real interest in matrimony, since she would come into control of a comfortable inheritance on her twenty-fifth birthday and since she had turned down any and all proposals directed her way.

Would Miss Carlisle still be unmarried today if Freddie hadn't fallen head-over-heels in love with Gigi's art collection? Freddie believed he and Gigi to be kindred spirits who felt keenly the passage of time, the loss of a gently fading spring, and the inexplicability of life's joys and pains, when ironically she had bought the paintings solely in the hope of pleasing and mollifying Camden.

Why had she never told him that she preferred the future to the past and rarely bothered about the meaning of life? She felt a rush of guilt. If she had, today Freddie probably would be engaged to Miss Carlisle, a woman with a clear conscience, rather than to Gigi, who, behind his back, allowed another man to have his way with her.

Could she claim martyrdom and higher purpose when she didn't unequivocally hate the swift coupling between Camden and herself? She hadn't even thought of poor Freddie until this morning.

She found Freddie pacing in the middle of the diminutive garden, having left his roost behind the rose trellis.

"Philippa!" He came forward and placed his evening jacket about her shoulders, enveloping her in his generous warmth and a strong waft of turpentine.

She glanced at him. "Have you been painting in your good clothes again?"

"No, but I spilled some sauce on myself at dinner," he answered sheepishly. "The butler cleaned it. Did a very decent job too."

She slid her knuckle against his cheek. "We really should have some jackets made out of oilcloth for you."

"Wouldn't you know it?" he cried. "That's what my mother used to say."

She started. Had she been patronizing? Or condescending? It hadn't felt that way.

"Do you know what Angelica said to me?" Freddie asked her gleefully. "She said a man my age ought to have more care. She also said that I'm dawdling because I'm scared my next work won't turn out any good, that I should get off my lazy posterior and put paint to canvas."

They rounded the rose trellis and sat down on the discreetly placed bench, the one on which Miss Carlisle was supposed to receive her wedding proposals. Freddie chuckled. "I know you said she thinks well of me. But she certainly doesn't sound that way tonight."

Gigi frowned. The only painting Freddie had finished in '92 hung in her bedchamber. She always asked about his progress on his next painting, but she'd never paid any substantial attention to his creativity, considering it little more than a hobby, a gentlemanly amusement.

Miss Carlisle saw it differently. Miss Carlisle saw Freddie differently. Gigi was happy to indulge Freddie's absentmindedness and artistic hesitations—as long as he adored her, she didn't care if he lolled on the chaise longue and ate bonbons from sunrise to sunset. But Miss Carlisle saw a diamond in the rough, a man who could make quite something of himself if he but put in the effort.

Was Gigi's affection for Freddie purer or more self-serving? Or perhaps, more to the point, wouldn't Freddie prefer to have made something of his talents?

Freddie rested his head against her shoulder and they fell silent, inhaling the moist air, heavy with the sweetness of honeysuckle. She'd always felt peaceful like this, with him leaning into her and her fingers combing through his fine hair. But today that tranquillity eluded her.

Was Camden right? Was Freddie's adulation of her all construed on mistaken assumptions? She shook her head. She would not think of her husband when she was with her beloved.

"Lord Tremaine was most charitable toward me yesterday," sighed Freddie, instantly dashing her resolution. "He could have abused me a thousand ways and I'd have submitted to it."

Gigi sighed too. Camden had garnered nothing but praises since his return. He was said to possess the refinement of a true aristocrat and the elegance of a Renaissance courtier. And it certainly didn't hurt that he looked the way he did. If he remained in England for much longer, Felix Wrenworth would need to surrender his honorary title of the Ideal Gentleman.

She wanted to warn Freddie about Camden. But what could she say? In the official version of their history, which Freddie accepted without question, she and Camden had agreed to live separately from the very beginning. She could not utter a word against Camden without exposing herself.

"Yes, that was very considerate of him," she mumbled. *And then he came home at night, set me against a bedpost, and stuffed me, dear Freddie.*

"But are you certain he will agree to a divorce?" asked Freddie, with the innocent puzzlement of a child being told for the first time that the world was round.

Gigi immediately tensed. "Why shouldn't I be? He said so himself."

"It's just that..." Freddie hesitated. "Don't mind me. I'm probably still flustered, that's all."

She pulled away from him so she could speak to him face-to-face. "Did he say or do anything? You must not let him intimidate you."

"No, no, nothing of the sort. He was a complete gentleman. But he asked me questions. He...tested me, if you will. And I, well, I don't know. I couldn't read him all that properly. But I thought—not that I'm often right in my thinking—I thought he didn't look like he'd be happy to let you go."

Gigi shook her head. This was so far out of her perception of reality that she had no choice but to deny it. "No one is ever happy about a divorce. I don't think he regrets letting me go. He is simply peeved that I couldn't leave well enough alone and had the temerity to interrupt his orderly life for the unworthy cause of my own happiness. In any case, he's already given his word. One year and I'm free to do as I choose."

One year from last night. She still couldn't think about it without being engulfed in vile heat.

"Amen to that," Freddie said fervently. "You must be right. You are always right."

When he looks at you he sees only the halo he has erected about you.

"I think I should return to the ballroom," she said, rather abruptly. "People will start to talk. We don't want that."

Freddie obligingly shook his head. "No, no, certainly not."

She wished for once he'd grab her by the shoulders, damn all the people in the ballroom, and kiss her as if the whole world was on fire. This was all Camden's fault. She had been perfectly happy with who Freddie was before he got here.

She stood up, kissed Freddie lightly on the forehead, and gathered her skirts to leave. "It'll do you no harm to pay some mind to Miss Carlisle. Resume 'Afternoon in the Park.' I'd like it for a birthday present."

A garden party was in full swing. Set against a profusion of red tulips and yellow jonquils was a kaleidoscopic parade of women, the edges of their creamy skirts blurring like a distant memory. In the middle of this swirl of colors, an oasis of calm. A man sat at a small table by himself, his cheek in his palm, his gaze enthralled by someone just outside the frame of the painting.

Lord Frederick was a far more talented and vivid

painter than Camden had guessed. The painting radiated warmth, immediacy, and charming wistfulness.

A Man in Love, said the small inset on the bottom of the frame.

A man in love.

At his sister Claudia's house in Copenhagen, there was a framed photograph of Camden, taken the day after New Year's Day 1883. He'd been waiting for his mother and Claudia to finish their primping in advance of a family portrait, and the photographer had captured him in a pose nearly identical to that of Lord Frederick's man in love—daydreaming in an armchair, his head propped up in his hand, smiling, gazing somewhere beyond the range of the camera.

He had been looking out the window in the direction of Briarmeadow and thinking of *her*.

The photograph remained Claudia's favorite, despite all his efforts to persuade her to get rid of it. *I like looking at it,* she'd insist. *I miss you like that.*

Some days he, too, missed it. The optimism, the headiness, the feeling of walking on air. He knew perfectly well now that it'd been based on a lie, that he'd paid for those few weeks of unbridled happiness by never being able to feel anything like that again, and still he missed it.

He might divorce her, but he'd never be free of her.

Gigi's sitting room was dark, but light flowed out of her bedroom, casting a long, narrow triangle the color of old gold coins along the angle of the bedroom door, which had been left slightly ajar. Strange, she was certain she had switched off the light before going out.

When she reached her bedroom, she discovered the light to be from Camden's apartment. The connecting door between their bedrooms was wide open. But his bedroom, though lit, looked empty, his bed undisturbed from when it had last been made.

Her heart rate accelerated. She had deliberately stayed out very late to avoid a repeat of last night. Surely he wouldn't bother waiting up when he still had three hundred sixty-three nights left to impregnate her.

But where was he? Fallen asleep in his chair? Or possibly still out on the town somewhere, seeing to his own amusement? But what did she care what he did in his own time? She should simply close the door—very quietly—and get herself to bed.

Instead, she walked into his bedroom.

The sight of the fully restored room still made her throat tighten. It took her back to the time when she used to flop down on his bed and weep at life's unfairness.

The day she emptied the bedchamber was the day she took charge of her life. Three months later she met Lord Wrenworth and began a torrid affair that further boosted her confidence. But this was where it all began, the decoupling of her life from Camden's, the choice to move on, no matter how lonely and uncertain the future.

His personal effects were nowhere to be seen, except for a watch on a silver chain that lay on the demilune table opposite the bed, an intricate timepiece from

Patek, Philippe & Cie. She turned the watch over. On the back was an inscription wishing him a happy thirtieth birthday from Claudia.

She put down the watch. The console table stood not far from the half-open door to the sitting room. A bright light washed in, but the sitting room itself was as silent as the bottom of the ocean.

She pushed the door open and saw rolls of blueprints, dozens of them, on chairs and tables. On the writing table, held open by a paperweight, a slide rule, and a tin of bonbons, was a sheet of white draft paper.

She saw Camden only after she had opened the door fully. He was seated in a low-slung Louis XV chair, clad in the black dressing gown that brought out the dark flecks in his green eyes, turning them the color of summer foliage at dusk. A book lay open in his lap.

"You are up early," he said, taking his sense of irony out for some exercise and fresh air, no doubt.

"Must be that Protestant work ethic I keep hearing so much about," she said.

"Did you do well at cards tonight?" His gaze dipped to the décolletage of her gown. "I'd guess you did."

She had worn one of her less modest pieces. It was, to be sure, a cheap trick to divert attention at the gaming tables, but she disliked idling her assets when she could make use of them. "Who told *you* about it?"

"You. You told me that once you were married, you planned to never dance again and to spend all your time at balls separating English fops from their cravat money."

"I don't remember ever saying anything like that."

"It was a long time ago," he said. "Let me show you something."

He rose and walked over to her, opening the book in his hands to an oversize page. The page was folded into quarters. He unfolded it. "Take a look."

She immediately recognized the large illustration as a rendering of Achilles' shield. Mrs. Rowland adored Book 18 of the *Iliad*, and many a night, as a child, Gigi had gone to sleep listening to the description of the great shield Hephaestus had wrought for Achilles, the five-layered marvel that depicted a city at peace and a city at war, and just about every other human activity under the sun, all surrounded by the mighty river Oceanus.

She had seen other imaginings of the shield, most of which, too faithful to Homer's depictions, were crammed with details of dancing youths and garlanded maidens, resulting in a filigree so fine that it could not possibly outlast the vigor of even one battle. But this particular interpretation was lean, shorn of minutiae, yet muscular and menacing in its austerity. The sun, the moon, and the stars shone down on the wedding procession and the bloody slaughter in equal serenity.

"It is the *oeuvre* of the man whom your mother would like you to marry," Camden said as he restored the page to its folded state. "If you can't hang on to me."

Gigi was surprised enough that she took the book from Camden and inspected its spine. *Eleven Years Before Ilium: A Study of the Geography, Logistics, and Daily Life of the Trojan War* by L. H. Perrin. The family surname of the dukes of Perrin was Fitzwilliam, but by custom a peer signed his title.

"Fancy that." She gave the book back.

Camden set it aside. "Since you are here, have a look at some of my designs."

He'd done nothing to indicate the slightest sexual interest in her. Yet the hairs on her neck abruptly stood on end. "Why should I be curious?"

"So you'll know whom to blame when Britain loses the next America's Cup Challenge."

She was dismayed despite her preoccupation. "You are helping the American side?"

Some forty years before, an American yacht had raced fourteen yachts from the Royal Yacht Squadron around the Isle of Wight and won by a whopping twenty minutes. According to legend, the queen, watching the race, asked who was second, and the answer she received was "There is no second, Your Majesty." Ever since then, English syndicates had been trying to best the Americans and win back the cup. To no avail.

"I'm helping the New York Yacht Club, of which I'm a member," he said.

He walked ahead of her to the writing desk and glanced back, waiting. The light of the standing lamp beside him caressed his hair, illuminating its sun-bleached locks. His expression was kind and patient—too kind, too patient.

She felt the tug of gravity on her feet. Only her refusal to reveal any weaknesses in herself forced her to move, one heavy heel at a time, to stand before the desk.

As she bent her neck to inspect the design, he moved behind her. "It's more of a preliminary drawing at this stage," he said.

He spoke next to her ear. A filament of pleasure zigzagged through her, acute and debilitating. She felt his hand brush aside the tendrils of hair that had escaped from her low chignon. Then his fingers settled on her nape.

"I see," she said, her voice tight.

"I can do the detailed scale drawing myself," he murmured, undoing the top button of her gown. "But mostly these days I have a draftsman do it for me."

She stared down at the designs. At the center was a yacht, appearing as it would at sea, sails fully deployed. To the side he had drawn a cross section of the hull and a view of the vessel in dry dock.

He reached around her and pointed at a deep, narrow protrusion from the keel halfway down the length of the yacht, while his other hand unmoored her buttons easily, languidly, and all too swiftly.

"I hope the fin keel will give the yacht greater lateral stability," he said, as if he were addressing a group of engineering students, even as he opened her gown all the way to her hips. "You want the yacht to ride as high as possible, to increase hull speed. But a vessel barely in the water would capsize that much more readily."

"Been capsizing boats lately?" she said, hoping her voice dripped enough tartness.

"Not for a while I haven't. But I did once. The first yacht I ever owned. I worked on the design for years, built her with my own hands, and she tipped over two leagues into her maiden voyage." He eased the gown off her shoulders, disengaging her arms from the bodice, his touch as light as the first breeze of summer. "Serves me right for calling her the *Marchioness*."

Her heart suddenly pounded. He named his first yacht after *her*? "What possessed you to do something like that? Did you forget that you couldn't stand me?"

"I was told I should either name my boat after my wife or my mistress," he said, as her dress crumpled into a heap of coppery satin and tulle. "I towed her in, rebuilt her from scratch, rechristened her the *Mistress*, and she's been sailing fine ever since, one of the fastest racing yachts on the Atlantic.

"You see," he whispered, loosening her corset laces and lifting the corset over her head. "You are trouble even from three thousand miles away."

"Truly, is there no depth to which I won't sink?" she asked sarcastically, even as she gripped on to the desk.

Her petticoats slipped off to join the discarded gown. He easily deprived her of her chemise, his accidental touches scalding her skin. "I think I still have a photograph somewhere of me waving from the *Marchioness*, idiotically overjoyed, just before she sailed."

"I'd have preferred seeing you in the frigid Atlantic. I should have liked to sail right by and not fish you out."

He retorted by divesting her of her drawers and trapping her naked body—naked but for white satin evening gloves and white silk stockings—between his body and the edge of the desk.

His fingertips skimmed over her bare bottom and headed slowly yet inexorably for the junction of her thighs. She closed her eyes and bit her lip but refused to clamp her legs together despite her nervousness.

"Are you always this wet?" he whispered. "Or is it just for me?"

She wanted to say something biting, something that would puncture his masculine pride so completely that he'd never be able to gloat again. But it was all she could do to suppress the whimper in her throat as he slowly pushed inside her. His dressing gown caressed her back, cool and silken against the burning sensations of his entry. He withdrew, then rammed inside her with a vigor that forced a gasp from her larynx and lifted her to her toes.

He sank his teeth into her shoulder. Nothing painful, just a strong bite to punctuate the hot, smooth glide of his body into hers. She could not silence a small moan.

Despite her desperate attempt to recite the alphabet backward—she reached only as far as V before she could no longer think—her body drowned in sensations. She was full, so full, and deliciously pummeled. The pleasure gathered and swelled. She gripped the edge of the desk tighter, her mind unable to comprehend anything except the need to extract ever greater, sharper, thicker pleasure from their mating.

That pleasure erupted in a quivering, imploding climax. She was vaguely aware of his final thrust, of the spasm of his body, of his labored breath in her ear and the heavy thudding of his heart against her back, plainly discernible through the thin layer of silk that separated them.

His cheek nuzzled against her neck. His hands were on either side of hers. They stood, practically in an embrace, with him leaning into her, surrounding her.

"Oh, God, Gigi," he murmured, the syllables barely audible. "Gigi."

She froze, the spell of the moment shattered. He had uttered that exact phrase on their wedding night, over her, under her, beside her, in what she had believed to be exultant bliss.

She disengaged herself, turned around, and slammed her palms into his chest. Her abrupt ferocity did not budge him, but his eyes widened in surprise. He moved aside. Not caring that she looked like a woman who made her living gracing pornographic postcards, she bent down, gathered an armful of her garments, and pivoted on her heels.

"Wait." He followed after her. She thought he meant to hand her an item of clothing she had forgotten. But instead he draped his dressing gown about her. "Don't catch a chill."

She had felt angry, mortified, humiliated. She still did. But his solicitude unearthed pain of the kind she thought she had resolutely put behind her when she cleared out his bedchamber: the pain of what might have been.

"I won't thank you," she said. She had only surliness left for defense.

"I've done nothing worthy of a thank-you," he said. "Good night, Lady Tremaine. Until tomorrow night."

Chapter Eighteen

25 May 1893

Mrs. Rowland greeted Langford, His Grace the Duke of Perrin, with a welcome that was noticeable for the absence of the effusive, sycophantic warmth she plucked out of thin air so easily. Not that one could find fault with her hospitality. But whereas she had once been eager—indeed, greedy—for any furtherance of their acquaintance, this evening she'd metamorphosed into a walking embodiment of correct politeness. Even the soft, pastel gowns she favored had been replaced by a relentless black, like the crepe of a widow in first mourning.

She received him in a parlor lit as brilliantly as the Versailles. So many candles blazed that he wondered if some parish church wasn't missing its altar. The windows facing the country lane were open, the dimity curtains only half drawn. Any passerby could clearly see the entire interior of the room.

Was she so eager to advertise her increasing familiarity with him? Possibly. But the path outside was lightly used during the day and barely trod at night. She might as well have painted herself a sign—*The Duke of Perrin calls at this estimable residence*—and then planted it face-down in her garden.

"Would you care for something to drink?" she asked. "Tea, pineapple water, or lemonade?"

He was fairly certain that no one had offered him lemonade since he turned thirteen. And it did not escape his attention that she gave him no choice of spirits.

"A cognac would do very well."

Her lips thinned, but she apparently couldn't quite summon up the wherewithal to deny a duke a simple request of beverage. "Certainly. Hollis," she said to her butler, "bring a bottle of Rémy Martin for His Grace."

The servant bowed and left.

Langford smiled in satisfaction. There, that was better. Lemonade indeed. "I trust your trip to London was rewarding?"

She laughed, a sound both startled and inauthentic. "Yes, I suppose it was."

She touched the cameo brooch she wore at her throat. He could not help staring at the contrast of her white fingers against the stark, light-devouring crepe. The skin on her hand, though delicate, lacked the succulence and translucency of first youth. He was reminded that she was, indeed, several years older than him, a woman approaching fifty. Granny Snow White.

But damned if she wasn't more beautiful than a bevy of nubile girls, more beautiful even than herself at age nineteen. As a rule, gorgeous women aged worse than plain ones—they had the greater fall. She, however, had acquired, somewhere along the way, a self-worth that had little to do with her beauty yet adorned her better than pearls and diamonds—an underpinning of substance beneath her still-lovely skin.

"I had the unexpected pleasure of meeting your cousins at the theater," she said. "Lady Avery and Lady Somersby were kind enough to invite me to sit in their box."

The significance of her statement did not immediately register. So she ran into Caro and Grace—a lot of people did, to their delight or chagrin, depending on whether they received juicy gossip or were probed three fingers deep for it. Then it dawned on him. Mrs. Rowland here hadn't had any idea at all of the person he had been before his present incarnation as the reclusive, practically asexual scholar.

And what would they have told her? Probably the bitch fight, the fire, and the time he hired all of Madame Mignonne's girls. They were far from the worst sins he had ever committed, but they ranked high in notoriety. And the virtuous—though opportunistic—Mrs. Rowland was shocked and dismayed enough to temporarily shelve her idol-worshipping mien and her breathless voice.

Truly, as if he could be deterred from more nefarious intentions by a few open windows and fifteen yards of reproachful black crepe, he who had successfully lifted a number of mourning skirts in his day, and sometimes before open windows too.

Not that he entertained any such designs concerning Mrs. Rowland. Had they met twenty years previously, well, it would have been quite another story. But he had changed. He was now aged and tame.

On most days.

"I trust they regaled you with stories of my youthful indiscretions," he said. "I'm afraid I haven't led the most exemplary life."

Obviously she hadn't expected him to confront the issue head-on. She attempted a nonchalant wave of her hand. "Well, what gentleman is without a few peccadilloes to his name?"

"Just so." He nodded with grand approval at her sudden insight. "The intemperance of summer leads to the ripe maturity of autumn. Thus it has always been, thus it always will be."

He almost laughed at the confusion his philosophizing caused in her. But her manservant came to the rescue with the delivery of the cognac, an excellent blend composed of fine eau-de-vie that had been aged fifty years in old Limousin oak barrels.

They moved to the card table she had set up and she tentatively inquired if they could, at this early stage, play for something other than one-thousand-pound-a-hand stakes. "My daughter and I played for sweets, butterscotch, toffee, licorice . . . you see what I mean, Your Grace."

"Certainly," he said magnanimously, especially given that he had played thousand-quid hands no more than three times in his life, after which even his vice-laden heart could no longer tolerate the awfulness of losing a year's income in a single night.

She rose and retrieved a large golden embossed box.

"My daughter sent me these Swiss chocolates Easter last. She knows I'm very fond of them."

The chocolates were packed in several trays, with most of those on the top tier already eaten. She discarded the top tray, then set one full tray before herself and one before him.

"What games did you play with your daughter?" he said, shuffling the decks of cards on the table.

"The usual games for two—bezique, casino, écarté. She is an excellent card player."

"I look forward to a few games with her when she arrives," he said.

Mrs. Rowland did not answer immediately. "I'm sure she would be delighted."

It would appear that while Mrs. Rowland could best a Drury Lane professional when it came to premeditated fabrications, she wasn't as smooth when a spontaneous instance of barefaced lying was required. Managing a husband and a fiancé at the same time was no mean task. He could see very well why Lady Tremaine refused to participate in her mother's harebrained schemes to add a third man to the already combustible mix. A few beats of silence passed as he dealt the cards faceup.

"Perhaps you'd rather play a few hands with her husband," said Mrs. Rowland. "She is not yet sure of her itinerary, so he might come in her stead."

"She is married?" He feigned great surprise.

"Yes, she is. She has been married to the Duke of Fairford's heir for ten years." Pride still informed her answer. Pride and a trace of despair.

The first ace landed in his lap. He shook his head slightly as he collected the cards, shuffled them, and held the deck out for her to cut. "I confess myself baffled, Mrs. Rowland. When you recommended your daughter to me, I had assumed her unattached and your gentle interest in my person intended to bring about a friendship between your daughter and myself."

She stared at him as if he'd asked her to undress. Well, he *was* stripping her bare, in a way. She tugged at the cameo brooch as if her collar was buttoned too tight. "Your Grace, I assure you—the mere thought of it! I—"

"Now, now, Mrs. Rowland"—he had not yet completely forgotten how to be smarmy—"a mother's machination to marry her daughter off to a man of consequence might not be the loftiest of human endeavors, but it is a time-honored one. Yet here I find that your daughter is a woman already safely and advantageously wed. For what purpose, then, have you sought out my company so assiduously, to the extent that you were willing to chase me down outside your house and promise to engage in activities that you otherwise despise?"

Her response was a resounding silence.

"Your bet, madam," he reminded her.

Mutely, she set three pieces of chocolate on a doily at the center of the table. He dealt her card facedown and his faceup. A measly five of spades. Next he dealt both of their cards facedown.

She placed her hands over her cards but did not lift them. Her cheeks flushed wine-dark. "I should like to answer your question now, sir. The answer is one that would embarrass both you and me—mortify me, in fact—but you deserve to know it."

She ran her tongue over her lower lip. "The truth is I've had quite enough of widowhood. And I've looked about my vicinity and come to the conclusion that you would make a fine husband for me."

He nearly dropped both his jaw and his cards. She had caught him as flat-footed as a five-hundred-pound man.

"I've watched you walk past my house every day these past five years, on fair days and foul," she continued, gazing at him with her beautiful eyes. "Every day I wait for your appearance at the bend of the road, where the fuchsia tree grows. I follow your progress until you can no longer be seen beyond Squire Wright's hedge. And I think about you."

He knew she was lying as surely as he knew that there had been something going on between the queen and her late manservant John Brown. But somehow he couldn't quite prevent her words from affecting him. Images came to mind of Mrs. Rowland in her bed at night, her hair and breasts unbound, bemoaning her loneliness, wanting, needing, pining away for a man. For him.

"But it isn't until now that I've plucked up the courage to do something about it," she said, her voice soft as a spring night. "I'm not a young woman anymore. So I've decided against a young woman's wiles in favor of a more direct approach. I hope I've not offended you with my forwardness."

It wasn't often that he didn't know up from down,

east from west. But he had to try damned hard to remind himself that when she thought of him, it was only with the intention of providing her daughter that elusive coronet of strawberry leaves, as she had so bluntly informed her fur ball of a cat.

"Why me?" He cleared his throat when he realized his voice sounded closer to a croak. "Pardon my observation, but you are a well-looking woman of independent means. If you would but put out the word—"

"But then I'd have to wade neck deep amongst sycophants and fortune hunters. My desire to be free of them was one of the reasons that motivated my return to Devon," she said quietly, reasonably. "As for why I have set my cap on you, sir, I suppose it's because I've been influenced by Her Grace your late mother."

"My mother?"

His mother had perished of pneumonia four months after his father passed away. Had she lived longer, he probably would have led a more upright life, if only to protect her from the likes of Caro and Grace.

"I'm sorry to have misled you, Your Grace, by pretending not to know your identity the day we met." At last she looked down at her cards and turned them over. An ace and a jack, a natural twenty-one. "The truth is, though we have never been introduced, I've known you for many years. I lived in this house in my youth, and I remember well catching sight of you from these windows when you were home from school on holidays."

He took the sugar tongs she offered and paid her

three chocolates from his tray. "How did you meet my mother?"

"When I helped to run the charity bazaar in sixty-one, she was the honorary patroness. She took a liking to me and invited me to a weekly tea at Ludlow Court." Mrs. Rowland smiled wistfully. "In private she was both gracious and ordinary—ordinary in that her concerns were the same as any other woman's: her husband and her son. I didn't realize it at that time, but looking back, I think she was quite lonely, stranded in the country because of the late duke's poor health, with few friends and even fewer diversions that she could indulge in without appearing callous to His Grace's illness."

He stared at her, no longer sure whether she was still fabricating tales but desperately hoping she wasn't. He had not spoken to anyone about his poor mother—his parents—in years. No one ever thought to ask him how he felt about being orphaned. They merely assumed, by his subsequent behavior, that he was all too glad to have his parents out of his profligate way.

Mrs. Rowland picked up a piece of chocolate wrapped in translucent paper and rolled it between her fingers. The paper crinkled and scrunched softly. "She didn't mention His Grace's illness much. She already knew it was only a matter of time. But she did speak at length about you. She was proud of you and looking forward to your First in Classics. She even showed me a letter that Professor Thompson at Trinity College had written to you, answering your question concerning a point raised in the *Phaedo* and complimenting you on your grasp of ancient Greek. But she was also worried. She said you were wild as the jungles of South America and a conundrum to her. She fretted that neither she nor your father could keep you in line. And she feared that your unruliness would only grow without the influence of a strong, steady wife."

If Langford were any closer to speechlessness, he'd personify it. Mrs. Rowland's revelations shocked him far more than he had thought possible or even likely. Five minutes ago he had been smugly certain that he knew more about Mrs. Rowland than she could ever guess. But now exactly the reverse was true. She had observed him as an adolescent, she had been a confidante to his mother, she had even read the prized letter from Professor Thompson.

"Why did we not meet if you were, as you say, a frequent visitor to Ludlow Court?"

"Because I stayed no more than half an hour for each visit, and because you were always away somewhere at teatime even when you were home on holiday. In summer you'd have gone to Torquay for seabathing, in winter, out stalking a deer or visiting a classmate in the next county."

Because he never had any time for his mother. He dined with her when he was at home and thought that simple act discharged all his duties and responsibilities as a son.

"As you might imagine, my conversations with a loving mother left a lasting, positive impression of her son, leading to my current intentions...."

"Until you were waylaid by Ladies Avery and

Somersby and informed of the more sordid aspects of my past."

"Actually, my daughter was the first to tell me." She smiled wryly. "She disapproves of you. But I think a judgment of you based only on your prodigal years is perhaps as biased and incomplete as that made solely on what one knows of you before and after those years."

She raked in the chocolates, set them in a neat pile before her, and cleared the cards. "Your turn to wager, Your Grace. Though I'd understand perfectly should you no longer wish to stay, now that I've revealed myself as both a fraud and a schemer."

No, she hadn't merely revealed herself to be a schemer. She was still a schemer. She was still weaving fact and fiction together in order that her daughter could rise from the ashes of her divorce more socially prominent than ever.

Yet something bound him to her now. Thirty years ago, when the young Mrs. Rowland had been respectfully attending the late duchess, he had been silent and sullen at dinner, ignoring his mother to the best of his capability. He had hardly known the woman who gave him life. Even the death of his father hadn't imparted to him any urgency to better acquaint himself with her. She had been the healthy one. He'd assumed that she'd be around to wring her handkerchief and frown upon his infractions for decades to come.

He put up five pieces of chocolate. "Please deal."

Chapter Nineteen

31 May 1893

A s you can see, sir, we have outstanding vehicles that would meet your every need," said the wiry Scotsman, proprietor of Adams's Fine Carriages, For Sale and For Let.

"Indeed," said Camden. "Most excellent wares. I will be out of town for a day or two. When I return, I will decide on one in particular."

"Very good, sir," said Adams. "Allow us the honor to conduct you home in one of our fine conveyances."

Camden smiled. He regularly hosted sorties on his yacht, and guests who had not seriously considered owning a yacht before had been known to commission one from him before they disembarked. So he appreciated the Scotsman's acumen. "It would be my pleasure."

"This way, please."

A sumptuous black-and-gold landau was already fitted to a team of four and ready to go as they approached the courtyard.

"Ah, Mrs. Croesus is here today, I see," said Adams, with evident pleasure.

"Pardon?" said Camden, certain he'd misheard the man. Mrs. *Croesus*? He couldn't help imagining a small female pup with a gold leash and a diamond-encrusted collar.

"Won't you excuse me for a moment, Mr. Saybrook?" said Adams.

He rushed forward to greet the woman about to mount the carriage. Rope upon rope of perfectly matched pearls rambled across her shapely front. The rest of her was swathed in brocade shot through and through with gold threads. Beneath her oversize and wildly beplumed hat, the chin-length veil that concealed her face sparkled in the sun—tiny diamonds sewn into the netting.

The woman appeared exactly as a human Mrs. Croesus should. He ought to ask Gigi, Camden thought dryly, why she, one of the richest women in England, rarely dressed the part. Next time he saw her, that was. After their last coupling the night of the Carlisles' ball, she had sent him a tersely worded note the next morning, informing him that she'd be unavailable for procreation-related purposes for the following seven days. And he'd hardly seen her since.

Today was the eighth day.

Adams fussed over Mrs. Croesus. She received his attention with a grand condescension that he quite obviously relished. At last he handed her into the open carriage, bowed, and returned to Camden.

"Don't much care for fancy ladies usually," he said.

"But there is something about that one. Magnificent, eh?"

The magnificent one raised the lapdog she'd held on the side away from Camden and lifted it to her face. "Magnificent indeed," said Camden, recognizing the corgi.

Gigi. What was she doing hiring a carriage from Adams's? Didn't she have barouches and broughams enough of her own? And why was she suddenly dressed like some American millionaire's mistress?

"On second thought," he said to Adams, "I've decided that a cab will be all I require this morning."

Gigi's hired landau went east, across Westminster Bridge, past Lambeth, into Southwark. Shops lined the thoroughfares. Vendors milled about the curb, hawking ginger beer and West Country strawberries. Sandwichboard men, wearily watching out for yobos who tipped them over for fun, advertised everything from tobacco to female pills.

The houses looked decent, some even well-to-do. But the prosperity did not extend beyond the main boulevard. The landau turned off onto a side street, and within a few blocks the neighborhood hung on to respectability by its fingernails.

The carriage stopped before a small establishment set between a grimy cookshop reeking of sausage and onion and the office of a doctor promising to not only cure common diseases and female ailments but also to regenerate hair and banish corpulence.

Half a dozen women stood on the sidewalk, two car-rying small children, all waiting. They smoothed skirts and hair with ungloved hands, trying to not stare at the grand lady in the landau and not entirely succeeding.

The coachmen leapt down, unfolded the steps, and held open the door. Gigi alit, looking richer than God and colder than Persephone in Hades' bed, her green-and-gold-striped day dress an almost shocking display of color and brilliance amid the women's faded blues and duns. As she approached the door, it was opened from within by a middle-aged, neatly attired woman.

From across the street in his hired cab, Camden watched in fascination. What was Gigi doing on a Bermondsey street barely one rung above seediness?

One waiting woman bent down to speak to her child, clearing Camden's line of sight at last to the small bronze plaque affixed to the left of the door.

Croesus Lending Co.
For Ladies Only

Gigi had dealt with this young girl and her young child a hundred times—different faces, different names, but always the same story. She'd been in love, she'd thought it would last, but it didn't. And here she was, at her wits' end, with only a ha'penny to her name, throwing her-self at the mercy of a stranger.

The story still sent chills down Gigi's spine. Had she been a poor, friendless seamstress, might she not have fallen for the handsome apprentice baker next door?

Had she been in service, perhaps she, too, would have believed the sweet nothings proffered by the son of the house.

She'd made all the same mistakes. She knew what it was like to be lonely and desperately in love. What it was like to willingly abandon all good sense.

Miss Shoemaker had been a promising apprentice florist in Cambridge when she lost her head over a young professor who came into her employer's shop every morning for a fresh boutonniere. The rest was mundane tragedy. He refused to marry her or even support her. She lost her position when her pregnancy could no longer be hidden. No other reputable florist would hire her. To keep herself and her child alive, she turned to prostitution.

It seemed that her prayers had been answered when a fellow apprentice florist, Miss Neeley, wrote for her help. Miss Neeley had left Cambridge to open her own shop in London before Miss Shoemaker's disgrace and still thought her a reputable young woman. Miss Shoemaker worked under Miss Neeley for two years, socking away every spare penny for the day when she could open her own shop. But just when she thought she had put her past behind her, in walked Miss Neeley's brother one fine morning and recognized Miss Shoemaker from her streetwalking days.

The outline of Miss Shoemaker's difficult young life took up all of one typed page from the private investigator Gigi kept on retainer for Croesus Lending. Those applicants with good references and character letters were handled by Mrs. Ramsey. The irregular cases came to Gigi.

She listened impassively as Miss Shoemaker stuttered her way through her unhappy story, her cheeks stained a dark red.

"I'm sorry I've no character, mum. But I know all about flowers. I can read some and I'm real good with numbers. Miss Neeley used to let me keep the books for her too. And she gots all sorts of compliments on them big arrangements I made for weddings and dances and such...." Miss Shoemaker's voice trailed off, finally cowed into silence by Gigi's glacial magnificence.

And it wasn't just her overdressed self; it was the room too. After the shabby anteroom and the narrow, dark hallway, the opulence of her office dazzled without fail. Lavishly framed paintings by Lawrence Alma-Tadema, brimming with the dazzling white marbles and the impossibly blue skies of a lost antiquity, drew forth astounded gasps. Furniture as fine as any found in aristocratic drawing rooms routinely made the applicants round-eyed with fear, afraid to soil the posh vermilion-and-cream brocade upholstery with their humble posteriors.

"You said you wish to open a shop of your own," Gigi said. "Do you have a location chosen?"

"Yes, mum. There is this small shopfront just off Bond Street. The rent is dear, but the location is good."

Miss Shoemaker had ambition and daring. Gigi liked that. "Bond Street? Getting ahead of yourself, Miss Shoemaker?"

"No, mum. I've thought and thought about it. It's

the only way. The people in trade, their wives wouldn't use me, not if they've heard anything from Miss Neeley. But the grand ladies, they might not care so much if I do real good work."

There was some truth to that. "Even so, I would advise you to become a very proper widow."

"Yes, mum."

"And before you become too thrilled with your blue-blood patrons, find out which pay their bills and which think you should pay them for the privilege."

"Yes, mum." Miss Shoemaker could hardly speak for her rising excitement.

"And keep your eyes peeled for any rich Americans coming to town. Get their business as fast as you can."

"Yes, mum."

Gigi wrote out a cheque and placed it in an envelope. "You may take this to Mrs. Ramsey in the next room down the hall. She will handle the rest."

Mrs. Ramsey would take Miss Shoemaker through Croesus Lending Co.'s standard contract, tell her what to do with the cheque, and, at the end, show her out through the back door. Gigi did not want the applicants to share their successes with one another or for it to become common knowledge that she granted the vast majority of their requests.

"Oh, mum, thank you, mum!" Miss Shoemaker curtsied so deep she nearly fell over.

"More sweet," her son, who'd been completely silent, suddenly chirped loudly.

"Shhh!" Miss Shoemaker dug out a pretty tin, opened

it, and quickly shoved a piece of bonbon into the boy's mouth.

The tin. Good God. From Demel's of Vienna. An identical one had been there right next to Gigi's hand, on Camden's writing desk, the last time he'd taken her.

"Where'd you get that?" she asked sharply.

"From a gentleman outside, mum," answered Miss Shoemaker, looking at Gigi uncertainly. "He gave it when Timmy wouldn't stop crying. I'm sorry, mum. I shouldn't have taken it. It was very wrong of me."

"It's all right. You did nothing wrong."

"But, mum—"

"Mrs. Ramsey is waiting for you, Miss Shoemaker."

Gigi searched all around, but there were no signs of Camden anywhere outside Croesus Lending Co. She rode the landau back to Adams's and allowed the Scotsman to hail her a cab, which took her to Madame Elise's, where she had fifteen minutes to choose fabric for a new shawl before her own brougham arrived outside, having unloaded her two hours earlier.

She arrived home and found Camden in his bedchamber, dropping a stack of starched white shirts into a traveling satchel.

"What were you doing following me?"

"Curiosity, my dear Mrs. Croesus. I happened to be at the carriage place when you came around," he said without looking at her, a small smile about his lips. "If you saw me dressed like the king on coronation day, calling myself Lord Bountiful and going about on mysterious business, what would you have done?"

"Gone about my own affairs, of course," she said, not very convincingly.

"Of course," he murmured. "But rest assured, your secret is safe with me."

"It's not a secret. It's but anonymity. The women who come to Croesus Lending for help aren't exactly what the holier-than-thou set would call 'the deserving poor.' I don't want to have to explain anything to anyone, that's all."

"I understand."

"No, you don't understand." What could he possibly understand, Mr. Mighty-and-Perfect? "These are hardworking, enterprising women who happen to have a less-than-spotless past. All they need are a few quid to get them on their feet again."

"How much money did you lend out today?"

She hesitated. Was he expecting a numerical answer? "Sixty-five pounds."

His brow lifted. "A goodly sum. Did any of it go to Miss Shoemaker?"

"Ten pounds." Ten pounds was a significant amount of money. It was not uncommon for working girls to earn two quid a month.

"What about Miss Dutton?"

"Eight pounds. Miss Dutton is an unusually talented calligrapher. She will have a secure future if she keeps her more destructive tendencies in check."

He placed three cravats in the satchel and looked up.

"On the strength of her own words? I assume Miss Dutton didn't have a character either."

"I have a private investigator on retainer. In six years I've had only three women default on me, and one of them was run over by a carriage."

"Admirable."

"Do not condescend to me." She grew angry at his facile comment. "Croesus Lending may operate outside conventional boundaries, but it is legitimate and honorable. I sleep better at night for it."

He buckled the satchel and came to her. "Calm down," he said, placing his hands on her shoulders. And when she jerked away from his touch, he took one more step toward her and placed his palms on her cheeks.

"Calm down. I think what you do *is* admirable. I'm glad someone remembers the forgotten. And I'm glad it's you."

She could not be more astonished had he announced he was nominating her for sainthood. He dropped his hands and ambled to the demilune table to wind his watch, but her cheeks remained hotly imprinted with his touch. "I just want to give someone a second chance," she mumbled.

She'd never received one from him.

His fingers paused in their motion. He glanced once at her before resuming the winding of his watch. He said nothing.

She suddenly felt she'd stayed too long. Said too much. "Well, then, I'd better let you get on. A pleasant trip to you."

"I'm going to Devon to dine with your mother and the Duke of Perrin. My train leaves Paddington in an hour. Have the kitchen pack you a sandwich. You can come with me."

A dozen thoughts raced through her head. He wanted her conveniently nearby so he could get on with impregnating her, so that Mrs. Rowland couldn't pester him about the divorce, so that it'd be less awkward at dinner with the duke. But the quake of pleasure brought on by his invitation refused to subside.

"I already told her I wouldn't come," she said.

"Give her a second chance," he said, slipping the watch into his pocket. "She'd like that."

Chapter Twenty

Copenhagen
July 1888

Camden liked being his nephews' favorite uncle,
that infrequent, mysterious visitor whose spectacular arrivals etched indelible, miracle-bright memories
upon impressionable young minds, forever remembered as an endless source of chocolate, clever toys, and
shoulder rides.

He'd had a rough crossing. His liner docked thirty-
six hours behind schedule. He arrived at Claudia's
house to only the boys and the servants, Claudia and
her husband having gone out for the evening. He had
his dinner brought up to the nursery and ate it with
two-and-a-half-year-old Teodor babbling away on the
chair next to him and five-month-old Hans snuggled
on his lap.

Teodor received his new kaleidoscope with terrific
enthusiasm. But he broke it after only a quarter hour.
He stared at the wreckage for a moment, then burst
into howls of inarticulate disappointment. Camden,
no neophyte when it came to bawling toddlers—he was

seven years older than Christopher—distracted Teodor with a few magnets. Once the boy realized that the small black blocks were "magical," he happily settled down to stick them to one another and to spoons and butter knives. Hans, on the other hand, comported himself with perfect gentlemanliness, chewing on his new rattle contentedly, occasionally emitting a happy gurgle.

Teodor, who no longer took afternoon naps, wore out earlier. His nanny carted him off to bed. Hans, after his bottle, fell asleep with his cheek against Camden's shoulder, his little mouth spreading a spot of warm drool against the cambric of Camden's shirt. Camden kissed his tiny ear with a swell of avuncular affection. And a vague sense of loss.

He'd left for the United States directly after he received his *diplôme* from the Polytechnique. The years that passed had brought him more wealth than he'd ever imagined. But fortune, as delightful and welcome as it was, did not warm his bed or populate a house with the children he wanted.

Claudia came into the nursery then. She kissed Camden on the cheek, Hans on his head, and went to kiss Teodor, already asleep in his crib.

She came back in a minute. "He's grown big, hasn't he?" she said, caressing Hans's hand.

"You don't see a baby for a few months, and he doubles in size," answered Camden. "Had an amusing evening?"

"Amusing enough. Pedar and I dined with your wife," said Claudia.

His wife, whom he had not seen since May of '83, more than five years ago. Camden rolled his eyes. "Yes, of course you did."

"I'm not making it up," said Claudia. "Your wife is in town. She called on me three days ago. I called on her the next day and invited her to dinner. And she returned the invitation tonight. We dined at her hotel."

It was to Camden's vast credit that he did not drop Hans on his head. "What is she doing in Copenhagen?"

"Sightseeing. A tour of Scandinavia. She's already been to Norway and Sweden."

"Alone?"

The moment the treacherous syllables escaped, he wished he'd torn out his tongue instead.

"No, with her personal harem," said Claudia, beginning to observe him too closely for comfort. "How am I to know? She hasn't introduced me to a paramour, and I haven't had her followed around. Find out for yourself, if you are curious."

"No. I meant if she had her mother with her." He handed Hans to the nanny. "Besides, Lady Tremaine's doings are none of my concern."

"In case you haven't noticed, Lady Tremaine discharges *her* familial duties. She calls on Pater and Mater once a week when they are in London. She sends presents for my children for Christmas and their birthdays. And when Christopher mismanages his allowance, she is the one who compels him to adopt austerity measures," said Claudia. "I think you should call on her. What's the harm? She is staying at the—"

He set a finger over her lips. "Remember what you said? I'll find out for myself, if I'm curious."

Later that night his good sense turned to ash, much like the Cuban cigars he smoked with Pedar. He managed a splendid silence during the ride to Mrs. Allen's hotel. He managed to walk away from Claudia's carriage when he arrived there. He almost managed to enter the hotel, its doors already held open by two respectful doormen. It defeated him then, this absurd inquisitiveness concerning his wife's presence.

He had Claudia's carriage stopped, on the pretext of an errant cuff link. While conducting the make-believe search, he found out obliquely from the coachman to which hotel Claudia and Pedar had gone for dinner. And then, instead of calling on Mrs. Allen—a young, wealthy, attractive widow from Philadelphia who'd been strongly hinting all throughout the Atlantic crossing that they should repair somewhere private posthaste—he took himself across town to his wife's hotel.

He was assured that she was indeed alone, attended by an entourage that consisted of precisely one maid. That the only guests she'd received were Claudia and Pedar.

The driving question behind his restiveness answered, he should have been satisfied. Yet he found himself speaking to the hotel clerk of kroner, as in how many kroner the clerk stood to gain if he'd discreetly pass along information of interest concerning Lady

Tremaine. Setting up clandestine arrangements to spy on her, to put it bluntly.

It was not difficult to discover her itinerary, as she relied on the hotel to supply her with transport. The very next morning he began receiving reports of her comings and goings. Within a few days he knew what she ate for breakfast, which monuments she'd visited, at what hour she took her evening bath, even where she'd stopped to buy some embroidered linen table-cloths.

Yet the more he knew, the more he had to know. How did she look? Had the years been kind to her? Was she the same woman he'd left behind? Or had she changed into someone unrecognizable?

He broke an engagement to dine with Mrs. Allen when he learned that Gigi would make an evening visit to Tivoli Gardens, Copenhagen's premier amusement park. He had enough control left to not go anywhere near her during the day. But perhaps, just perhaps, he could catch a glimpse of her at night and still remain in the shadows.

He walked the acres of Tivoli Gardens until he thought he must already be in his dotage. At last he spotted her on the grand carousel. She was laughing, holding on to the gilded post of her wooden horse for dear life, her long white skirts streaming with the rotation of the carousel and the summer breeze off the sea.

She looked well. Better than well. Delighted.

In the bright orange glow of the park's artificial lights, she was something out of an old Norse fairy tale, elemental, dangerous, and downright crackling with sensual energy. More than a few men in the crowd stared at her, eyes round, mouths half open.

He gazed at her until he could no longer stand the asphyxiation in his chest. He didn't know what he'd been thinking. Somehow he had thought—had hoped, in the baser chambers of his heart—that she might appear wan and wretched beneath an impassive facade. That she yet pined for him. That she was still in love with him, despite all evidence to the contrary.

This woman did not need him.

He turned and walked away. He stopped the reports and the lunacy. He tried to forget that he'd gawked at her like a hungry mutt with its front paws upon the windowsill of a delicatessen. He made up to Mrs. Allen for his neglect and inattentiveness.

And then came the encounter on the canal.

Mrs. Allen looked very fetching in her peach-and-cream Worth gown. The scenery behind her, however, held its own. The houses that lined the canal were painted in unabashedly spirited colors, the hues of a fashionable Englishwoman's wardrobe: rose, yellow, dove gray, powder blue, russet, and puce. As the sun approached its zenith, the canal glittered, ripples of silver beneath the boats that plied the waterways.

"Oh, my goodness gracious!" exclaimed Mrs. Allen, latching on to his elbow. "You must look at that!"

He turned away from the storefront display of model ships he'd been perusing and looked in the direction she pointed.

"That open window on the second story. Can you see the man and the woman inside?" Mrs. Allen giggled.

Obligingly, he scanned the windows on the opposite bank, until he felt the weight of someone's gaze on him.

Gigi!

She sat at the bow of a pleasure craft a stone's throw away, under the shade of a white parasol, a diligent tourist out to reap all the beauty and charm Copenhagen had to offer. She studied him with a distressed concentration, as if she couldn't quite remember who he was. As if she didn't want to.

He looked different. His hair reached down to his nape, and he'd sported a full beard for the past two years.

Their eyes met. She bolted upright from the chair. The parasol fell from her hand, clanking against the deck. She stared at him, her face pale, her gaze haunted. He'd never seen her like this, not even on the day he left her. She was stunned, her composure flayed, her vulnerability visible for miles.

As her boat glided past him, she picked up her skirts and ran along the port rail, her eyes never leaving his. She stumbled over a line in her path and fell hard. His heart clenched in alarm, but she barely noticed, scrambling to her feet. She kept running until she was at the stern and could not move another inch closer to him.

Mrs. Allen chose that moment to link her arm through his and lay her head against his upper arm, rubbing her cheek against his sleeve like a well-scratched kitty.

"I'm famished," said Mrs. Allen. "Won't you take me to a restaurant that serves cold buffet?"

"Of course," he said dumbly.

Gigi didn't move from her rigid pose at the rail, but she suddenly looked worn down, as if she'd been standing there, in that same spot, for all the eighteen hundred and some days since she'd last seen him.

She still loved him. The thought echoed wildly in his head, making him hot and dizzy. *She still loved him.*

All at once, he could not even recall what had been her trespass against him. He knew only, with absolute certainty, that he had been the world's premier ass for the past half decade. And all he wanted was everything he'd sworn would never tempt him again.

He sleepwalked through lunch and rushed Mrs. Allen back to her hotel for her afternoon beauty nap, turning down her invitation to join her as if she exhibited symptoms of the bubonic plague. He raced about Copenhagen, to the barber's, the jeweler's, then back to Claudia's house for his best day coat.

He walked into his wife's hotel with a freshly shaven jaw and a wilting bunch of hydrangea bought from an elderly flower vendor about to go home for the day. He felt as nervous and stupid as a pig living next door to a butcher. Standing before the hotel clerk, he had to clear his throat twice before he could get his question out.

"Is . . . is Lady Tremaine here?"

"No, sir, I'm sorry," said the clerk. "Lady Tremaine just left."

"I see. When is she expected to return?" He would

wait right here. He would never go anywhere again without her.

"I'm sorry, sir," said the clerk. "Lady Tremaine is no longer with us. She vacated her suite and departed for the harbor. I believe she was trying to board the *Margrethe*, leaving at two o'clock."

It was five minutes past two o'clock.

He raced out of the hotel, flagged down the first carriage for hire, and promised the cabbie the entire contents of his wallet if the cab but reached the harbor before the *Margrethe* left. But when he arrived, all he could see of the *Margrethe* was three columns of smoke in the distance.

He gave the cabbie double the usual fare anyway and stared at the horizon. He could not believe it. Could not believe that all his hopes of a future together would come to aught, so swiftly and pitilessly.

For the first time in his life, he felt lost, hopelessly rudderless. He could follow her to England, he supposed. But being in England would crush them with all the weight of their infelicitous history. Would remind him incessantly of why he'd left her in the first place. In England neither of them could be spontaneous. Or forgiving.

Perhaps it just wasn't meant to be.

It took hours, but in the end he convinced himself that his guardian angel must have toiled on his behalf. Imagine if she had actually been there. Imagine if he had actually thrown all caution to the wind. Imagine if he had actually gone back to her, a woman he could never again trust.

He told himself he could not imagine any such thing. He really couldn't. Not a sensible man like him. His fingers closed over the velvet box that contained the diamond-and-ruby necklace he'd bought, all fire and sparkling beguilement, like her. Mrs. Allen would have one hell of a parting gift from him.

The blue hydrangea he threw into a canal, watching the bouquet drift in the water until it disintegrated. Who'd have believed that after all these years, she still possessed the power to shatter him without even once touching him?

Chapter Twenty-one

Gigi wished she could better predict this man who was her husband.

She'd been infinitely certain that he'd demand love-making in the confines of her private coach on the way to Devon—so certain, in fact, that she'd taken precautions. And suffered erratic heartbeats from the moment they left the house together.

He, on the other hand, began working on the designs of some mechanical contraption before the train even departed Paddington Station, leaving her with little to do other than watch the world hurtle by at sixty miles an hour, feeling entirely daft.

And self-conscious. And a little light-headed.

He'd paid her a compliment, an unadulterated compliment, on something that genuinely mattered to her. She felt like a green debutante at her first ball after an unexpected dance with the most extraordinary, notorious rake of them all: She knew perfectly well that the fizzy warmth in her was unreciprocated, unwise, and uncalled for, but there wasn't a damned thing she could do about it.

He wrote in a quick, slanted hand, unraveling reams of equations that would look to the uninitiated as incomprehensible as the hieroglyphs before the discovery of the Rosetta Stone. Even she, having been extensively tutored in higher mathematics and mechanics—so that she wouldn't be hampered by ignorance when dealing with her own engineers—could understand only parts of it, looking at the numbers and symbols upside down.

She deciphered that he was working on something about the heating and exchanging of gases. When his calculations moved on to angular momentum, she further deduced that he was refining the design for an internal combustion engine.

She had her doubts about the automobile. Certainly it was wonderful and novel and—nowadays—feasible. But who other than the most adventurous and the most wealthy would want to own and operate one, when carriages were so much simpler and more convenient in town and trains a great deal faster and more reliable over long distances? At least one's horses were not likely to die three times going from London to Brighton.

But she was curious enough to have paid a visit to Herr Benz in Mannheim the previous summer and was about to negotiate a license to build Benz engines in her own factory. The internal abacus she'd inherited from her Rowland ancestors swiftly calculated the savings she'd realize if she could use Camden's design—if it worked.

And if he were truly her husband.

"What's the matter with your engine?"

"It can't expel exhaust gases fast enough when its rotational speed exceeds one hundred revolutions per minute," he said, without looking up. Without expressing any surprise at her familiarity with subjects outside the grasp of the overwhelming majority of women—and men, for that matter.

But then, he knew all about the Honorable Mr. Williams, who'd been her tutor before he became her lover.

The partial vacuum created by the exodus of exhaust gas drew fresh air and fuel into the cylinder. The expanding gas created from the ignition of the air-and-fuel mixture powered the engine, but residual exhaust gases that were not expelled would reduce its efficiency.

"You should begin the expelling cycle at an earlier point in the crankshaft's rotation," she said. "That would sacrifice a bit of power but improve your efficiency."

"Correct."

"The trouble comes in determining at which precise point, doesn't it?" she said. Her engineers had agonized over the voltage of the third rail they had designed for London's new underground tubes.

"Always," he answered. "The design can be refined only to a certain point. I've narrowed it down to two possibilities and determined their angles to within one point two degrees. Now my engineers in New York will modify the engine and test it."

"Good thing you won't get your hands dirty."

"But getting my hands dirty is half the fun. I always build my own designs. I can build anything." He glanced at her and smiled. Her heart thudded to a stop. The sun really did shine brighter when he smiled. "Would you like to be the first English lady to rumble down Rotten Row in a horseless carriage?"

She smiled despite herself. That fizzy warmth—half effervescent elation, half heedlessness—spread unabated within her. "I know you really *can* build anything. I know your little secret."

He was puzzled. "Secret?"

"Claudia's gown that she wore to her first ball."

"Ah that," he said, relaxing. "That's not my secret so much as hers. She was rather mortified, if I remember correctly, that other people had ball gowns made by Monsieur Worth, while hers was cobbled together by her brother."

"So modest."

"When I say cobbled, I mean cobbled. I had no idea how to manufacture the kind of neckline she wanted without the bodice falling off her. So I took apart one of my mother's mesh bustles and wired the entire décolletage. She was terrified during the ball that the gown would either kill her or poke some handsome swain in the chest."

"She showed it to me when she came to England in 1890," said Gigi. "I couldn't believe that *you* made it until she swore it on the lives of all her children."

"It was my first and last foray into haute couture," he said dryly. "I was nineteen and thought there was nothing I couldn't do. When Claudia wept for hours on end because there was no room in the budget for a new gown for her first ball, I thought, how hard could it be? After all, couture was just the softer side of engineering, and I'd cut and sewn plenty of sails for my model ships."

"She said you were a wizard."

"Claudia has rose-colored hindsight. I never knew what panic was until the ball was two days away and I still hadn't figured out how ten yards of skirts should gather and drape under the bustle. All the non-Euclidean geometry in the world couldn't have dug me out of that hole."

She thought of the gown, lovingly packed in layers of tissue, kept in Claudia's old chamber at Twelve Pillars. *I have the best brother in the world,* Claudia had said that day, a not-so-subtle reminder that Gigi should get on a transatlantic liner posthaste.

"You did all right in the end."

"I wired the skirt too," he said.

They both burst out laughing. The corners of his eyes crinkled in mirth, laugh lines that she'd never seen before—lines that had come from the sun and the salt of the sea, marks of a man in his prime.

He stopped and looked at her. "Your laughter is the same," he said. "I used to think you all sophisticated and worldly, until you laughed. You still laugh like a little girl getting tickled, all hiccupy and breathless."

What did one say to something like that? If he were anyone else, she'd consider it a declaration, not necessarily of love but of great fondness. What was she to make of it when it *did* come from him?

He quickly changed subjects. "Before I forget, I've never thanked you for keeping Christopher in line, have I?"

Christopher had gotten himself into a few scrapes over the years. Nothing terribly alarming—no illegitimate children, ruinous debts, or criminal friends—but his parents worried and wrung their hands. After Saint Camden and Mostly Sensible Claudia, Their Graces were ill equipped to deal with a more temperamental offspring. So Gigi had stepped in dutifully, extricated Christopher from potentially harmful situations, unleashed stern lectures Their Graces were too softhearted to deliver, and ruthlessly choked off his allowance whenever he deserved it.

"No need to thank me," she said. "I enjoyed keeping him in line."

"He complained about you in his letters. He said you were harsh as the Gorgons and twice as deadly. That you meant to ship him to Vladivostok and leave him at the port penniless. That you threatened to bankrupt anyone who dared to loan him money when you stopped his allowance."

There was such relish in his voice that the dangerous warmth infecting her at last turned into a conflagration of recklessness. "Did you miss me?" she heard herself ask.

Suddenly the only sound in the coach was the low roar of the train's engines and steel wheels clacking on steel tracks, going a mile a minute. She looked out the window, feeling as stupid as a stampede of lemmings.

He, too, looked out the window. For a long time he didn't speak, until she almost had herself convinced that they were both going to pretend that her question had never been uttered.

But then he did answer. "That was never the point, was it?"

They arrived at Mrs. Rowland's cottage a little after teatime. The weather had turned dour and wet in London just before they departed, but a gentle sun shone upon this part of Devon, though the soil was drenched and rain dripped off leaves still.

The roses were at their peak. Mrs. Rowland's cottage, with its bright white walls and vermilion trim, was all pastoral charm. Gigi half-expected her mother to fall down in a faint upon seeing Camden and herself together. But Camden must have had a telegram sent ahead, because though a note of curiosity wended through Mrs. Rowland's welcome, she was not taken by surprise.

"This is a lovely house," said Camden, kissing Mrs. Rowland on the cheek. "The photograph you sent didn't quite do it justice."

"You should see Devon in spring," said Mrs. Rowland. "The wildflowers are incomparable in April."

"I will come in April then," said Camden. "I should still be in England at that time."

Gigi felt her mother's gaze on her back as she stood looking out at the garden, strewn with petals from the earlier shower. He'd said nothing new, of course. Their deal was for one year, and that one year didn't conclude until next May. But for some reason she could not see them going on like this for another eleven months, or even another eleven weeks.

For ten years things had remained frozen in place, because he'd made it abundantly clear the circumference of the earth was not enough distance between the two of them. When he first returned, he not only personified antagonism, he took it to hitherto unscaled heights. But things had changed. This thawing of enmity put them on terra incognita, before dangerous possibilities, possibilities that she dared not even think of in the light of day, because they led to utter madness.

"I shall look forward to it," said Mrs. Rowland. "We don't see enough of you."

"I believe I have issued invitations beyond number for you to visit New York City, dear madam," Camden said, a smile and a challenge in his voice. "And you've always found reasons to demur."

"But don't you see, my dear lord Tremaine," said Mrs. Rowland sweetly, "I could never call on a man who would not speak to my daughter."

Gigi almost turned around in her astonishment. Somehow she'd never thought of her mother as an ally in this matter. She'd always believed, perhaps because of her substantial culpability, that Mrs. Rowland blamed her for the silent disaster that was her marriage. That her mother's letters had given Camden the wherewithal to blackmail her had further contributed to her conviction that Mrs. Rowland would enter into a sexual union with the devil himself if Camden would only bestow his blessed forgiveness on Gigi.

"Of course, I really shouldn't have corresponded with you either," said Mrs. Rowland. "But I always fall so maddeningly short of perfection."

This time Gigi did turn around. Was that an apology? From the woman who'd never done anything wrong in her life?

Hollis entered with the tea service, and the conversation took a sharp turn to Mrs. Rowland's latest charity gala. Camden, it turned out, was intimately acquainted with Mrs. Rowland's charitable efforts.

"Isn't that quite a bit more than what you usually raise at these events?" he asked, once Mrs. Rowland had named a sum.

"It is, I suppose." Mrs. Rowland hesitated. "His Grace honored us with a large contribution."

"The same duke who's coming to dinner tonight?" said Gigi.

Good Lord, was that a blush on her mother's face? To be certain, they'd had some cross words over the Duke of Perrin the last time Mrs. Rowland was in London. But the colors staining Mrs. Rowland's cheeks did not seem to have originated either in consternation or embarrassment.

"The very same." Mrs. Rowland was once again the closest approximation of the Madonna this side of the Italian Renaissance. "An admirable figure of a man. A classical scholar. I'm quite pleased that you will be making his acquaintance."

Camden raised his cup. "I, for one, am looking forward to dinner with trembling anticipation."

Camden left within minutes for the scenic ride down to Torquay that Mrs. Rowland had apparently promised him. Gigi had felt uncomfortable with him in the room, with her mother's sharp eyes assessing their every interaction, as if all their recent dealings could be deduced from a "Would you please pass the creamer?" But without his presence as a buffer, the awkwardness between the two women immediately came to the fore, as strong and unmistakable as the scent of vinegar.

"I visited Papa's grave last Friday," said Mrs. Rowland, after nearly three minutes of unrelieved silence.

Gigi was surprised. They didn't speak of John Rowland very often. Grief was a private matter. "I saw your flowers when I went on Sunday." John Rowland would have turned sixty-eight on Sunday had he survived the typhoid fever that took him at age forty-nine. "He always did like camellias."

"Because you gave him a handful from the garden when you were three. He adored you," said Mrs. Rowland.

"He adored you too."

Her father had taken her along whenever he shopped for a present for his wife. Nothing was ever too good for his beautiful missus. He loved big, showy things—perhaps the reason behind her own flamboyant taste in jewelry, though she rarely wore any—but in the end he bought only cameos and modest pearls, because he didn't want his wife to have to wear anything she'd consider garish.

"We were married ten years and five months when he passed away." Mrs. Rowland took a small cream cake, set it before her, and cut it into perfect quarters. "You'll be married ten years and five months in a fortnight. Life is uncertain, Gigi. Don't throw away your second chance with Tremaine."

"I would rather we not speak of him."

"I would rather we do," said Mrs. Rowland firmly. "If you believe that I have schemed only because Tremaine is in line for a dukedom, then you are greatly mistaken. Do you think I never came upon the two of you together in the sitting parlor at Briarmeadow, holding hands and whispering? I'd never seen you so alive and happy, before or after. And I'd never seen *him* that way, completely without his reserve, for once acting his age, when he'd always carried the burden of the world on his shoulders."

"That was a long time ago, Mother."

"Not long enough for me to have forgotten. Or you. Or him."

Gigi took a deep breath and finished her tea. It was already cold, and too sweet—because Camden's ungloved hand had brushed hers when he passed the sucrière, and she didn't know two from four in the minute afterward. "What good does it do any of us to remember? I loved him then, I would not deny it. And perhaps he loved me too. But that is all in the past. He no longer loves me and I no longer love him. And if there are second chances going around, no one has offered me any, least of all Camden."

"Don't you see?" cried Mrs. Rowland, exasperated, setting down her teacup with an uncharacteristic *thud*. A glob of milky brown liquid sloshed over the rim of the cup and spread into an astonishingly perfect circular stain on the embroidered tablecloth that Gigi had purchased during her ill-fated visit to Copenhagen. "That he is here in England, living in your house, being civil to you, persuading you to come with him to see me—all this, does it not mean anything to you? Does it have to be stated in so many words or carved on a stone tablet, for heaven's sake?"

Was it not enough that she had to struggle with it by herself? She did not need to hear it spelled out item by item by her mother, as if she were a dimwit chit from some Oscar Wilde play.

"Mother, you forget why he is here in the first place," she said coolly. "We are divorcing. I have pledged my hand to Lord Frederick."

Mrs. Rowland rose abruptly. "I will rest for a short while. It would not do for me to appear haggard before His Grace. But if you think that you love Lord Frederick a fraction as much as you love—not loved, but love—Tremaine, then you are a greater fool than any Shakespeare ever wrote."

Gigi remained in the parlor long after Mrs. Rowland had swept out, trailing a faint wake of rose attar behind her. Slowly, absently, she finished the cream cake Mrs. Rowland had left behind, as well as the two small jam tarts that still remained on the three-tiered platter.

If only she could be certain that her mother was dead wrong.

Chapter Twenty-two

The duke, upon first glance, did not appear either a scholar or a reprobate—no book dust or buxom doxies clung to him. But he was certainly imposing as an aristocrat of the highest rank, with none of the golly-would-you-believe-my-good-luck mellowness that characterized the current Duke of Fairford, her father-in-law. No, this was a man born to lord over lesser beings and who'd done it authoritatively for the entirety of his adult life. A man who could cow half of society into hushed awe with his sheer ducalness.

Gigi was not immediately impressed. Despite an upbringing focused exclusively on becoming a duchess, she seemed to have inherited a democratic streak from her plebeian ancestors. "Good evening, Your Grace."

"Lady Tremaine, you have decided to join us after all." His corresponding wry amusement made it evident that he was not without a clue as to the purpose behind the dinner.

The surprise was her mother, who did *not* have a

democratic bone in her body. Gigi would have expected some reverence on her part—and triumph that she'd finally maneuvered Gigi and the duke into the same room—but Mrs. Rowland's demeanor was rather one of grim determination, as if she were on a mission to Greenland, a grueling journey with nothing but barrenness at the end.

Equally intriguing was the duke's deportment toward Mrs. Rowland. A man such as he did not know how to be *nice*. He probably tolerated his friends and treated everyone else with condescension. Yet as he complimented Mrs. Rowland on her flower arrangements, he displayed a solicitude and a delicacy Gigi hadn't sensed in him before.

Camden arrived late, his hair still slightly damp from his bath. He'd returned from the seashore only thirty minutes ago.

"May I present my son-in-law, Lord Tremaine," said Mrs. Rowland, in a rare bit of archness. "Lord Tremaine, His Grace the Duke of Perrin."

"A pleasure, Your Grace," said Camden. Despite his hurried toilette, he seemed more settled into the role of affable, oblivious host than anyone else. "I've had the pleasure of reading *Eleven Years Before Ilium*, a most illuminating work."

The duke raised one black brow. "I had no idea my modest monographs could be found in America."

"As to that, I wouldn't know either. I received a copy from my esteemed mother-in-law, when she was in London last."

The duke turned his monocled gaze to Mrs. Rowland.

He'd have resembled a *Punch* caricature if it weren't for his commanding presence and his sardonic self-awareness.

Mrs. Rowland shifted her weight from one foot to the other, then back again. Gigi's eyes widened. The men in the parlor might not understand the significance of that seemingly unremarkable motion. But Gigi knew that Mrs. Rowland *never* fidgeted. She could hold as still as a caryatid, and for about as long.

"My mother is a learned acolyte of the Blind Bard," said Gigi. "You will find few women, or men for that matter, sir, more thoroughly knowledgeable concerning all things Homeric."

This revelation startled the duke again, in a way that felt more complicated than simply a man's surprise that a woman would know something in his field of expertise. He inclined his head in Mrs. Rowland's direction. "My compliments, madam. You must tell me how you came to develop a passion for my arcane subjects."

Mrs. Rowland's response was a high castle wall of a smile. Camden glanced Gigi's way. Apparently she wasn't the only one to have noticed something highly irregular.

Hollis announced that dinner awaited. Mrs. Rowland, with almost obvious relief, suggested that they pair off and proceed to the dining room.

For Victoria, about the only silver lining to the cumbersome evening was that the duke didn't immediately succumb to Gigi's charms.

She'd fretted about Gigi's looks throughout her daughter's girlhood, as the child stubbornly refused to blossom into the kind of flawless beauty Victoria had been but instead grew unfashionably tall, with wide shoulders and a challenging gaze that was Victoria's despair. Then, a few years ago, after Victoria at last realized she no longer needed to train her eyes on the girl's gown and coiffure for signs of imperfection, she noticed something quite confounding.

Men stared at Gigi. Some of them gawked. At balls and soirées, they had their eyes glued to her as she walked, talked, and occasionally—largely with indifference—glanced their way. When Victoria mentally distanced herself and studied her daughter as a stranger would, she was shocked to realize just how obscenely attractive Gigi might be to the masculine sex.

She had no words to describe the kind of primal allure Gigi exuded, an incandescent sensuality that surely didn't come from Victoria. It made Victoria feel old, past her prime, her vaunted beauty a distant second place to Gigi's youth, luminosity, and glamour.

Gigi looked as well as she ever did in a dinner gown of vermilion velvet, the skin of her throat and arms glowing in the lambent light like that of a Bouguereau nymph. The duke spoke to Gigi as he ought to, making the obligatory grunts concerning the relative proportion of precipitation to sunshine in recent days in both London and Devon. But unlike Gigi's husband, who glanced at her over his wineglass with every other forkful, Perrin kept most of his attention on the plate before him, gravely tasting the successive courses of *soupe d'oseille, filet de sole à la Normandie,* and duck *à la Rouennaise.*

"Allow me to compliment you, madam, on your chef," the duke suddenly looked up and said. "The food is nowhere near as terrible as I expected."

Victoria was absurdly pleased. Ever since the night when they'd gambled over chocolates and she'd practically told him to drag her upstairs and ravish her lonely old bones, she'd been on pins and needles.

She could repeat to herself only so many times that, in desperate embarrassment at being found out, she'd made up the whole thing on the spot. The only problem was that she was a terrible impromptu liar. Without hours and days of prior preparation, she either blurted out the truth or bungled so badly the odor of her mendacity could be scented a furlong away.

Had she told the inadvertent truth instead? Was this whole exercise in folly simply an opening for her to grab the duke by his lapels and make him take notice of her at long last? He hadn't entirely believed her, but he didn't disbelieve her enough. There was something about truth, the visceral ferocity of it, that seeped under and around incredulity, no mattter how well-founded and watertight.

"Thank you," she said, "though I cannot return the compliment on your tact."

"Tact is for others, madam." As if to underscore his point, he glanced at Gigi and Camden and said, "Forgive the curiosity of a dotard who retired from Society many years ago, but is it commonplace nowadays for a couple about to divorce to be on such apparently friendly terms?"

"Quite so," answered Camden, his tone as smooth and creamy as a dish of flan. He looked at Gigi. "Wouldn't you say, my dear?"

"Without a doubt," said Gigi dryly. "We do loathe scenes, don't we, Tremaine?"

Even the duke was left momentarily speechless by this bravura performance. He moved on to a safer topic. "I understand you've quite the Midas touch, Lord Tremaine."

"Hardly, sir. It's Lady Tremaine who has the head for business. I but try my best to reach financial parity with her."

Victoria glanced at Gigi, hoping she'd heard the admiration in Camden's words. But the quick shadow of confusion in Gigi's eyes suggested that she heard something else instead.

"I'd always thought it otherwise," said Victoria. "Lady Tremaine builds upon the success of her forefathers. But you started with nothing."

"I wouldn't say so, madam. I'm no Horatio Alger, hero beloved of the American imagination," replied Camden. "My first acquisitions were made with substantial loans obtained against Lady Tremaine's inheritance."

Gigi choked on her wine. She coughed into her napkin as Hollis rushed to her side with a fresh napkin and a goblet of water. She took a long draft of water and promptly resumed her ingestion of the slices of duck on her plate.

Victoria took it upon herself to ask the question that Gigi didn't. "I had no idea. How were you able to do that?"

Camden, like his cousin before him, had signed a marriage contract that prohibited any direct access to Gigi's fortune. "I proved to them who I was and who she was. I had the marriage papers and the announcement from the *Times*. The Bank of New York decided quite on its own that my wife would come to my rescue should I be in danger of defaulting," he said, his smile subtly feral.

Good grief. Dazzled by his polish and finesse, Victoria had never observed this brazen side to her son-in-law. She'd always thought the once-upon-a-time affection and friendship between the calculating heiress and the urbane marquess endearing but odd, as the two could not be more different one from the other. How she'd underestimated Camden by equating his burnish of faultless manners with a lack of inner ferocity.

The duke took an appreciative sip of his Burgundy, a fourteen-year-old Romanée-Conti. Victoria was rather shocked to see that he was smiling a little.

He was not classically handsome, his features more rough-hewn than refined, with unruly brows and a Mont Blanc of a nose—a face that lent itself easily to terrifying scowls. But his smile—a slight, underdeveloped one at that—was utterly transforming. It illuminated his fine chestnut-brown eyes, animated his lips, and melted his hauteur with surprising warmth and earthy machismo.

She did not use the word lightly—in fact, she'd never applied it to any living man—but he looked nigh on *irresistible*. Suddenly she saw why otherwise properly reared ladies fought over him like harpies.

"There are few things I loathe more than small country dinners," he said. "But, madam, had you only informed me that such remarkable diversion lay in store for me, I would not have compelled you to provide additional entertainment."

A moment of absolute silence. Victoria was too disoriented to feel embarrassed. She hadn't yet grasped that the focus of the conversation had abruptly shifted from the Tremaines to her dealings with the duke.

"Dear sir," said Gigi wryly, "pray do tell."

"Oh, Gigi, please, none of that unseemly interest," Victoria huffed. "His Grace but requested that I play a few hands of cards with him, which I gladly obliged."

"Sir," Gigi addressed the duke, a sly smile on her face. "I've heard that you were a scoundrel. I see that you are at least a rascal."

"Gigi!" Victoria cried, mortified.

But the duke seemed amused rather than offended. "I *was* a scoundrel in my youth, to put it kindly. As for my rascally demands, let's just say I could have stipulated a great deal more and still received compliance."

Victoria felt her face flame a color as bright as Gigi's gown. Oh, how she hated to blush in public, so inelegant and infantile. Camden, bless him, was eating with gluttonous zest, as if he hadn't heard a word of the conversation in the last five minutes. Gigi, taking a cue from her husband, gave the remaining slice of duck breast on her plate another good poke. The duke, however, wasn't done.

"Young lady," he addressed Gigi. "I hope you realize how fortunate you are, at your age, to still have a mother who would dance with the devil for you."

It was Camden's turn to cough into his napkin, though in his case it sounded more like choked laughter than actual choking. The dinner, up to that point a parody, if a rather barbed one, was now a farce.

She'd known the dinner to be a bad idea for a while now, hadn't she, thought Victoria wildly. Why, oh, why hadn't she called it off? Why had she persisted as if the duke were Moby Dick and she the crazed Captain Ahab, who would either harpoon him or die trying?

Gigi was not one to take lectures sitting down. "Sir, I hope you realize that, while I am eminently grateful, I have also reminded my mother, pointedly, that no dancing with the devil is necessary on my behalf. I already have the affection and the fealty of a good man. My future happiness after my divorce is already assured."

The duke sighed exaggeratedly. "Lady Tremaine, I do not profess to know the marvelous qualities of this other man. But why wage—and waste—a divorce when it's more than evident to me that you and your husband haven't even tired of each other yet?"

Having silenced Gigi and strangled Camden's mirth, His Grace turned to Victoria and smiled again, a full smile this time. She nearly melted into her chair, leaving nothing behind but a whalebone corset and an assemblage of skirts.

"Madam"—he raised his glass in a toast—"this is the most sublime Burgundy it has ever been my privilege to enjoy. You may be assured of my everlasting gratitude."

Chapter Twenty-three

The silence of a house settling into the night was first disturbed as Camden stood brushing his teeth over a basin of water. Then came a loud crash to his left, a heavy vibration that traveled up his ankles to his knees, followed by a muffled shriek.

The cottage had six bedchambers upstairs—Mrs. Rowland's at the eastern corner and five others, of southern exposure, lined in a row. Camden was in the chamber closest to Mrs. Rowland's and Gigi in the one furthest away.

The shriek came from Gigi's direction.

He spat the tooth powder out of his mouth and pulled open the door. Mrs. Rowland's door opened a second later. "Good heavens, what was that?" she cried.

"The ceiling, probably," he said.

Gigi, too, was in the hallway, her face very pale against the midnight blue of her peignoir. "What's the matter with your house?" she said tightly to her mother.

Camden began opening doors. The room next to his

seemed fine, except that several pictures had fallen off the wall. He opened the door to the middle chamber. A gust of debris greeted him. Almost the entire ceiling had collapsed, blanketing the floor and the furniture in dust-ridden chunks of plaster and timber. Above him gaped the cavernous void of the attic.

"Good heavens! How did this happen?" Mrs. Rowland moaned. "This is a most sturdy house."

"I don't think anyone should sleep on this floor until the ceiling is repaired and the integrity of the entire structure inspected," said Camden.

"You and I can share the governess's room on the ground floor," said Gigi to Mrs. Rowland. "Do you have a spare cot for Camden?"

"Nonsense!" cried Mrs. Rowland. "Lord Tremaine is a first-time visitor to this house. I will not have him spend the night on a cot in the parlor like hired help. I will ask to be put up at Mrs. Moreland's cottage down the lane—she has two daughters who visit her, so she always has a spare chamber made up. You and Camden take the governess's room."

"I will take the cot and sleep in the parlor," said Gigi. "I'm not a first-time visitor. It doesn't matter where I sleep. Or I can come with you to Mrs. Moreland's."

"Absolutely not to either of your mad propositions!" Mrs. Rowland recoiled in grandiose horror. "I will not have that kind of gossip bandied about. The two of you may divorce up a storm in London, but here I have my reputation to consider. I will not have people asking why my daughter would not share a room with her lawfully wedded husband. There, I think I hear

Hollis coming up. I will confer with him about the arrangements. Mind that you do nothing to embarrass me, Gigi. No cots whatsoever."

After Mrs. Rowland hurried down the steps with surprising energy and bounce, Gigi cursed under her breath. "Arrangements my foot," she said, her voice seething. "She arranged for the ceiling to cave in! This house was inspected from top to bottom only a year ago because I was worried that it might be getting a bit decrepit. It *is* sound. Ceilings in sound structures do not just fall in like that, and certainly not so beautifully, exactly in an unoccupied room so that nobody gets hurt."

"We have underestimated your mother's determination."

"She should be having an affair with the duke, that's what she should be doing," Gigi huffed. "Look at her, she is sacrificing the roof over her head to herd us into the same bedchamber when we already—never mind."

Camden felt his heart beginning to pound. He hadn't planned on paying Gigi a conjugal visit, this being Mrs. Rowland's house and all. But if they were going to be stuck in the same—and chances were, fairly cramped—room and forced to share a bed, well...

"Do you have anything that needs to be carried?" he asked.

She shot him a suspicious glance, but in the light spilling out from all the open doors, he noticed she was no longer as pale as she'd been a minute ago. "No, thank you. You go on."

He went down the stairs. Hollis showed him to the

governess's room. Camden found himself in a chamber both larger and prettier than the one he had been given, its walls covered in a cream damask with elegant persimmon-and-moss arabesque patterns. Pink and white ranunculus in painted Limoges vases stood on each nightstand. The bed itself was quite large, the white summer bed linen already invitingly turned down.

"Mrs. Rowland uses this chamber for afternoon repose in the summer," Hollis informed him. "It is cooler than the upstairs chambers."

Camden turned off the lamps and opened the window shutters. Night air wafted in, cool, moist, and heavy with the scent of honeysuckle. A waxing moon was on the climb, its light pale and lucid. He discarded his robe, and, after a brief hesitation—Who was he trying to fool? Napoleon wanted Russia less badly than he wanted to lie with her—he removed the rest of his clothing too.

Gigi came only after a good quarter hour. Her footsteps stopped outside the door. Then nothing happened. The silence unfolded and unrolled, shrouding him in its oppressive strata, chafing at his patience and nerves.

The doorknob finally turned, softly. She closed the door behind her but advanced no further, standing with her back against it, her feet just beyond the imprint of moonlight. He was reminded of a night long ago, in a different house that also belonged to Mrs. Rowland, where a similarly lustrous moon also silvered a long swath of the room—the beginning of the end, the end of the beginning.

"Like old times, isn't it?" he said, after a full minute had passed.

More silence. "What do you mean?" she said at last, her voice slightly creaky.

"Don't tell me you've forgotten."

She shifted, barely audible sounds of silk sliding on flesh and against the panels of the door. "So you were awake," she said accusatorily.

"I'm a light sleeper. And I was on an unfamiliar bed, in an unfamiliar house."

"You took advantage of me."

He chuckled. "What did you expect, after you felt me up and down? I could've done more and you'd've let me."

"I could've done more too. I almost climbed back into your bed that night. Would have been a short path to the altar."

"You don't say," he murmured. "What stopped you?"

"I thought it was dishonorable. Something beneath me. Ironic, isn't it?" She pushed away from the door and advanced until she stood by the bed, on the farther side from him, her silhouette limned against a nimbus of moonlight, the dark curves of her body just barely visible inside the diaphanous shadows of her peignoir.

He swallowed.

"I should have gone ahead and done it that night," she said. "You'd have married me, knowing you'd been had. But you wouldn't have been infuriated enough to run to America, only disgusted enough to not be happy with me. We'd have been like every other couple in Society—a normal life, you see."

"No," he said, his voice harsher than he'd intended. "You should have done the honorable thing. Theodora married one day before we did. Had you a little more patience, when I returned to England for Easter, you could have had your cake and eaten it too."

The bed dipped beneath her weight. She slid under the covers, safely on her side of the bed. "I think I've learned my lesson already."

"Have you?"

She didn't answer. Instead, she asked a question of her own. "Why do you place so much importance on reaching financial parity with me?"

Because I am married to you, the richest woman in England after Victoria Regina, you idiot. What's a man who still dreams of fucking you to do?

He reached under the cover, grabbed her by the front of her peignoir, and yanked her toward him. She gasped. And gasped again as his teeth scraped the crook of her neck.

He rolled on top of her... groaning with the heavenliness of her under him. Since his return, he'd seen her naked. He'd climaxed inside her. But he had not allowed himself to feel her, the dense, smooth texture of her skin, the firm undulation of her body. He grabbed a fistful of her peignoir and pushed it upward. "Take it off."

"No. You can do what you want perfectly well with it in place."

"What I want is you naked. Without a stitch."

"That wasn't part of our deal. You never said I had to disrobe for you."

"What's the matter?" he said softly into her ear, enjoying her quiver. "Afraid to be naked under me?"

"It's not right. I'm not going to dishonor Freddie by allowing you any more liberties than I must."

Suddenly he was enraged, at her obduracy and her obtuseness. Lord Frederick would make her about as happy as a clam in a bowl of bouillabaisse. He gripped her peignoir at her throat and tore it down its length, the shrill *sszzzzz* rudely rending the somnolent darkness. "There. Now if Lord Frederick asks, which is none of his business, you can tell him in all honesty that you didn't *allow* me any liberties."

She panted, the sound of a woman unable to get enough air, her exhalations drowning out the muffled chirping of sleepless crickets in the garden.

He lowered himself onto her, the sensation of her skin against his at once shockingly familiar and unnervingly new, as if he'd never left her bed all these years, as if this was only the second night of their honeymoon and he'd been staring at her all day, dying for the sun to set and a blessed, endless night to descend.

He was a fool. A fool to fall for her the first time. And a fool to come back now, when he already knew his weakness all too well, having wrestled with it every day of these past ten years.

Too late.

He drowned himself in the velvety feel of her, marveling at the way her skin slid over her clavicles with her every breath, kissing a trail along the top of her shoulder, reluctant to leave each square inch of her glorious skin, impatient to savor all of her.

She placed her hands against his upper arms, but she didn't push. She only emitted a sweet, despairing sound as he kissed the base of her throat. The gloom in his heart lifted a bit, though he knew it was madness to think this was anything but madness.

He kissed his way to her chin, to the soft spot just under her lips. There he hesitated. To kiss her on the mouth was to inform her, in exactly so many words, that she'd marry Lord Frederick over his dead body.

Beneath him, he felt her heartbeat, as rapid, erratic, and uncertain as his own. Did he want to go down that path? Did he dare? And what awaited him at the bitter end if he were to walk this avenue of folly?

"There is something I have to tell you," she said suddenly, rupturing the moment of suspense. "There is no point to your sleeping with me. None at all. I am using a Dutch cap. I have been using one all along. You stand no chance of getting me with child, so you might as well leave me alone."

When he was six years old, during an exuberant game of chase in the corridors of his grandfather's house, he'd run into a wall. The next thing he knew, he found himself flat on the floor, too stunned to understand what had just happened. He felt like that now. He didn't know what to make of her outburst, her abrupt decision to push things to the brink.

He gazed down at her. Her features were only half visible in the faint illumination of the moon, a shadow of a high cheekbone, a dark fullness of lips, and eyes like water at the bottom of a deep well, black with pinpoints of refracted starlight.

"Then why do you tell me? Why not go on duping me? That would have served your purpose better."

"Because I can't take it anymore," she said, lying very still. "I'm sure you are happily vindicated in your opinion of me. But it doesn't matter. I can't go any further."

"Why?" He ran his fingers through her hair, the ultimate luxury. Her hair was heavy, smooth, glossy, and cool as morning dew. He never remembered another woman's hair the way he remembered hers. "What happened to your legendary ruthlessness?"

She closed her eyes and turned her face away from him.

His fingers felt ridiculously comforting against her skull. They moved with reassuring gentleness, coming to rest for a moment next to her temple, then sliding lower along her ear, her jaw, and finally her lips. The pad of his thumb skimmed over her bottom lip, rolled it down slightly so that he touched the moist membrane just inside her mouth.

His reaction confused her. She wanted to ask him, loudly, whether he'd heard anything she'd said—that she hadn't changed, hadn't learned her lesson at all, and had tried to deceive him again. But his touch hypnotized her. It was warm, curious, and utterly without rancor. She could not speak. She was all awareness—all deprived, hungry, unbearably keen awareness.

He kissed the lobe of her ear, the bone that hinged her jaw, the tip of her chin. He kissed her neck, her shoulder, and the indentation of her clavicle. She kept her eyes tightly shut. In that absolute darkness, he was all heat and sensation to her, his lips a source of cool fire that burned everything they touched, spawning jolts of desire that spiked through her body, leaving her mindless and weak.

Suddenly his mouth closed around her nipple. She gasped, a flabbergasted sound of pleasure. He licked her. She wanted to thrash and gyrate and beg for more. Her nails dug into the counterpane. His hand found her other nipple and rubbed it between his thumb and forefinger, with just enough force to make her abandon all efforts at quietness. She moaned out loud.

His hand moved lower, down her side, coming to rest a fraction of a second against her hip and then on to pry her legs apart. She made a feeble attempt to keep them together, but he only had to swirl his tongue slowly once around her nipple for her to forget everything.

He found her, probably the easiest thing in the world—he but had to go to the source of her wetness. And then his finger, no, fingers were inside her.

"Tell me to stop, and I will," he said, just before he took her other nipple into his mouth.

Somewhere in the back of her mind, she realized what he was doing: dislodging and removing the Dutch cap. She might have objected had she been capable of coherent speech. But she wasn't, and the only sounds she emitted were choked whimpers of arousal.

He easily extracted the Dutch cap from her and tossed it to the side of the bed. She shivered.

"Now there's nothing between us," he said.

A sudden flash of terror paralyzed her. She was utterly exposed to him—her womb, her future, her entire life. And just as suddenly, an overwhelming swell of desire inundated her. She wanted him inside her, to possess her, to shatter her, to fill every emptiness and destroy every defense.

With a moan of despair she grabbed hold of him and pulled him down to her, kissing him so hard that their teeth banged and ground together. He pulled away slightly, restrained her face between his hands, and kissed her his way, slower, more gently, and much more thoroughly.

She opened her legs wide and he came into her, thick and hot, as he kissed her. She wrapped her legs about him, urging him, wanting something fast, furious, and utterly obliterating. But in that he refused to oblige her.

He tormented her with long, slow strokes, teasing her nipples as he drove into her at a leisurely pace. He made her beg for each delicious thrust. He made her thrash and gyrate and wail and whimper. And only when she was wholly vanquished, desperate, convinced that she would exist forever in this state of trembling, feverish arousal, only then did he give in and pummel her to her incoherent, wild, joyous, and vocal satisfaction.

* * *

If only she could make time stay still. If only she need never depart the warmth of his embrace and the euphoria of their lovemaking. If only her world consisted of just this one dark room drenched in the sweet muskiness of sex, protected from tomorrow and the day after tomorrow by impregnable walls of forever-night.

Were she to have a guinea for every if-only of her life, she could pave a highway of gold from Liverpool to Newfoundland.

His breath still quick and erratic, her husband pulled away from her to lie on his back, not quite touching her. She bit her lower lip, the cold, clammy tentacles of reality already creeping up her limbs toward her heart.

He would not say anything unkind. But his silence was enough to remind her of everything she'd vowed never to do when he first returned. And all her declarations of love for Freddie, were they no more than words, and empty words at that?

"I called on you at your hotel in Copenhagen," he said.

It took her an entire minute to decipher what he'd said. And even then she didn't understand. "You...you didn't leave a card?"

"You'd already left, for the *Margrethe*."

A blaze of elation swallowed her, only to be replaced by a bleak disbelief, an impotent amazement at Fate's capriciousness. "I didn't catch the *Margrethe*," she said, dazed. "It'd already sailed when I arrived at the harbor."

"*What?*"

She'd never heard him say "What?" before. He was

too perfect for that; he'd never failed to use the more correct and more polite "Pardon?" Up until this moment.

"Where did you go, then?"

"Back to the same hotel. I left only the next day."

He laughed, with bitter incredulity. "Did the hotel clerk not tell you that a fool came for you, with flowers?"

It was like finding out she was with child, then bleeding all over the place three weeks later. Only it was happening all in one searing moment. "The day clerk must have been gone by the time I decided I needed a place to stay for the night."

He'd come for her. For whatever reason, he'd come for her. And they'd missed each other, as if Shakespeare himself had scripted their story on a day of particular misanthropy.

"What flowers did you bring?" she asked, because she couldn't think of anything else to say.

"Some…" His voice faltered, something else she'd never heard from him. "Some blue hydrangeas. They were already wilted."

Blue hydrangeas. Her favorite. Suddenly she felt like crying.

"I wouldn't have minded." She kept talking, to keep the tears at bay. "I was so upset I went to Felix as soon as I came ashore in England, only to find out he'd gotten married during the time I was away. I made a fool and a nuisance of myself anyway."

He made a sound halfway between a snort and a grunt. "I almost hate to ask."

"You've nothing to worry about. He didn't succumb to my advances. I came to my senses. End of story."

"I came to my senses too, after a while," he said slowly. "I convinced myself that what was done between us could not be undone, could never be undone."

"And there is no such thing as a fresh start. Not really," she concurred, her tears welling, the room a dark blur.

For the first time in her life, she saw exactly what she'd thrown away when she decided to have him by means fair or foul. For the very first time she truly understood, deep in her bones, that she'd not saved him but wronged him by consigning to him all the ability of a box turtle to make his own choices. She had been—just as she hadn't wanted to admit—impetuous, shortsighted, and selfish.

"I should not have done what I did. I'm sorry."

"I wasn't exactly a paragon of rectitude myself, was I? I should have had the frankness to confront you, however unhappy that encounter would have been. Instead, I retreated to subterfuge and confused vengeance with justice."

She laughed bitterly. For two intelligent people, they'd certainly made all the wrong choices that could have been made. And then some.

"I wish—" She stopped herself. What was the point? They'd missed their chance already.

"I wish the same. That I'd caught you that day, somehow." He sighed, a heavy sound of regret. He turned toward her and turned her toward him, his hand clasped firmly on her upper arm. "But it's still not too late."

For a long moment she didn't understand him. Then a thunderbolt crashed atop her, leaving her blind and staggered. There'd been a time in her life when she'd have walked barefoot over a mile of broken glass for a reconciliation with him. When she'd have expired from joy upon hearing those exact same words.

That time was years and years ago, long past. Her imbecilic heart, however, still leapt and burst and rolled around in clumsy cartwheels of jubilation.

Right into a wall.

She was promised to Freddie. Freddie, who trusted her unconditionally. Who adored her far more than she deserved. She'd reaffirmed her desire and determination to marry him every time she'd met him, the last time only two days before.

How could she possibly slap Freddie with such a gross betrayal?

"I tried not to," said Camden, his eyes the most brilliant pinpoints of light in the night. "But all too often I wondered what might have happened, back in eighty-eight, had I not given up. Had I the nerve to come look for you in England."

Why didn't you? she cried silently. *Why didn't you come for me when I was lonely and heartsick? Why did you wait until I'd committed myself to another man?*

She covered her eyes, but her head was still babel and bedlam, feral thoughts cannibalizing each other, emotions in a pandemonium of roundhouse and fisticuff. Then suddenly a siren song arose above the din, sweet and irresistible, and she could hear nothing else.

A new beginning. A new beginning. A new beginning. A new spring after the dead of winter. A phoenix arising from its own ashes. The magical second chance that had always eluded her futile quests now presented to her on a platter of gold, on a bed of rose petals.

She had but to reach out and—

It was this very same insatiable craving for him that had overcome her a decade ago, this very same impulse to damn everything and everyone else. She'd surrendered her principles and acted out of expediency and untrammeled self-interest. And look what had happened. At the end of the day, she'd had neither self-respect nor happiness.

But the siren song descanted more beautifully still. Remember how you giggled and prated together about everything and nothing? Remember the plans you made, to hike the Alps and sail the Riviera? Remember the hammock you were going to crowd in warmer weathers, the two of you, side by side, with Croesus stretched atop the both of you?

No, those were mirages, memories and wishes distorted through rose-tinged lenses. Her future lay with Freddie—Freddie, who did not deserve to be ignominiously cast aside. Who deserved the best she had to give, not the worst. He had entrusted his entire happiness to her. She could not live with herself were she to trifle with that trust.

What about—

No. If she must endure the siren song, like Odysseus, thrashing and flailing in temptation, then she would. But she would not abandon Freddie. Nor her own decency. Not this time. Not ever again.

She looked at Camden. "I can't," she said, her voice barely above a whisper. "I'm pledged to another."

His fingers on her arm tightened infinitesimally. Then the coolness of the night replaced the warmth of his hand. His eyes did not leave hers, but she could no longer see the light in them. Only an infinite darkness met her gaze. "Why did you tell me about the Dutch cap exactly?"

Why exactly? "I was"—if there was a riding crop nearby, she'd gladly have used it on herself—"I thought you'd be so disgusted you wouldn't want anything more to do with me."

"I see, preserving your loyalty to Lord Frederick still."

His voice had gone chill. As had her heart. A frozen expanse except for one white flame of anguish.

"Why, then, did you not object when I exposed you to a very real risk of consequences?"

And what could she say? That she'd ever been so? That he had but to display the slightest sweetness and approval for her to forget everything otherwise important? That she was a hopeless imbecile in his bed?

"I wasn't thinking. I'm sorry."

The bed creaked. For a fleeting second she saw the deep channel of his back as he sat with his hands braced to either side of him, his head bent. Then he left the bed altogether.

"I wish you'd have remembered all those scruples a little sooner," he said, a current of anger churning beneath his seamless politeness. He shrugged into his dressing gown and tightened the sash in a savage motion.

She sat up, clutching the bedspread against her chest. *Stay,* she wanted to say. *Stay with me. Do not leave.* Instead, she mumbled in arrant daftness, "You said yourself that what happened between us cannot be undone, can never be undone."

"And would that I had heeded my own sage advice," he said curtly, marching toward the door.

"Wait!" she cried. "Where are you going? The rooms upstairs aren't safe. You don't know what other damages could have been done."

"I'll take my chances," he said. "There's bound to be a bed in this house that's less dangerous than yours."

Camden lay abed in the chamber that had been first assigned to him. He stared at the ceiling and half-wished it would collapse on him and knock him senseless.

Not that he had a full implement of sense left. *I wasn't thinking,* she'd said. She most certainly wasn't alone in it. He probably hadn't had a properly lucid day since the first letter from her solicitors arrived the previous September, requesting an annulment.

He'd long referred to his marriage as "that tolerable state of being." Tolerable because as long as the legalities were ironclad and ineluctable, she was still wedded to him, with a chance that one day, in a faraway, golden-misted future, they might yet rise above their youthful *Sturm and Drang* and achieve some sort of passable happiness. Not that he willingly admitted any such wishful thinking to himself, but fourteen-hour working days translated into nights too weary for self-censorship.

When she moved to officially dissolve their marriage, with flocks of letters from her lawyers darkening the sky like so many swarms of Egyptian locusts, the stasis on which he depended descended into chaotic disequilibrium. He found himself a stunned observer, unable to do anything other than toss the letters into the fireplace with increasing grimness and alarm.

Annulment was one thing. Divorce, however, quite another. When she'd actually gone ahead and petitioned for divorce, he'd been jolted with wrath, a massacre-the-peasants-and-salt-the-earth blood rage. This marriage was their devil's pact, begun in lies and sealed in spite. How dare she try to break free of this chain of acrimony that bound them? Neither of them deserved any better.

How injudicious he'd been to not understand the eruption of years of pent-up frustration. And how blind, when he'd calmed down during the Atlantic crossing, to think that he'd arrived at a reasonable, mature solution in his demand for an heir as a condition for releasing her from their marriage.

All he'd achieved was the unleashing of the beastly attraction that had taken him years to tame. But whereas once the beast had devoured her, this time it consumed *him*.

He didn't know whether it was courage or madness that made him ask her outright to not throw away everything they'd ever had. He only knew the black pain of her rejection, a sense of loss through which he could barely breathe.

Somehow he couldn't believe that this was it, that their story would end with such wretchedness, as if Hansel and Gretel had become the witch's dinner after all, or Sleeping Beauty's prince a pile of gnawed bones in the Enchanted Forest. But her voice, though barely audible, had been firm and clear. She might cling and writhe beneath him—and lose her head momentarily—but she kept her larger goal firmly in sight. And that goal was to sever all ties with him.

Perhaps she was right. Perhaps he was still stuck in 1883. Perhaps this was indeed how their story would end, she as another man's radiant bride, and he but a dusty footnote in the annals of her history.

She was in the dining room, staring at an already cold cup of tea, when he appeared at her side, in riding gear, his hair windblown.

"I imagine we should know, in a few weeks, whether there will be consequences from our action last night," he said without preamble.

"I imagine so." She looked back to her tea, all too aware of his presence, of the scent of morning mist still clinging to him, and already panicking over what news the end of her cycle might bring. Either way. "If there aren't any consequences, would you let me go to Freddie?"

"And if there are, would you still insist on marrying him?"

"If there are"—she pushed the words out past the lump in her throat—"I would hold up my end of the bargain, and I should like you to honor your part of it."

In response, he chortled softly, a sound without warmth or emotions. He took her chin in hand and slowly tilted her face so that she was forced to look at him. "I hope Lord Frederick does not live to regret his choice," he said. "Your love is a terrible thing."

Chapter Twenty-four

"No, no, it won't do. Get me the green one instead," said Langford. He unbuttoned the claret-colored waistcoat—the third he'd rejected—and handed it back to his valet.

A scowling, middle-aged man stared back at him in the mirror. He'd never been exactly handsome, but in his prime he'd been quite something to behold, always impeccably coiffed and garbed, always with the most desirable women of the upper echelon draped over his arms.

Fifteen years in the country and suddenly he was a bumpkin. His clothes were a decade out of fashion. He'd forgotten how to pomade his hair. And he was fairly certain that he no longer remembered how to seduce a woman. Seduction was a matter of mind. A man one hundred percent certain of himself had women eating out of his hand. A man eighty percent certain of himself had only pigeons eating out of his hand.

And this eighty percent man, for reasons listed only

on the devil's tail, had invited Mrs. Rowland to tea—tea!—as if he were some fluttery little old lady looking forward to a bit of crumpet and gossip.

Or, worse, as if he were some sentimental sap seeking to turn back the clock thirty years.

His valet returned with a deep-green waistcoat, the color of a densely wooded valley. Langford shrugged into it, determined to stick with this particular selection whether he looked a prince or a frog. He looked neither, just a perturbed, confounded, and slightly apprehensive man who hadn't exactly let himself go nor exactly kept himself up.

It would have to do, he supposed.

Her landau pulled up before the manor at Ludlow Court at exactly two minutes past five. Beneath her lace parasol, she looked as dainty and prim as the queen's own teacup. Her choice of attire—an afternoon gown of pearl and pale blue—pleased him. He liked the creams and pastels that predominated her wardrobe, colors of an eternal spring, though had someone asked him during his man-about-town days, he'd have decreed such hues much too pedestrian.

He welcomed her himself, presenting his ungloved hand for her support as she alit from the carriage. She was both pleased and somewhat nonplussed—good, that made two of them.

"I called on you a few weeks ago, Your Grace," she said, half coyly, half challengingly. "You were not home."

They both knew he'd been home. But only he knew

that he'd watched her from the window of an upper floor, in a mixture of exasperation and fascination. "Shall we to tea?" he said, offering his arm.

By ducal standards, Ludlow Court was more than modest, it was downright humble. A long time ago, in his twenties, Langford had been invited to Blenheim Palace. As his carriage approached that great edifice from a distance, he'd been consumed by an overwhelming sense of inadequacy: Compared to the colossus that was the Marlboroughs' ancestral estate, his own seat seemed merely a glorified vicar's cottage.

Blenheim Palace's facade of grandeur, however, quickly proved just that, a facade, or, to be more precise, an illusion. For as his conveyance drew near to the house, the facade itself turned out to be in a state of advanced ill-repair. Inside the great mansion, the curtains were molded and full of holes, the walls dark from badly maintained flues, and the ceiling water-stained in practically every room—this after the family had sold the famed Marlborough gems to help matters. A few years after his visit, the seventh duke had had to petition parliament to break entail so that the whole contents of the house could be auctioned off to defray family debts.

In contrast, the manor at Ludlow Court was a jewel box, a diminutive but perfect example of Palladian architecture with lucid, elegant lines, beautiful proportions, and an interior that Langford had been able to maintain—and occasionally update—with relative ease.

But as he passed through the anteroom and the

grand entrance, with Mrs. Rowland's hand barely touching his arm, he wondered what she thought of it. Her current residence might be little larger than a hunting lodge, but he understood that she'd previously lived in a much grander place, one larger than his own and likely more modern and more lavishly furnished, given her late husband's fortune.

"You have rebuilt the terrace," said Mrs. Rowland, almost as soon as they entered the south drawing room. One side of the room overlooked the terraced slope at the rear of the house, leading down to the spread of formal, geometric gardens and the small lake beyond. "Her Grace used to fret about it."

"Did she?" Yet something else he didn't know about his own mother.

"Yes, rather. But she chose not to repair it so as not to disturb your father in his illness," Mrs. Rowland said. "She was a very good woman."

That, he'd realized only too late. In his proud adolescent years, he'd secretly thought his mother too frumpy and countrified, possessing none of the regality and glamour befitting the consort of a prince of the realm. Her anxious love he'd borne as if it were a millstone about his neck, little suspecting that he'd be adrift without it.

"She never said anything to me about it. And I fear I was too obtuse and self-occupied to guess it of her. I had it repaired only when I began giving weekend parties here."

"It is very pretty," she said, gazing out the window at the exuberant apricot-gold roses blooming along the balustrade. There were roses on her wide-brimmed hat, roses confected from ribbons of pale blue grosgrain. "She would have liked it."

"Would you prefer to take tea on the terrace instead?" he asked impulsively. "It is a beautiful day without."

"Yes, I would, thank you," she said, smiling a little.

He ordered a tea table set up outside under an extended awning, with a white tablecloth and a few cuttings of the roses she was just admiring set in a crystal vase.

"I think it's high time I apologized," she said, as they settled into their seats, side by side on a wide angle so that they each enjoyed an uninterrupted view of his gardens.

"That is hardly necessary. I thoroughly enjoyed myself at the dinner and found both the food and the company fascinating."

"I don't doubt that." She laughed, rather self-consciously. "For theater you couldn't do much better. But I wish to apologize for my entire scheme, from the very beginning, when I sent away all my servants and stranded my kitten in a tree so that I could demand your assistance."

He smiled. "I assure you I did not participate in your scheme as an unwitting dupe. I knew what I was getting into when I agreed to be your temporary and rather churlish Sir Galahad."

She colored. "That much I've surmised, believe me, from later events. But it still behooves me to apologize for my original deceit."

Tea arrived amid much pomp and ceremony. Mrs. Rowland took both sugar and cream, the little finger of her right hand held just slightly extended, a delicate curl like a petal of oriental chrysanthemum.

"As much as I approve of your acknowledgment concerning this 'original deceit,' it's your subsequent tale that concerns me more," he said, ignoring his tea and watching her stir hers with a languid, creamy daintiness. "Would you apologize for that too?"

"Only if it were a blatant fabrication."

In his distraction he took a sip of tea. He still disliked it. "Do you mean to tell me it wasn't a blatant fabrication?"

She went on stirring her tea. "After much thoughtful reflection, I've decided that I don't know anymore."

He cursed his curiosity. And his lack of tact. A more circumspect man would not have asked the question and would not have to deal with the wide-open vista of her answer.

"Perhaps you could help me decide," she said. "I'd like to know you better."

I'm not a young woman anymore. So I've decided against a young woman's wiles in favor of a more direct approach. That, at least, was no fabrication. "What would you like to know?"

"Many things. But, most pressingly, how and why did you come to be the person you are today? I find it an intriguing mystery."

His heart thudded. "No mystery there. I almost died."

But she wasn't so easily satisfied. "My daughter almost died at age sixteen. That experience only made her more of what she already was, not a different person altogether—which you, by all accounts, have become."

She raised her teacup and let it hover just below her lips, her wrist as steady as the pound sterling. "My instincts tell me that I cannot understand you until I know the story behind your transformation. And that your story is more than a man's brush with death. Am I wrong?"

He considered a variety of answers and rejected them all. Having enjoyed the privilege of bluntness his entire life, he was ill-suited to suddenly take up prevarication.

"No," he said.

The teacup continued to linger in the vicinity of her chin, a shield almost, a disguise too, to hide her dangerous perspicacity behind a bit of glazed fine bone china painted with ivy and roses. "If I may be so forward, was there a woman?"

He didn't *need* to answer her question. But then, he didn't need to invite her to tea either. He didn't know his plans any more than she did hers, possibly a lot less.

"Yes, there was a woman," he answered. "And a man."

Her features froze in momentary shock. Carefully, she set down her teacup. Presumably the stability of her wrist was no match for the excitement of her rather salacious imagination.

"Goodness gracious," she mumbled.

He laughed a little, with rue. "Would that it were that kind of uncomplicated sordidness."

"Oh," she said.

"You have probably heard about the hunting incident. I was shot, bled profusely, was put into surgery for six hours, and barely survived," he said. "But you are right. That in itself had no more life-changing effect on me than a hangover or a bad case of indigestion."

A week after Langford was out of danger, Francis Elliot, the man who'd shot him, came to see him. Elliot had been a classmate at Eton, the one whose house in the next county Langford had frequently visited when he was home on holiday. Over the years, their once-close friendship had gradually cooled, and they saw relatively little of each other, Langford living fast and footloose, Elliot settling down to be the staid, responsible, unimaginative landowner in the mold of his forefathers.

That particular morning, Langford, highly peevish from both pain and ennui, had lambasted Elliot on his shoddy marksmanship and slandered his manhood in general. Elliot held his tongue until Langford ran out of pejoratives—no easy feat, as Langford, trained to be a man of letters, possessed a near-infinite supply of belittling words.

Then, for the first time in his life, Langford heard Elliot shout.

"It turned out that the man who shot me did so deliberately, though he hadn't meant to almost kill me.

That was the result of nerves and bad aim—because I'd seduced his wife."

Mrs. Rowland had lifted a cucumber sandwich. She went still. He'd shocked her without even getting to the worst part of it.

"I had no idea what he was talking about. I'd never met his wife as far as I was concerned, until I remembered, very vaguely, an encounter at a masked ball given by another friend of mine six months previously. There'd been a woman, a young matron with a forlorn air about her.

"What had been an evening's diversion for me, nothing more, had precipitated a domestic crisis for my friend. He loved his wife. They were going through a difficult phase, but he loved her. Loved her deeply, passionately, if also awkwardly and inarticulately."

At first, Elliot's tale invoked in Langford nothing but contempt. He would never let a woman, any woman, matter half so much to him. Any man who did so had only himself to blame for such an idiotic attachment.

Then, after his initial outburst, Elliot did something startling: He apologized. Through gritted teeth, he apologized for everything—for his lack of character, his lapse of judgment, for taking his despair out on Langford when it was his own fault that his wife was unhappy in the first place.

Langford, still irked, accepted his apologies with no pretension of graciousness. But after Elliot's departure, he couldn't get the man out of his head, couldn't stop seeing the expression on Elliot's face as he apologized, an expression that held only self-reproach and a determination to do the right thing despite the avalanche of scorn he was sure to trigger.

With this unconditional apology, Elliot had proved himself, despite his earlier action, to be a man of fortitude, conscience, and decency—everything Langford scorned and despised as too plebeian for his exalted self.

"I didn't want to change or be changed," said Langford. "The way I'd lived was a highly pleasurable, highly addictive way to live. I was loath to give it up. But the damage was done. I was shaken. In the subsequent days of my convalescence, I began to question everything I'd taken for granted about my choices in life. How many others had I hurt in my mindless quest for amusement? What worthy use, if any, had I made of my talents and my vast good fortune? And what would my poor mother have thought of it all?"

Mrs. Rowland listened with grave concentration, her eyes never leaving his. "What happened to your friend and his wife?"

It was a question that still plagued him in the dark of the night. From what he'd learned, they seemed to be fine, with no reports of shameful squabbles or unseemly fondness for the bottle. "I understand they have produced three children together. The eldest came along about a year after he shot me."

"I'm glad to hear that," she said.

"But that doesn't really tell us anything in and of itself, does it?" A man and his wife could very well procreate in mutual abhorrence. He wanted to picture for himself a family in harmony, but his mind would only paint images of silent, frightened children walking on eggshells around parents locked into a hideous bitterness. A bitterness for which Langford was responsible.

"Marriages are curious things," said Mrs. Rowland. "Many are exceedingly fragile. But others are exceptionally resilient, able to recover from the most grievous injuries."

He would like to believe her. But the marriages he'd known had been by and large indifferent. "You speak from personal experience, I hope."

"I do," she said firmly.

"Tell me more," he said. "I demand something at least halfway sensational in return for the divulging of my own unspeakable past."

She picked up her teacup and then, rather resolutely, set it down again. "Sensational it wouldn't be. The most sensational thing I've ever done in my life was blurting out to you that I wished to marry you. But it should come as no surprise now that I had indeed wished to marry you, more than thirty years ago."

It was still a surprise to hear her speak of it so candidly.

"I believed I had the looks, the comportment, and your mother's approval. The only obstacles were your youth and your certain disinclination to marry a girl handpicked by your mother, but I considered neither insurmountable. When you were done with university, I'd still be of a marriageable age. And in the meanwhile I would educate myself in the classics, so as to distinguish myself from other women who would be vying for your hand.

"My plan no doubt strikes you as both arrogant and simpleminded. It was. But I believed fervently in it. In hindsight, I can see that we'd have dealt disastrously together—I'd have been dismayed by your promiscuity and you in turn repelled by my sanctimonious meddle-someness, as my daughter has called it. But in those heady days of 1862, you were mythologically perfect and I was fixated on you.

"Needless to say, when Mr. Rowland began his court-ship, I was not thrilled with his attention. I craved rank and disdained money made in sooty ways, whereas he possessed nothing but the latter. I didn't understand why my father welcomed his calls, until I did as well. Believe me, having to marry him for such a mortifying thing as my family's ruinous finances did not further endear him to me."

There was regret in her voice. Suddenly Langford re-alized that the regret wasn't for him but for the long-departed Mr. Rowland. He felt an odd pulse of jealousy. "You mean to tell me your marriage eventually recov-ered from that grievous injury?"

"It did. But it took a long time. When I married Mr. Rowland, I decided to be a right proper martyr. While I refused to lower myself by seeking out your news or succumbing to affairs, I also refused to see him as any-thing other than a legal entity to whom I sacrificed my dreams for the sake of my family. Even when my senti-ments finally changed, I didn't know what to do. It seemed ridiculous that I should feel something other than duty and obligation toward a man I'd called only Mr. Rowland for so many years."

Her voice trailed off. She finally lifted the cucumber sandwich to her lips again. "We had three good years before he passed away."

He didn't know what to say. He'd always considered happy marriages to be the stuff of fairy tales, about as likely as fire-breathing dragons in this mechanized age. He found himself ill qualified to comment on her loss.

In the silence, she ate the cucumber sandwich with great daintiness. When she was done, she shook her head and smiled wistfully. "Now I am reminded why polite society does not engage in rampant honesty. Awkward, isn't it?"

"Not so much as it is thought-provoking," he answered. "I don't think I've had a more frank conversation in my entire life, on things that mattered."

"And now we've nothing left to talk about except the weather," she said wryly.

"Allow me to correct your misconception here, madam," he said, with equal dryness. "I understand that beneath your facade of ideal femininity, you are a bluestocking who just might be learned enough to appreciate my vast erudition."

"Oh-ho, watch that arrogance, Your Grace," she said, grinning a little. "You might find it to be exactly the other way around. While you were out carousing nightly, I read everything that was ever jotted down during classical antiquity."

"That may very well be. But have you an original thought on it?" he challenged.

She leaned forward slightly. He noted, with pleasure, the gleam in her eyes. "You have a few days to listen, sir?"

Chapter Twenty-five

... Picnic ... capture ... light ... tree ... shadow ... purple ..."

Gigi stared at Freddie's moving lips, her concentration stranded somewhere beyond the Cape of Good Hope. What was he talking about? And why was he speaking so earnestly of such incomprehensible and inconsequential things when barbarians had broken through the gate, torched the bailey, and were about to storm the keep?

They were in trouble. They were in trouble so deep and wide that the best alpinists broke down and wept halfway up and the greatest sailors turned around and headed home long before reaching the other shore.

Then she remembered. He was talking about "Afternoon in the Park," and he was talking about it because she'd asked him to, so that they could carry on a decent conversation and that she could pretend, at least for the duration of his call, that all was well, that the smoke darkening the sky was merely the kitchen roasting a few boars for the evening feast.

She blinked and tried to listen more attentively.

Two days after their return to London, Camden had left to visit his grandfather in Bavaria. But the damage was done. He'd been gone more than a month now, and not one of the nearly eight hundred hours had gone by without her revisiting their last night together and catching her breath anew at his intrepid offer. Everything reminded her of him. The details of her own town house, which she'd barely noticed anymore, had suddenly become a narrative of all her once-fervid hopes: the piano, the paintings, the Cyclades marble she'd selected for the floor of the vestibule because it matched the color of his eyes exactly.

Had she made the right choice?

She knew what it was like to have made an unethical choice. She knew the fear and the corrosive anxiety that bled into and adulterated every joy, every delight. In this instance, she was fairly sure she hadn't come down on the wrong side of the moral divide.

But where was the sense of inner strength conferred by the right choice? Where was the peaceful slumber and the clear sense of purpose? Why, if she'd made the right decision, did it feel oppressive and, on some days, palpably suffocating?

She gave Freddie permission to resume his daily calls, to silence the gossip that the trip to Devon had generated. Freddie's renewed visits quelled the rumors but did nothing to soothe her agitation. The rapport they shared was still there, but the sense that they belonged together was becoming as frayed as a tenth-century tapestry, on the verge of disintegrating altogether with the least exposure to the elements.

"Freddie," she interrupted him.

"Yes?"

She broke the moratorium on physical contact that had been in place since the day of Camden's return and kissed him.

It was always nice kissing Freddie. Sometimes even very nice. But she needed more than nice. She had to have something surpassingly ardent—a veritable conflagration—to erase the burning imprints her husband had left on her, to eradicate from memory her response to him, all hungry abandon and desperate need.

The kiss was very nice.

And she spent the entirety of it thinking of the very person she was hoping to forget.

She pulled back and pasted on a smile. "Forgive the digression. Go on, tell me more about the painting."

Freddie looked to the door as if expecting to see tweeny maids giggle and then run off with news of what they'd espied. When the corridors remained silent, he leaned forward and tried to kiss her again.

"No." She stopped him. She didn't want any more reminders of her vastly different reactions to the two men. Or of the fervor Camden effortlessly fomented in her. "We still shouldn't. That was my fault."

Disappointment dimmed Freddie's eyes. But he nodded slowly, ceding to her wishes. "Three hundred and nine days to go." He sighed. "I swear, the days are thrice as long as they were before."

In this, at least, they were in perfect accord. She turned to his art again, since it was one of the few safe topics left to them. "I'm glad, then, you've been able to keep yourself busy. I hear Lady Wrenworth is pleased with her portrait."

Freddie revived a bit at her compliment. "I had dinner at the Carlisles' two days ago. Miss Carlisle asked me to paint her portrait too. We will probably start next week."

"It seems she has a high enough opinion of your skills, at least."

"Well, she did warn me she would be highly critical if it didn't meet her standards." Freddie smiled a little. "Did you know that she's been to an Impressionist exhibition? All this time I thought you were the only person in my acquaintance who knew anything about the Impressionists."

Gigi bolted straight up. Freddie, startled, rose too. "Is everything all right? Is it Miss Carlisle? I should have asked you about it fir—"

"No, it isn't Miss Carlisle." Oh, if it only were. If only Freddie and Miss Carlisle had been up to some mischief. "It's me. I should have told you long ago: I don't know anything about the Impressionists."

"But you have the most marvelous collection I've ever seen. You—"

"I bought them wholesale. I bought out three private galleries. Because Tremaine liked the Impressionists."

Freddie looked as if she'd just told him that all nine of the queen's children were illegitimate. "But—does this mean—were you—"

"Yes. I was in love with him. I wanted him for more than his title. But I overstepped and my marriage withered on the vine." She took a long breath. "I'm sorry I didn't tell you earlier. Very sorry. I apologize."

Freddie swallowed, gamely trying to digest the past she'd suddenly dumped on him. Then he cleared his throat, and she tensed. Dear God, what would she say if he asked her whether she still loved her husband? She could not lie to him, not at this juncture. Yet she could not bring herself to face the truth. Could not handle the abject terror of being in love—the kind of love that had already once before derailed her life.

Freddie looked as conflicted as she felt. He glanced down at his shoes, stuck a hand in his pocket, drew the hand out again, and fiddled with the fob of his watch. "You—you really don't know anything about the Impressionists?"

She didn't know whether to laugh from relief or to weep. Perhaps Freddie loved her only for her paintings. Perhaps he was as afraid of the question as she.

She pointed at a canvas directly behind him, a landscape of blue sky, blue water, and a French village with ochre roofs and porridge-colored walls. "Do you know who painted that?"

Freddie turned to look. "Yes, I do."

"I don't. Or at least I don't recall anymore. I bought it along with twenty-eight other pieces." She touched his cheek. "Oh, Freddie, forgive me. I—"

She stopped cold. Slowly, as if expecting a knife-wielding assassin, she removed her hand from Freddie's face and turned toward the door. Her husband stood there, leaning against the doorjamb.

Her heart gave a leap of pure, startled joy.

"Lady Tremaine." He nodded. "Lord Frederick."

Her pleasure instantly decayed into self-recrimination. How could she be so vile? She'd completely forgotten about Freddie, as if he wasn't there, as if he'd never been there.

Freddie bowed awkwardly. "Lord Tremaine."

She could return neither Camden's greeting nor his gaze. She only vaguely recalled the time when she'd been dead certain that a divorce was the key to unlocking her happiness, when she'd fully, confidently anticipated putting him behind her once and for all.

Why hadn't she seen it? Why hadn't she realized sooner that she had been seeking that one last battle, a titanic clash, one for the ages?

And why must Camden have turned everything on its head? To go so far as to suggest that he bore an equal share of the culpability. To ask her if she wanted to start afresh, a new life together. Was he mad?

Or was she?

"I was—I was just about to leave," said Freddie.

"Please, Lord Frederick, do not discommode yourself on my behalf. Lady Tremaine's friends are always welcome in this house," said Camden, all gallantry and graciousness. "I've had a long journey; if you will excuse me."

As soon as Camden was out of earshot, Freddie turned to her, half in shock, half in panic. "Do you think he saw us—"

"No." She'd have known. He couldn't have been there for longer than a few seconds.

"You are sure?"

"Tremaine is no more a threat to my physical well being—if that's what you are worried about—than you are."

Freddie took her hands in his. "I guess—I guess that isn't what I'm really worried about. I'm only afraid that the more time he spends around you, the less willing he will be to let you go."

No, it was the other way around. The more time she spent around Camden, the more impossible it became for her to let *him* go.

She patted Freddie's hand. "Don't fret, darling. No one can take me away from you."

She'd made the right choice. She had.

If only the reassurances she offered Freddie didn't sound to her own ears like so much mendacious drivel.

Camden ripped off his necktie and threw it on the bed. He crossed the chamber, rinsed his face, and buried it in a towel. She was touching another man, with tenderness and affection. What else was she doing with him?

Camden slapped down the towel and caught his own reflection in the mirror above the washbasin. He looked about as happy as the citizenry of Paris on the eve of the Storming of the Bastille, primed for violence and mayhem.

He dipped a hand in the washbasin and flung a constellation of water drops against the mirror. The drops rolled down the glassy surface, obscuring the face that stared at him in unblinking belligerence.

Her obstinacy angered him. To be sure, he'd been too abrupt in proposing a new beginning. But now she'd had a whole month to think things through. That she belonged with him and not with Lord Frederick was so obvious to Camden that he couldn't even begin to understand how she could choose otherwise.

His own obstinacy, however, angered him even more. So she'd made a stupid choice. At least it was consistent and honorable. She'd said over and over again that she would swim the Channel in January for the chance to marry Lord Frederick. Why couldn't he accept it? Why did he dream and hope and plot still?

He walked to his steamer trunk and wondered whether there was any sense in even opening the thing. He hadn't returned to England on some random date. The *Campania* would leave for New York City within the week. And he'd seen enough this afternoon.

The image surfaced again in his mind, her hand against Lord Frederick's cheek, the infinite care in her touch. *Oh, Freddie, forgive me,* she'd said. And she'd looked at Camden and immediately looked away.

Camden frowned. He hadn't thought of it before. Why was Gigi asking Lord Frederick to forgive her? Except for that brief interlude when she'd forgotten herself, she'd been unwavering in her loyalty to him. And Camden couldn't imagine her divulging the intimate details of her conjugal relations to anyone, least of all Lord Frederick.

His head remained blank for another minute. Then his world turned upside down. It could have meant only one thing: There had been consequences to their lovemaking. He was going to be a father. They would have a child together.

He gripped the bedpost, unsteady on his feet, as if he were drunk on the very best champagne. A child, dear God, a child. A baby.

She'd agreed to his conditions only because she never intended to conceive. He knew her well enough to know that she would not give up her firstborn to marry Lord Frederick. She would stay with Camden and they would become a family. And given their propensity for ending up in bed together, that family would grow.

He could scarcely comprehend it; absurdly maudlin images inundated his mind. A family of his own, full of stubborn, naughty brats with bright eyes and cunning smiles. Puppies running through the house. Chubby arms held out to him for hugs. And her, regally, confidently at the center of it all.

It was all he wanted. It was everything he'd ever wanted. He pulled off his travel-crumpled coat and flung open the trunk to search for another. In the back of his mind he was vaguely aware that this wasn't how he'd wished to be chosen: by default. But he didn't care anymore. A whole new life was open before him and he was dizzy with the possibilities of it all.

Goodman entered to deposit a batch of letters and departed with the coat Camden had picked out, to be pressed. While Camden waited impatiently for his coat to return, he riffled through the stack of mail.

There was a letter from Theodora. Ironically, she'd become a frequent, faithful correspondent after their respective marriages. He'd gone from merely *Monsieur* to *Cher Monsieur*, then *Très Cher Monsieur, Cher Ami,* and now *Mon Très Cher Ami.*

He skimmed through the pages. She was well. The twins were well. The winter in Buenos Aires continued mild and humid. She contemplated moving back to Europe, for the sake of the children, now that her husband, may God rest his soul, no longer needed the benefit of southern climes. And in other news, she planned to visit New York late in summer. She'd be delighted if he would call on her. She had missed him greatly these past two years.

Not long after Theodora married her grand duke, they relocated to Buenos Aires for his health. Most winters—June, July, August—they traveled to Newport, where they kept a house. Camden was usually too busy with his ventures to join the summer circuit for long stretches of time. But he occasionally sailed up, attended a few functions, and called on her, with presents for Masha and Sasha.

He'd like to see her and the twins. But not this summer. Something far more important and wonderful would keep him in England for quite a while, something called fatherhood.

Goodman returned. Camden shrugged into the newly pressed coat and wound a necktie about his collar. It took him a minute to realize the butler was still hovering about discreetly, waiting for Camden to address him.

"What is it, Goodman?" he asked, knotting the tie.

"Her ladyship would be dining at home this evening. Would your lordship be joining her?" asked Goodman.

Camden paused. There was something different about Goodman's tone. It was almost . . . wistful. Where was that quiet indignation Camden had come to expect, that sense of righteous reproach on behalf of his mistress?

"Yes, I would," said Camden.

He was home at last. He would never leave again.

She didn't hear him as he entered the back parlor. She lolled on a chaise longue, cocooned in a gown the color of the Mediterranean at only a few feet of lucid depth, her head tilted back, her eyes lashed to the eight-foot-wide plaster medallion at the center of the ceiling.

He rarely saw this side of her, still, almost drowsy, languorous and voluptuous as a nymph on a sultry spring afternoon after a night of bacchanalia. The half of her skirts trapped under her weight pulled at the layers on top, tightening the spread of taffeta about the roundness of her hips and the mouthwatering length of her legs, long enough to connect Dover to Calais.

He feasted on her, drinking in her somnolent sensuality. But all too quickly she perceived him. She swung her unshod feet off the chaise and sat up straight.

"You look well," he said.

His compliment took her aback. Uncharacteristically, her hand crept to her coiffure and tucked a tiny escaped strand of hair behind her right ear. "Thank you," she replied, her tone almost diffident. "So do you."

That was not a bad beginning. "I apologize for my earlier intrusion."

"Oh, that. Freddie was just about to leave."

"Did you tell him?"

"Tell him . . . of what?"

He blinked. She didn't sound coy. She sounded baffled.

She was not pregnant.

Suddenly he felt unsteady again, this time as if someone had swung a very large object at the back of his head.

"Nothing," he said. "Nothing."

He walked to the grandfather clock and pretended to check the time on his watch, when he wanted to grab the poker next to the grate and smash everything in the room. The children they were going to have. The life they were going to share. Everything slashed and burned in a vicious assault by reality. And her, oblivious to his pain, throwing away their happiness as if it were last week's bread.

For a while, as he wound a watch that needed no winding, nobody said a thing. Then he heard her deep breath and knew, from the way his heart suddenly splintered, what she was going to say.

"There are no consequences," she said. "Will you let me go?"

Every single cell inside him screamed no. He would most certainly not let her go. In fact, he was feeling downright nostalgic for those terrible old days when a woman had no choice whatsoever in those matters, when he could laugh cruelly, hang Lord Frederick by his ankles in the dungeon, rip her chemise to ribbons, and have her right on the dais of the great hall, under the scandalized eyes of the local bishop.

The period they'd agreed to was far from over. That she refused his entreaty did not release her from the conditions he'd set. That every touch would be fraught with peril did not diminish the allure of holding her fast to the pact.

His heart pounded. He had to close his eyes to control his ragged breath. True, there were all sorts of ways he could bludgeon her, with the diminished but still powerful husbandly prerogatives granted him under English law. But in the end, what would it accomplish?

He recognized much of his younger self in her stubborn clinging to the idea of a "good" love, in her deep, sincere, if vastly misplaced sense of personal responsibility toward Lord Frederick.

Ten years ago she'd clearly perceived the ill suit between Theodora and himself. But she hadn't enough faith to let him discover it for himself. If he were to impregnate her with the express goal of keeping her bound in matrimony, he'd have made exactly the same mistake she had.

But what if she doesn't come to her senses, or doesn't come to her senses in time? howled some primal part of him, all but trembling in angst. His entire person seized, recoiling in dread. That was a distinct possibility. He could not allow that to happen. He could not. His world would fall apart.

Was this how she'd felt all those years ago? The anxiety. The simmering frustration. The corrosive fear that if he didn't do something, she would be lost to him forever.

Had he been nineteen, he'd have embarked on the same wrong path. At thirty-one, even having lived through the aftermath of that debacle, he was still tempted almost beyond endurance.

Only pride and his last shred of good sense saved him in the end. He wanted her to remain his wife not because he'd put an erotic spell over her or because she loved her infant too much to give it up but because she couldn't imagine her life otherwise, because she saw every breath she took intertwined with his, for better or for worse, in sickness and in health, for as long as they both should live.

"As you wish," he said.

"What?!"

She couldn't have heard it right. She couldn't.

"Break open that bottle of champagne. This time next year you could be Lady Philippa Stuart."

She didn't know why she should be so stunned. Yet she was dazed with distress, barely keeping herself together, as if all these weeks she'd been holding her breath, waiting for him to return and reclaim her, vowing never to let go of her again.

He came close, too close for comfort, and sat down next to her, the light worsted wool of his summer trousers socializing insouciantly with the layers of her skirts. She became aware of the subtle scent of starch from his shirt, the spice and citron of his soap. A small part of her wanted to move away. The rest of her wanted him to trespass further, to push her down, hold her immobile, and do whatever he willed with her.

He did something even more shocking. He took her hand in his and said, "I've been a cur, haven't I? Coming here and subjecting you to this impossible situation."

He played with her fingers absently, running the pad of an index finger across the inside of her knuckles. His hands were cool and faintly moist, as if he'd just washed and toweled them dry. The skin of his fingertips scraped her palm ever so slightly, reminding her that he did more than playing piano and rendering scaled drawings with those hands.

She wanted to kiss his hand, every roughened finger pad, every knuckle. She wanted to suck on the ball of his thumb and lick the lines and wrinkles of his palm.

If only she'd conceived. If only. If only. If only.

She had desperately wanted it. With the relentlessness of garden weeds she had wished it, dreamed it, desired it. It would have been an answered prayer, a clarion call, a catalyst around which all future courses of action would instantly crystallize.

But it didn't happen.

"You'll be returning to New York City, then?" she said, careful not to choke.

"On the next steamer, I would imagine. My engineers are quite excited about the progress of our automobile. My accountants salivate at the investment opportunities, given the current upheaval in the stock market," he said, as if his departure had nothing to do with the end of their union. "If you are in the mood for acquiring some rail lines, you should come to the States end of this year or beginning of next."

"I will keep that in mind," she said numbly.

He rose. She stood up too.

"You'll need to watch out for fortune-hunting young ladies now," she said, wondering whether her awkward chuckle sufficiently hid her unhappiness.

"And title-hunting ones too." He smiled. "And those who are simply dazzled by the way I walk and talk."

"Oh, yes, especially watch out for those."

Don't cry. Don't cry now.

Suddenly she realized that she was now the one holding on to him, not the other way around. He but allowed his hands to remain in her panicked grip. He was done. He'd said everything he wanted to say to her.

Let go, she thought. *Let go. Let go. Let go.*

When she at last did what she commanded, it was not through force of will. Her hands slackened and slid off his because it was not her place, nor her privilege, to touch him of her own volition.

"Good-bye, then," she said. "And a safe crossing."

"I wish you every happiness," he said, with grave formality. Then, with a swift peck to her cheek, "Parting is such sweet sorrow."

She didn't know what was so sweet about a sorrow that felt like her still-beating heart impaled upon the fangs of Cerberus. She could only watch hopelessly as he disappeared from her view, from her life.

This time for good.

Chapter Twenty-six

London
25 August

My dearest Philippa,

I apologize for my letter arriving late yesterday. The light these past couple of days, though thinner and cooler than the light of high summer, has a wonderful golden quality, especially late in the day. Miss Carlisle thinks I've made tremendous progress on "Afternoon in the Park."

People are trickling back into London. Last night I had dinner at the Carlisles' and revealed myself a bounder when I admitted that I'd been in town for two weeks. Everyone else boasted that he'd spent the whole of August grousing in Scotland or sailing off the Isle of Wight.

I'll be overjoyed to see you tomorrow. I wish we were already married.

I enclose, as always, a thousand loving thoughts.

Yours ever devoted,
Freddie

Camden's departure had not gone unnoticed. Such was the newsworthiness of the event that within thirty-six hours the whole of London knew he'd vacated his apartment and taken everything with him. The telegraph—indeed, the telephone—paled before the swiftness and efficacy of mouth-to-ear gossip transmission.

What did it mean? Everyone had wanted to know. Had Lady Tremaine won her battle? Had Lord Tremaine permanently withdrawn from the war? Or had he only temporarily retreated to regroup?

Gigi paltered, fudged, and equivocated—when she could. When pressed hard, she lied outright. She didn't know, she repeated. Lord Tremaine did not communicate personal plans to her. She didn't know what he intended—didn't know, didn't know, didn't know—and therefore must curb her impatience just a bit longer.

The divorce papers were typed afresh, needing only her signature. She told the lawyers to sit on them. Goodman inquired whether the furniture and decor in Camden's bedchamber should be removed, covered, or polished daily in anticipation of his return. She had him leave everything alone. Her mother sent a fortune in telegrams. She ignored them en masse.

But she couldn't ignore Freddie. Freddie—bless him for having been so patient—showed mounting signs of distress. *Is there anything from Lord Tremaine's solicitors?* he asked every time they met. *I wish we could get married. Right away.* There was a fearful and almost frantic quality to his pleas. She gave the same carefully crafted answer each time and hated herself with ever greater venom.

Croesus was the only one who didn't pose questions she couldn't answer. But he looked dejected and listless in Camden's absence. She'd find him in the conservatory, napping on Camden's favorite rattan chair, the one with faded blue paisley cushions and cigar burns on the armrest, as if waiting for his return.

Maintaining this intractable status quo was like juggling flaming scimitars. She woke up tired and went to bed dazed with fatigue: parrying a thousand acquaintances' curiosity, keeping her mother at arm's length, cosseting Freddie as best as she could, and withholding the truth even from her few trusted friends.

The end of the season brought little relief. With rail travel as instantaneous as it had become, even her retreat to Briarmeadow provided no refuge. At the end of every week she hosted a three-day house party so that she and Freddie could see each other without any hint of impropriety. As a result, half of the time her house was swollen with people. Torrents of eager, unsatisfied inquisitiveness eddied and swirled, driving poor Freddie to distraction and making her as cross as a stranded dowager with a bladder full of tea and no place to empty it.

And guilt-ridden. And ashamed. And despondent.

She knew what she was doing, of course. She was doing her damnedest to postpone the moment of reckoning, the moment when she must either step forth to marry Freddie or at last face the fact that she could not, not even with Camden having completely removed himself from the melee.

But how could she tell Freddie that? He had been

her faithful friend from the very first. Never in all this chaos had he blamed her, explicitly or implicitly, for anything. He had stood by her with courage and humility, enduring gossip that painted him as either a fool or a fortune hunter of the highest order.

She owed him. He should be rewarded for his loyalty and his trust in her. He'd done so much for her, the steadfast Sancho Panza on her wild-eyed quixotic quest. How could she do any less for him?

The brook was clear and shallow this time of the year. It murmured and soughed, with the occasional burble of a sunlit splash. The willows languidly trailed the tips of their soft branches on the surface of the stream, like a coy woman flaunting the luxuriance of her unbound hair with slow, teasing turns of her head.

Gigi didn't know what she'd expected to find here. Camden flying down the hill like a Cossack and sweeping her up, perhaps. She shook her head, amazed at her own persistent idiocy.

Still she didn't leave. In ten and a half years she'd forgotten how pretty this spot could be, how quiet, with no sounds except for the soft laughter of the brook, the rustle of the morning breeze as it skittered between leaves and branches, the lowing of sheep in the meadow behind her, grazing on a high green carpet of lucerne, and...

Hoofbeats?

Her heart ricocheted against her rib cage. The horse

was coming from her own property. She whirled around, picked up her skirts, and sprinted up the slope.

It was not Camden but Freddie. Her surprise was almost stronger than her disappointment. She didn't even know Freddie could ride. He had an awkward seat but hung on stubbornly, somehow zigzagging the horse forward on a prayer.

She ran toward him. "Freddie! Be careful, Freddie!"

She had to help him untangle his boot from the stirrup as he dismounted, the heel having caught on the way down.

"I'm fine. I'm fine," he reassured her hastily.

She glanced at her watch. Freddie usually arrived on the 2:13. But it was not even eleven o'clock yet. "You are early. Is everything all right?"

"Everything is as it should be," he answered, as he inexpertly tethered the horse to a salt lick. "I didn't know what to do with myself. So I caught an earlier train. You don't mind?"

"No, no, of course not. You are always welcome here." Poor Freddie, he'd become thinner each time she'd seen him. She felt a pinch in her heart. Her darling. How she wanted him to be happy.

She kissed him on his cheek. "Did you paint well yesterday?"

"I'm almost done with the picnic blanket."

"Good," she said, smiling a little to herself, enjoying his enthusiasm the way a parent enjoyed a child's. "What about the items on the blanket? The picnic basket, that one remaining spoon, the half-eaten apple, and the open book?"

"You remember?!" Freddie looked to be in shock.

So he'd noticed her preoccupation. She supposed it would have been too much to hope that he hadn't. "Of course I remember." Though only vaguely. And only because she'd asked him repeatedly. "How are they coming along?"

"The book is giving me fits, half in the sun and half in the shade. I can't make up my mind whether the shadows should be tinged with ochre or viridian."

"What does Miss Carlisle think?"

"Viridian. That's why I'm not sure. I thought they'd be ochre." He took a few steps in the direction of the stream. "Are we still in Briarmeadow? I don't remember ever being this far from the house."

"That's Fairford land over there, beyond the water."

"Land that would have been yours one day."

She glanced at him but caught only his profile. "I've land enough."

Freddie sighed. "What I meant was, if you and Lord Tremaine had not had your falling out. Or if you'd managed to patch things up between the two of you."

"Or if the seventh duke had not died just before he was to marry me," she said. "Life does not proceed according to plans."

"But you probably don't very often wish that the seventh duke hadn't died."

She opened her mouth to say something that would put his mind at ease, as she'd done innumerable times in recent months. But suddenly, the conceit and stupidity of it struck her. Freddie knew. Even if he hadn't acknowledged it, he understood that everything had changed.

His anxiety could not be soothed away with mere words, nor eradicated even with a wedding ceremony. Like the phantom of a haunted house, it might recede into the woodwork when the sun was high and the day bright, only to return with a vengeance at the onset of long nights and howling storms.

Her lack of a response hung heavy in the air. Freddie looked a little shocked. Like her, he'd probably become accustomed to the elaborate reassurances she manufactured with the efficacy of industrial processes. But she was a sham. The castle on the hill she'd built them was no more real than a painted fort on a stage backdrop.

Freddie walked away from her, as if needing the distance to sort out his own thoughts. She could still coddle him, go on feigning that everything would be all right. But it would be an egregious lie.

It was a sad reflection on her arrogance—and naïveté, to some extent—that she remained convinced for so long that she could still make *him* happy, even if he couldn't do the same for her. There was no such thing as a marriage with one happy spouse. Both must be or neither.

She caught up with him at the edge of the meadow.

"The light is good here," he said halfheartedly. He looked like something out of one of his beloved Impressionist paintings, a pensive, melancholy figure *en plein air,* against a brilliant sky and a verdant landscape.

She pointed downstream. "See where the willows

grow close to the bank? That's where I first met Lord Tremaine."

Freddie scuffed the sole of his boot against an exposed rock. "Love at first sight?"

"Close enough, within twenty-four hours." She took a deep breath, and another. It was time to come clean. "In some ways I was a victim of my youth and inexperience: I'd never been in love before and I couldn't handle the intensity of my emotions. But mostly I was my own worst enemy—I was too selfish, too myopic, and too ruthless. I knew it was terrible to deceive him into thinking that his intended had already married someone else, but I went ahead and did it anyway."

Freddie gasped. It was the first time she'd ever told him—or anyone, for that matter—what lay at the core of her marital infelicity. Little wonder. It was an ugly story, full of what she liked least about herself.

"What I did bought me three weeks of happiness—rotten happiness at that—and then utter downfall." She sighed. "Life has its way of teaching humility to the arrogant."

"You are not arrogant," Freddie said stubbornly.

Oh, Freddie, beloved Freddie. "Perhaps not as much as I used to be, but still arrogant enough not to have informed you of the truth from the very beginning—about my marriage, about the paintings..."

Freddie turned toward her. "Do you really think I love you because you had certain paintings on your walls? I was already in love with you long before I ever set foot in your house."

She took his hands in hers, gazed at their linked

fingers, and slowly shook her head. "Alas, I'd hoped it was the paintings. That would make you and Miss Carlisle perfect for each other."

"Angelica wants to make me into something I'm not. She wants me to be the next Bouguereau, the most renowned artist of my day. But I'm not meant to be either famous or prolific. I'm a slow painter, and I don't mind it. I paint what I like and when I like. And I'd rather not second-guess whether a particular shadow is ochre or viridian."

She smiled ruefully. "I can sympathize with that. Though I'd have wished that between you and Miss Carlisle—"

"I love *you*."

"And I adore you," she said, fully meaning every word. "I know of no better man than you. But should we marry, there'd be three of us in this marriage, always. That is not fair to you. And in time it would become intolerable.

"I've agonized about it day and night. You have been the dearest friend. I kept asking myself, how could I let you down? How could I hurt you? But I've come to see that I would completely betray your trust were I to continue this pretense that we could go on as if nothing has changed. Things have changed, and I can no more undo these changes than I can make water flow uphill. I can only be honest with you, once and for all."

Freddie's head lowered. "Do you still love him?"

The question that she'd once dreaded, that he hadn't dared to ask six weeks ago. "Yes, I'm afraid. I don't know how I can apologize to you enough—"

"You don't need to apologize to me for anything. You've never let me down, and you didn't this time either." Freddie enfolded her in an embrace. "Thank you."

She was befuddled. "Whatever for?"

"For liking me as I am. I never much cared for myself until you came along. You don't know how wonderful the past year and a half has been for me."

Dear Freddie, only he could be so sweet to thank her at a time like this. She hugged him back fiercely. "You are the most wonderful person I've ever met, bar none."

When they let go of each other, his eyes were rimmed in red. She, too, had to fight the urge to cry, a sigh and a tear for something that simply wasn't meant to be, a lovely courtship that would have collapsed under the weight of a complicated marriage.

Freddie was the first to speak. "You'll be going to America now, I guess?"

She shrugged, trying to be nonchalant about it. "I don't know."

Camden had let her go with such ease and graciousness; he must have already come to the conclusion that he no longer wanted her, that the offer of reconciliation had been an aberration brought on by an emotional surge that could little withstand the force of reason.

He would have gone on with his life already, taken a new lover or two, perhaps even begun to pay some mind to those beauteous young American misses being paraded before him, with their perfect American teeth and perfect American noses. Would he really want her to show up and spoil all his brand-new plans?

"Come." She placed her hand on Freddie's elbow. "We'll walk back. It's time for lunch. My groom can get the horse later. Tell me what is it you will do, now that you have declined to be the next great, world-renowned artist?"

Gigi saw Freddie to the train station on Monday morning. She managed to have an agreeable time, conversing more frankly, affectionately, and easily with him than she'd been able to do in a long time. She even enjoyed her guests once she took the plunge and informed them that, though she esteemed Freddie more than ever, she had deemed it prudent to release him from his commitment.

When she arrived home, Goodman informed her that she had a caller waiting. "A Mr. Addleshaw from Addleshaw, Pearce and Company is here to see you, milady. I have him in the library."

Addleshaw, Pearce & Co. were Camden's solicitors. What was a senior partner doing paying her a visit far from the city?

Addleshaw was in his early fifties, shortish and natty in his tweed suit. He smiled as Gigi entered the library—not the tight, cautious smile she'd have expected from a lawyer but the delighted grin of a long-lost friend.

"My lady Tremaine." He acknowledged her with a neat bow.

"Mr. Addleshaw. What brought you all the way to Bedfordshire?"

"Business, I fear. Though I confess, your ladyship,

I've wanted to meet you in person ever since Mr. Berwald first contacted us with regard to the late Duke of Fairford."

Of course. How could she have forgotten? She had relentlessly driven Mr. Berwald, her head solicitor, against this very same Mr. Addleshaw, who had defended his client's interests with the ferocity of a mother lion.

She smiled. "Am I quite as fearsome in person?"

He didn't answer her question directly. "When Lord Tremaine informed me that he would marry you by special license, I'd half-expected it. Unlike his late cousin, however, he was all but counting the days. I can see the reason now."

Ah, the sweet yesteryear. Her heart ached anew. She indicated a chair. "Please, have a seat."

Addleshaw produced a rectangular box from his briefcase and pushed it across the desk. The scent of rosewood, sweet and heady, wafted to her nostrils. "This came to our office last week, by special courier. I ask that you please open it and verify that the contents have not been disturbed during the transit and my safe-keeping."

What could Camden possibly want to give her? She drew a complete blank. Inside the wooden box lay a velvet jewelry case. She lifted its lid and lost her breath.

Against a bed of cream satin sparkled a magnificent necklace, the chain of it done entirely in diamonds, one teardrop loop nestled against the next. Seven rubies, each surrounded by diamonds, dangled from the necklace, the smallest two the size of her thumbnails, the largest one at the center bigger than a quail's egg. There were also two matching earbobs, each with a ruby as big as the pad of her index finger.

She'd seen plenty of parure in her life. She owned a few gorgeous pieces herself. But even she rarely came across a set with such nerve and audacity. It would take a superbly self-assured woman to subsume its glitter in her own radiance, to not become a mere accessory to the necklace's splendor and costliness.

There was a note, undated and unsigned, in Camden's slanted hand. *The piano arrived in one piece, as out of tune as ever. Civility demands a return gift. I'd bought the necklace in Copenhagen. You might as well have it.*

In Copenhagen. He'd bought it for *her*.

"Looks like everything is here," she mumbled.

"Very good, ma'am," said Addleshaw. "I am also to inform you that you may, at your pleasure, re-petition for divorce. Lord Tremaine has instructed us to stand aside and do nothing to impede its progress. The divorce should be a fairly straightforward legal matter at this point, as you have no children and no entanglement of properties that isn't already clearly spelled out in your wedding contract."

For a moment, her heart stopped beating. "He has withdrawn all objections?"

"Yes, ma'am, Lord Tremaine stated his assent in a letter addressed to myself. I have brought the letter, if your ladyship would like to read it."

"No," she said quickly. Much too quickly. "That will not be necessary. Your word is good enough."

She rose. The lawyer got to his feet also. "Thank you, ma'am. There is, however, one last small matter."

Gigi glanced at him, surprised. She thought their interview concluded already. "Yes, Mr. Addleshaw?"

"Lord Tremaine requests that you return to him one small item, a ring with filigree gold work and an insignificant sapphire."

She froze. Addleshaw had described her engagement ring.

"I shall have to search for it," she said.

Addleshaw bowed. "Allow me to take leave of you now, Lady Tremaine."

The small sapphire glittered mutedly as Gigi turned the ring between her fingers. Camden had bought it for her. And she'd been floored. Not by the ring itself, but by him, by the overwhelming symbolic meaning of the gesture. *He loved her.*

Her wedding ring she'd donated long ago to the Charity for the Houseless Poor, but this ring she'd kept—out of sight, in a box that also contained the desiccated remains of all the flowers he'd ever brought her and a faded length of blue ribbon that had once been a sweet, crushed bow on Croesus.

Now he desired the ring back. Why revisit the most painfully sweet part of their past now? Why not demand that Croesus be returned too while the poor old dog still had a breath left?

Was he deliberately trying to provoke her?

But what if he wasn't provoking her? What if he

really just wanted the ring back? Well, then. He'd still get what he wanted. He only had to fish it out of her—

She clamped a hand to her mouth. It was hardly the most sexually shocking thought she'd entertained in her life. What astounded her was the waywardness and mischief of it, all ebullient optimism when she'd believed herself morose and listless.

She loved him. If she'd been willing to violate the principles of decency in her youth, why couldn't she do something that was perfectly within the bounds of good behavior—namely, showing up naked on his bed? Only think of the endless sexual possibilities.

She tittered a little into her hands. She was a naughty woman, assuredly. And Camden had adored her for it.

There. Nothing more to be said for it. She was going to New York City. And she would not return until she could inform Mrs. Rowland that she was at last going to be a grandmother.

Chapter Twenty-seven

2 September 1893

Victoria's weekly tea with the duke happened only twice. After that, it became two times a week. For a week and half. Toward the end of that particular week, somehow they ended up in animated conversation by the fence of her front garden as he walked past her cottage. Then he invited her to come along with him, she accepted, and they'd shared the walk each day thereafter.

There were advantages to being an almost hag, Victoria reflected. In her youth she'd been fervently concerned that everyone should perceive her perfection. She mouthed only the most agreeable platitudes and ventured not a single opinion that wasn't as bland as porridge for the invalid.

Amazing what changes thirty more years of life brought about in a woman. Why, only the day before, as they toured her private garden, she'd declared His Grace blind for not seeing that the friendship between Achilles and Patrocles was more than friendship—what man would be so grieved by a mere friend's passing that he'd refuse to let the corpse go to the funeral pyre?

He, on the other hand, dug in his heels and defended the thesis of friendship. Romantic love as Western civilization currently understood it did not emerge until the Middle Ages. Who was to say that masculine friendship, in an epoch before a man saw home and hearth as the anchor of his existence, couldn't have been deeper and more emotional?

Today, on a short stroll through his gardens, they'd disagreed on a host of topics already, from the merits of the metric system to the merits of George Bernard Shaw. The duke felt no compunction in calling a few of her opinions preposterous. She, to her own pleasant surprise, gave no quarter and labeled some of his views as downright asinine, in exactly so many words, to his face.

"I've never heard so many contrary opinions in my entire life," he remarked as they neared the house.

"Alas," she teased him, "what a sheltered life you've led, sir."

He looked startled for a moment. "A sheltered life? I suppose you aren't entirely incorrect. But still, shouldn't a genteelly raised woman such as yourself at least make an effort to agree with me?"

"Only if I'm out to ensnare you, Your Grace."

"You are not?" He turned a baleful gaze on her.

She batted her eyelashes. "Why would I want to put up with a man as disagreeable as yourself when I already have all the advantages of wealth *and* a future duke for a son-in-law?"

"For now."

"Oh, have you not heard, then? My daughter has released Lord Frederick from their engagement. Furthermore, she departed this morning on the *Lucania* for New York City, where her husband resides."

"And that has slaked your blood thirst for a duke of your own?"

"Temporarily," she said modestly.

He harrumphed. The duke had a soft spot for all things ludicrous. Between the two of them, her not-quite hunting of him had become an ongoing joke.

She smiled. Despite his dissolute past, his ever-present hauteur, and his great fondness for intimidating lesser mortals, he'd turned out to be quite a decent chap. His attention flattered, but the gratification extended far beyond the stroking of her vanity. She took genuine pleasure in his company, in the thoughtful, honorable man he had made of himself.

Inside the house, the tea service had been set out in the south parlor, with a footman ceremonially warming the teapot. A fire crackled in the grate, shedding a golden tinge on the walls.

"How remiss of me, Your Grace," she said as the servants retreated. "I have been so busy informing you of your intellectual shortcomings that I forgot to wish you a happy birthday."

"You and two hundred of my closest friends," he said wryly. "I used to throw a birthday bacchanal for myself every year, right here at Ludlow Court."

"Do you miss a good bacchanal?" How could one

not, she thought? She'd never had one and sometimes she still missed it.

"Occasionally. But I don't miss the aftermath. The wallpaper in this particular room had to be changed six times in eleven years."

She glanced at the walls. The damask wall covering was of a different pattern—acanthus rather than fleur-de-lis—but care had been taken to find a near exact match of the rich celadon green background she remembered, so that the room remained much as it was thirty years ago when she'd come for tea and wild dreams. "It's remarkable how little the wallpaper has changed, for all that."

"Trust me, it didn't look anything like this during my more debauched days. The wallpaper featured other...themes."

He smiled. Her heart thudded. Her almost hag-hood notwithstanding, she couldn't help being rampantly curious about the latent scoundrel in him. The least reference to his former wickedness had her in a lather. Accompanied by one of those alluring smiles...well, she could count on not sleeping much tonight.

"I had the old wallpaper duplicated exactly after I retired from Society. I had everything duplicated, from memory and old photographs. But I found I couldn't really stand it." He took a sip of his coffee—he'd given up the pretense of drinking tea several weeks ago, admitting that he couldn't stomach the stuff. "So I made a few changes to suit myself."

"The past does exert a terrible toll, doesn't it?" she said quietly.

He turned an unused teaspoon by its handle, down, and up again. His silence was his answer. In his self-imposed exile there was a strong element of punishment. But it needed not be that way. Not anymore.

"My daughter keeps a private investigator on retainer." Gigi and her modern, progressive ways. She hoped the duke didn't inquire too closely as to why. "I availed myself of his services on something that concerns you."

His eyebrow rose. "If you wish to know how Lady Wimpey's bed caught on fire, you've but to ask me."

A month ago she'd have blushed. Today she didn't even blink. "Actually, I'm more interested in those items of foreign manufacture and iniquitous nature to which Lady Fancot was apparently partial."

"They were only velvet-lined handcuffs—foreign-made, perhaps, but hardly iniquitous," he said.

"Good gracious, what is wrong with that woman?" said Mrs. Rowland indignantly. "Isn't a nice strong silk scarf good enough for her?"

He almost sprayed coffee all over the tablecloth. Good grief. *This* woman constantly forced him to reevaluate his opinion on what being a virtuous woman entailed. Apparently, sexual creativity in a proper, earnest English marriage was not half as dead as he'd believed.

"But I digress," she said, reverting to an impeccable demureness that hid God knew what other experiences and inclinations, a contrast rich in properties aphrodisiacal. His younger self would have expended enough wherewithal to wage three wars to possess her already.

His current self did exactly the same, but only in his mind.

"Now, where was I? Oh, yes. I had the detective look into the state of Mr. Elliot's marriage."

He wouldn't quite compare her announcement to being shot in the chest, having lived through the latter—but it came perilously close. He felt as he had then, standing dumbly in place, looking down at his hand clasped just to the right of his heart, blood seeping out between his fingers.

How could she, of all people, not understand that he could not bear to learn the truth of what had happened to the Elliots' marriage? That whatever peace and tranquillity he'd been able to derive from his hermit's life had depended on his not knowing, on hoping that he had not brought about the unhappiness of an entire family?

Perhaps she sensed the magnitude of shock in him. Her face turned somber. "I shouldn't have, I know."

He glared at her. "Lady, your specialty is undertaking that which you shouldn't. Rest assured you'll face vituperation such as you've never imagined." He could have gone on longer, informed her of his exquisite command of invectives, and depicted in graphic detail the shrunken, pockmarked state of her soul after he was done with her. He didn't. There was no point in postponing the inevitable, though God knew he wanted to. "Now tell me what your detective has learned."

"They are fine," she said, smiling sweetly.

His imagination was playing tricks on him. He

thought she said they were fine. "The truth, if you will," he said.

"My detective worked in the Elliot household for several weeks and reported with confidence that Mr. and Mrs. Elliot get along very well, not just with civility but with fondness."

"You are making it up, aren't you?" he mumbled. How could it be? How could any human association that had gone so wrong right itself? Was he in error after all and Man not quite as doomed as he'd long gloomily believed?

"You need not depend solely on what I say. The detective's name is Samuel Ripley. He worked for the Elliots for three weeks last month, under the name Samuel Trimble, as an underbutler. What I tell you is but a summary of his written report, which arrived yesterday on the late post. It is a richly detailed document, with all overheard exchanges and eyewitness accounts painstakingly recorded.

"My daughter is nothing if not prescient at employing people with the utmost dedication. It is clear to me that Mr. Ripley spent an inordinate amount of time at keyholes and upper-story windows. Why, there are sections of the report that I hastily skimmed over, to preserve my womanly delicacy."

His heart constricted. His throat constricted. The dark cloud of culpability had hung over his head for so long, he'd forgotten the pure, beatific light of a clear conscience.

"I've brought the report with me, if you would like to have it fetched from my carriage."

He rose, fetched the nearly half-inch-thick document himself, and, standing next to Mrs. Rowland's landau, read every word of the meticulously chronicled domestic life of Mr. and Mrs. Elliot, not skipping any sections, particularly not those in which the couple engaged in activities that they ought to have performed no more times than they had children. He especially enjoyed the lurid yet sweet endearments they had for each other. *My darling little dumpling. My lord of the battering ram.*

Langford Fitzwilliam, His Grace the Duke of Perrin, returned to the south parlor walking on air, blinded by the incomprehensible beauty of the world.

Mrs. Rowland had a glass of cognac waiting for him. "There, sir," she said. "You have not ruined a man's life. You may breathe easy again."

He drained the cognac. Fires of joy spread in him unabated. "I feel I can smile through a hundred small country dinners."

"That is exceedingly heartening news. I've at least that many people to impress by having a duke at my table."

"Only at your table?" He grinned. "Where have all your ambitions gone?"

"Not gone at all, only mellowed, Your Grace. I stand today quite satisfied to rub people's faces in our warm friendship."

He *tsk*ed. "I'd have expected more from you, Mrs. Rowland. You do know what your revelation means, do you not?"

The idea had been knocking in his head for some days. It had slipped in, like a determined lover, past all

gates and barricades to whisper by the fluttering curtains of the virgin bower that was his entire experience
with matrimony. And the idea was, he would be quite
happy to marry her, if she would have him.

But his past had weighed on his aspirations. What
right did he have, hissed some dank, sinister voice, to
the love of a good woman, any good woman, let alone
one as beautiful, accomplished, and wise as Mrs.
Rowland? What right did *he* have to happiness for himself, when he'd so casually despoiled the happiness of
others?

But that was no longer the case. He was an emanci-
pated man, liberated from the bondage of blame and
self-torment, at ease to enjoy the years remaining to
him, with her by his side and in his bed, if he was so fortunate.

The gleam in his eyes made Victoria's heart skip a
beat. "That there is still time left to plan a bacchanal?"

"No, that it frees me to propose marriage to you."

She felt as flabbergasted as she'd been when she discovered herself in love with John Rowland. "You wish
to *marry* me?"

"What in the world do you think I have been up to,
madam? Have I not followed the rules of courtship
most assiduously? Drinking tea, for heaven's sake. You
should be flattered. I'd rather drink from my horse's
trough."

"I thought you wished to speak of bygone years. Or,
at most, make me amenable to a liaison."

"I do want to reminisce. And I do plan to take you to
bed, madam. Neither, however, precludes marriage."

"But I am going to be fifty years of age in less than fifteen months!" she cried—and couldn't believe she gave away that carefully guarded secret.

"Excellent news. That makes you a few years younger than I'd thought."

Her eyes went round. "You thought I was *how* old?"

He laughed. "I didn't. I took our age difference into consideration and found that it didn't half-matter. Since you found happiness with a man nineteen years your senior, there is no reason for you to be undone by a man a few years your junior."

"I—I cannot give you any heir."

"For which my cousin's son would be intensely grateful." He took her hand, further disorienting her. "Allow me to assure you, madam, that the thought of infants at my age is profoundly distressing. My second cousin once removed is an upstanding enough fellow. I have no regrets about Ludlow Court passing to him."

She was tempted to say yes right away. Oh, how she was tempted. Not since the invention of chocolate gâteau had there been a greater temptation than what the duke dangled before her nose just now. *Her Grace the Duchess of Perrin.* These magical words exploded shivers of delight deep into her viscera. That at this stage in her life, with old age breathing down her neck like an overeager suitor, she could still gain all the prestige and social stature she'd ever craved, with the man once considered the most elusive bachelor in the kingdom. Why, what kind of fool could possibly respond in the negative?

She bolted out of her chair, jerking her hand away

from him. "No." She shook her head, her voice shaking just perceptibly. "No. Your marrying me would be little different from your efforts to restore Ludlow Court to a facsimile of what it had been when your parents were alive."

He frowned. "I fail to observe any similarity between the two."

"Don't you see? Like the wallpaper, I was your mother's choice!"

"Am I to understand that in following my heart's—not to mention my loins'—desire, I am but atoning for my adolescent negligence of my mother, by fulfilling her wish posthumously?"

She wished it were otherwise, but she wasn't blind. He liked her. He was physically attracted to her. But what separated her from the pack was that she provided a link to his lost youth. "Yes."

"You object to such a noble purpose?"

Oh, drat the man. How could he be flippant at a time like this, when she felt herself about to crumple, held erect only by the stiffness of her corset. "Because it is more wishful thinking than noble purpose. Your mother, bless her memory, would be proud of the man you are today. No further appeasement is necessary."

He nodded, at last appearing somewhat thoughtful. "I take it that is your primary and overwhelming objection."

"It is."

"Any others I should know about? My contrariness, for example? My distaste for tea?"

"No, none at all." She wished there were others. They would make it less painful to refuse his offer.

He smiled, a smile that twenty-five years ago would have left a wide swath of upended crinolines in its wake. "If that is indeed the case, then permit me to read something to you, my dear Mrs. Rowland."

He rose and walked to a satinwood writing desk that had belonged to his mother. More than once the duchess had gone to the desk to retrieve something to show Victoria, during her long-ago visits.

The duke brought out a large vellum-covered book from a lower drawer. "My mother's diary." He quickly turned it three-quarters of the way and then slowly flipped a few more pages, looking for an exact place. "Here's what she wrote on the eighteenth of November, 1862."

He lifted the diary, turned to face her, and read. *"Had tea with Miss Pierce today. Our last time, I suppose. She thanked me for my friendship and informed me of her engagement to a Mr. Rowland, a wealthy man with no antecedents of significance. A pity. Had planned to introduce her to Hubert. They would have made a pleasant match."*

"Hubert?" Was Hubert one of the duke's given names? She'd thought his full name was Langford Alexander *Humphrey* Fitzwilliam. "Who is Hubert?"

"A cousin of mine. The Honorable Hubert Lancaster, third son of Baron Wesport. Lady Wesport was my mother's eldest sister. Hubert would have been about twenty-six at that time."

"Her *nephew*?" Victoria reeled. She covered her

mouth with her hand. Merciful heavens. All these years, all these years . . .

"A nice enough man, with a very respectable name and a very minor fortune," said the duke. "You mustn't forget, I was all of what, fifteen, sixteen at the time? My marriage was far from foremost on my mother's mind. And for all her kindness, she was not unaware of our position. She herself had been the daughter of an earl. She probably expected at least as much pedigree in a daughter-in-law."

Victoria groaned. This was more mortifying even than having her daughter and son-in-law thinking that she'd engaged in illicit acts to lure the duke to her dining table. "If you will be kind enough to have your footman fetch me a spade, I would like to excavate a ten-foot hole outside for myself."

"And ruin my thoroughly beautiful gardens? I think not, my dear." She heard him shut the diary and return it to the drawer. "It's no shame to let your youthful imagination get carried away. Far worldlier women than you have lost their heads over me."

Oh, that man and his arrogance. Her skin must have thickened nicely with age, for she was already in retorting shape. "If you wish me for a bride, you shouldn't try so hard to have me expire from mortification."

He came so close that she could smell the lingering scent of his shaving soap. Her middle-aged heart began pounding. This was actually going to happen. This monumentally desirable, marvelous, and interesting man esteemed her enough to want her hand in marriage. Her!

"May I take your silence to signify that you've accepted my suit?"

"I've said no such thing," she said perversely.

"You should. I've proved, conclusively, that I'm not doing my mother's bidding from beyond the grave. And by your own words, spoken a bare two minutes ago, you have no other objections to marrying me, none at all." He paused, rather deliberately, his eyes sparkling with gleeful wickedness. "I see. You want me to exert myself further. Well then, seducing a woman should be right up my alley, if only I could remember how. Now, do I kiss you before I lie with you or only afterward?"

She summoned a pinch of mock outrage. "As I said before, what a sheltered life you've led, Your Grace. It is both. I'm shocked—shocked, I say—that you do not know better."

He grinned widely. "I don't know why I haven't taken up with virtuous women before. I'm delighted to be making up for lost time."

With that, he kissed her.

It was neither the lofty, delicate kiss she'd envisioned as a nubile girl, nor the sin-drenched osculation that had lately dominated her imagination. He kissed her with gusto and delight, a man at last achieving his heart's desire.

She melted accordingly, in complete contentment.

He pulled away after too short a time. "Now say yes," he urged, nuzzling at the corner of her lips.

"Hardly," she huffed. "I am not signing away my independence on the basis of one kiss, as delicious as it may be. Remember, Your Grace, I was a married woman. A *happily* married one. You, sir, will have to demonstrate ability beyond kissing to persuade me to the altar."

He laughed, a sound of robust delight. Glancing around the parlor, his gaze settled on a scroll-armed settee upholstered in cream brocade.

"All right." He kissed her again. "Be careful what you wish for, my dear Mrs. Rowland. Or you might just get it."

Chapter Twenty-eight

8 September 1893

New York City made Gigi's stomach churn.
Though she'd read that the city aspired to be the
new Paris, she hadn't expected a very near copy of it.
Certain sections of the city, with its solidly neoclassical
edifices, their friezes and cornices plastered in motifs
botanical and mythological, could easily have passed
for parts of the Right Bank. And one particular church
she passed on the way to her hotel had been an unabashed copy of Notre Dame.

She could scarcely control her labored breathing,
though she walked with all the speed of a reform bill
plodding through parliament. Steady traffic flowed up
and down the avenue, a percussive chorus of hooves
striking pavement and wagon wheels creaking under
their load. From a nearby street came the rumble of an
elevated train. The air, though less polluted than
London's, emanated the familiar notes of horseflesh
and industry, though it also hinted faintly, and ever so
exotically, of sausage and mustard.

She made sure to inspect all the hotels, the shopfronts, and all the millionaire manses that crowded lower Fifth Avenue. Still, the distance disappeared in no time. Suddenly she was at the right intersection, the right address. She clenched her fingers about the whalebone handle of her parasol and wrenched her gaze from the opposite side of the street.

No, she must be mistaken. Camden, in his perfect breeding, had always been so modest, so restrained in everything he did. There was nothing in the least modest about this gorgeous manor that looked as if it had been bodily lifted from some nobleman's estate in the heart of Europe. The facade was of pearl-gray granite, the jaunty, polygonal roof dark blue slate. The windows sparkled like the eyes of a flirtatious belle at her most successful ball. And every ornate line and sensuous curve spoke of high baroque and lavish wealth.

She felt like she had the first time she'd seen Camden naked: flabbergasted, speechless, and just about falling down with excitement. She had not come properly prepared. To storm this particular citadel, she'd need much more of the paraphernalia of her own wealth and station to convince a suspicious butler that she was the real Lady Tremaine and not some imposter out to steal the silver.

When the door opened, however, the butler recognized her nearly immediately, judging from his jaw bouncing off the black marble-tiled vestibule. He recovered quickly, stepped back, and bowed. "My lady Tremaine."

Gigi stared at him. The man looked vaguely familiar. She was sure she'd seen him before. She was—

"Beckett!" Amazement and guilt muddled her veins. When her scheme had fallen apart, she hadn't been the only one punished. As surely as the Empress of India was an Englishwoman of German blood, Beckett had abruptly left Twelve Pillars because Camden had discovered his role in the scam. How could he, then, of all people, head the staff in Camden's service?

"You are..." What could she say to him? And had he guessed, over the years, what her role had been in all this? "You are in New York."

"Yes, ma'am," Beckett said respectfully, as he took her parasol, but offered no elaborations. "May I offer you some excellent tea from Assam while we see to your luggage?"

The anteroom was glorious, the drawing room nearly rapturous in its opulence. She'd been in royal palaces that were less rich in furnishing and art—and what art, as if someone had taken a section of the grand gallery of the Louvre and made it into a living space. Not that she didn't find it perfectly to her taste, but what had happened to Camden's preference for understated houses and Impressionist paintings?

"I have brought no luggage," she said. Now, the all-important question. "Is Lord Tremaine home?"

"Lord Tremaine has gone sailing with a group of friends," said Beckett. "We expect him to return no later than five o'clock in the afternoon."

Surely they couldn't be speaking of the same Lord Tremaine. First a house in which a cake-loving Marie

Antoinette would have felt quite at home. And now this supposedly hardworking entrepreneur out frolicking when it wasn't even remotely Sunday?

"In that case, I will call another time," she said. She couldn't possibly sit in the drawing room and sip tea for the next five or six hours. It'd be too strange.

She was beginning to regret a little that she'd asked every person in England who knew Camden's whereabouts not to breathe a word of her Atlantic crossing to him. Perhaps she should have sent advance notice.

"Lord Tremaine is hosting a dinner tonight. Should I send around a carriage to fetch your ladyship from your hotel?"

Gigi shook her head. Before a crowd of strangers was hardly the way she'd envisioned their reunion. "I will arrange for my own conveyance, if I decide to attend. And you need mention nothing to Lord Tremaine."

"As you wish, ma'am."

"You should have your own children," said Theodora.

She stood in a pretty powder-blue frock against the foredeck rail of *La Femme,* the forty-footer Camden sailed for pleasure now that he used the *Mistress* mostly for business. Beyond the fluttering ribbons of her hat, a thicket of masts bobbed sedately—a thousand ships before the topless towers of the Financial District.

Camden looked up from the plate of lemon cookies he was sharing with Masha. "How do you know I don't?" he said.

Theodora blinked, then blushed. "Oh," she said.

He didn't, of course. He'd always been careful. But he probably should have resisted the urge to tease her. The dear girl was never one for jokes. He used to think her beyond adorable when she'd earnestly try to puzzle them out. But then he'd been all of fifteen.

"Forgive me, that was flippant of me," he said. "You are right, I should have children. I would dearly love a few."

"But how?" asked Masha. "Mama said you are to be divorced. How can you have children when you are not married?"

"Masha!" Theodora said sharply, her color heightening further.

"It's all right," said Camden. He turned to Masha, who had her father's sad eyes and long nose. But beneath the face of a lugubrious Russian Madonna lurked a spirit as rambunctious as a dozen sailors on shore leave. "My dear Maria Alekseeva, you are a very shrewd young lady. Indeed, that is my dilemma. What do you propose I do?"

"You must marry someone else," said Masha decisively.

"But who would marry me, Mashenka? I'm so old, as old as dirt."

Masha giggled and lowered her voice. "But Mama is even older than you. Does that mean she's older than dirt?"

Camden whispered, "Yes, it does. But don't tell her."

"What are you whispering about?" said Theodora, a little put out.

"I was just telling Uncle Camden that he should

marry you, Mama," Masha answered cheerfully. "Then you'd be too busy to lecture me."

Before Theodora could recover from her astonishment enough to say anything, Sasha cried from the aft deck of the schooner, "Masha, come here! I've got something tremendous."

Masha promptly dashed off to help her brother reel in his big catch.

"Oh, that girl," muttered Theodora. "She is going to be my despair."

"I wouldn't worry about her," said Camden. "She will fend for herself just fine."

Theodora said nothing. She closed her parasol, held it with both hands before her abdomen, then set its tip down on the deck. Her index finger traced what seemed to be random patterns on the parasol handle. But he knew she was unconsciously writing down her thoughts. *Gott. Gott. Gott.*

She was embarrassed and discomfited. In this she hadn't changed much. Camden helped himself to another cookie.

"I hope you don't think that I came to New York because . . . because you are about to be a free man."

"You didn't?" He'd never alluded to his marital woes. But Theodora was quite aware of them, judging by what Masha had said.

Theodora twisted her hands together, mortified. She was not accustomed to such directness from him. Mutely, she gazed at him, her enormous blue eyes beseeching him to assess the situation, infer what she wanted, and offer it to her without her ever having to speak a word—what he'd always done before.

He sighed. She'd come at a wretched time, when he desperately wanted to be either alone at sea or alone in his workshop. He hadn't the heart to disappoint the children, so he'd spent the past three weeks showing them a good time in the city. But he had no where-withal left to play guessing games with her. If she wanted something from him—and she did, *something*—then she could damned well come out and say it.

"Will you really divorce Lady Tremaine?" she asked timidly.

"She is the one who wants a divorce, therefore we are headed for a divorce," he said, more surly than he'd intended. A letter had arrived from Addleshaw this morning, assuring him that the engagement ring he had requested from Gigi would arrive forthwith.

He didn't want the damned ring. Wasn't it enough that he had to look at the cursed piano? He wanted *her* to come with the ring. But his ploy had failed. She would marry Lord Frederick. And he, what would he do?

"You will need another wife, won't you?" Theodora's voice had dropped so low that he barely heard the last few syllables.

He didn't need another wife. He wanted the one he already had. "That is a question for the future."

Gott hilf mir, her finger scribbled. Well, God help them all.

The children screamed in delight, breaking the uneasy silence. "Look what we got! Look what we got!"

hollered Sasha, running toward them with a striped bass that looked to be at least a five-pounder.

"Look at that!" exclaimed Camden, standing up. "I never caught anything half so big when I was your age."

He unhooked the vigorously thrashing fish and tossed it into a bucket of water. "Want to have it served with a lemon butter sauce for supper?"

"Yes!" the boy answered unambiguously.

"Right ho!" Camden lifted Sasha high in the air and spun him around.

"Me, me too! I helped," said Masha, raising her arms up to Camden.

He did the same with her, enjoying her high-pitched giggles. "My expert anglers, think you two can catch another one before we set sail?"

They ran off, leaving him again alone with Theodora. He opened the lid of the picnic basket to store the remainder of their lunch: half of a cold chicken pie, slices of roast beef, an almost empty dish of potato salad, and a few lemon cookies.

Theodora came to stand beside him as he returned a flask of lemonade to its place. "I've been thinking of the past, of St. Petersburg," she murmured. "Remember what you used to say to me then?"

"I haven't forgotten." He closed the picnic basket and stared down at it. "But the truth is, I'll be bitter over the divorce. A new wife would find me lacking in both affection and care, and I love you too well to subject you to that."

There, he'd finally admitted it. The divorce would devastate him. Would come just short of annihilating him. He dreaded the post deliveries, dreaded any and all letters from his English solicitors, dreaded the eventual cable from Mrs. Rowland decrying Gigi's irreversible folly.

"I see."

She sounded abysmally dejected, like a child being told that there would be no Christmas come December. He pulled her toward him. "But I will still take care of you, always. If you are ever in need, I'm just a cable away. And if, God forbid, something should happen to you, I'll raise the twins as my own."

He kissed the top of her straw hat. "I will take care of everything for you, you still have my word on that."

"I guess...I guess that's all any woman could ask for," she said slowly. The shadow on her face lifted. She smiled shyly and kissed him on the cheek. "Thank you. You are the best friend I ever had."

They stood thus for a minute, with his hand on her waist and her face resting against his sleeve. He sighed. Ironic that he should have his arm about Theodora on a boat that he'd again somehow named after Gigi—*La Femme*, the woman, the wife.

But the sun was warm, the breeze cool. It was still a beautiful day even if he couldn't have his wife. He returned a kiss to Theodora's cheek. "Shall we sail?"

Gigi saw the horseless carriage as soon as she stepped out of the Waldorf Hotel at five o'clock. The beautiful piece of machinery, built around a phaeton chassis, black with trims of crimson, rumbled its progress majestically. The liveried manservant who drove it couldn't have looked prouder had he been atop the queen's state coach.

His pride was reflected on the faces of two of the passengers he ferried. The children basked in the admiration and curiosity displayed on the sea of faces turned toward them. The third passenger's reaction was harder to gauge, as the long veil of her hat effectively hid all her features above her chin.

"To whom does the automobile belong?" Gigi asked a doorman.

"To the English lordship who lives ten blocks down, ma'am," said the doorman. "They say he's a viscount."

"No, an earl," said the other footman. "And that's his sweetheart the Russian grand duchess there. She's been coming up in his horseless carriage every day now."

Gigi felt herself petrify. Camden lived ten blocks south of the Waldorf Hotel. She'd counted it this morning. And hadn't the former Miss von Schweppenburg married a Russian grand duke?

She fumbled with the veil of her own hat as the automobile came to a quiet stop before the hotel. The passengers alit. The driver opened the boot and retrieved a heavy-looking bucket, which the children immediately took from him, causing their mother to issue a string of safety warnings in French.

The driver bowed. "I'll bring the carriage around at eleven, Your Highness."

"Thank you," said Her Highness.

And it was her, the former Miss von Schweppenburg. Who was going back to Camden's house at eleven o'clock at night, after the dinner crowd would have departed, for purposes that needed no clarification.

The bucket was passed to a doorman with instructions for the kitchen. Grand Duchess Theodora and her children entered the hotel and disappeared into a lift.

Gigi slowly walked to a corner of the lobby and sat down. She'd expected to fight for him, given that he might have already taken a lover, to physically remove the other woman, or women—she'd had far too much time to ponder it on the crossing—from his bed and his life, if necessary.

Any other woman.

What was she to do now?

Chapter Twenty-nine

"If you do not mind my forwardness, Lord Tremaine, I think my Consuelo would make you a splendid marchioness," said Mrs. William Vanderbilt, née Alva Erskine Smith.

"I do not mind at all," said Camden. "I've been known to be exceedingly fond of forward women. But I am, however, almost twice Miss Vanderbilt's age and still very much married, last time I checked."

"My, sir, you are such a gentleman," cooed Mrs. Vanderbilt. Her Southern-belle manners, however, did not quite disguise her flinty determination. "But I have heard from numerous trustworthy sources, on both sides of the Atlantic, that you may not remain married for much longer."

It's because you are young and you used to be a bit of an impoverished nobody. Expect the proposals to fly fast and thick now. After nearly eleven years, that prediction was coming true. This wasn't the first time Mrs. Vanderbilt had broached the issue in recent weeks. Nor was she the first, second, or even third matron with a marriageable daughter to suggest that her precious girl was just the perfect candidate for him.

All throughout the dinner, the first he'd held since his return from England, he'd felt on display, like a fattened goose about to be turned into foie gras. The smiles on the women were too bright, too ingratiating. Even the men with whom he'd shared cigars, whiskey, and business ventures for the past ten years regarded him differently, with the sort of hearty approval better reserved for sixteen-year-old mistresses.

"Well, then, milord, you will come for dinner next Wednesday?" drawled Mrs. Vanderbilt. "I don't think you've seen Consuelo for a good six months, and she has become ever so much more beautiful and swanlike and—"

The doors to the drawing room swung open—burst open, in fact, as if blown apart by a passing cyclone. In the doorway loomed a woman and a dog. The dog was small, well-behaved, and sleepy, snuggled in the crook of the woman's arm. The woman was tall, haughty, and ravishing, her voluptuous figure poured into a sheath of carmine velvet, her throat and breast glistening with a maharaja's cache of rubies and diamonds. And, ever so incongruously, she also sported a very humble sapphire ring on her left hand.

"Now, who is that?" demanded Mrs. Vanderbilt, at once peeved and fascinated.

"That, my dear Mrs. Vanderbilt," replied Camden, with a glee he couldn't and didn't hide, "is my lady wife."

* * *

Never in her entire life had Gigi felt so vulnerable, standing before a roomful of strangers—and a husband who had another lover arriving in an hour.

She'd already ordered a suite for her return voyage on the *Lucania* and telegraphed Goodman to have the house on Park Lane readied. A cable for Mrs. Rowland lay on the bureau in her hotel chamber—*Tremaine has taken up with the Grand Duchess Theodora, née von Schweppenburg*—but somehow she couldn't send it, couldn't admit that final defeat, not without one last gallant and largely foredoomed charge down the hill.

Now all eyes were on her, including Camden's. There was surprise on his face, a measure of amusement, and then a nonchalance that did not bode well for her chances. She waited for him to acknowledge her, to toss her at least a line of greeting. But other than a few inaudible words to the woman next to him, he said nothing, leaving her to jump off the cliff entirely by herself.

She let her eyes travel the drawing room. "Truly, Tremaine, I expected better from you. The decor is obvious to the point of atrociousness."

A collective gasp reverberated from the high ceiling.

He smiled, a cool smile that nevertheless ignited her hopes anew. "My lady Tremaine, I distinctly remember informing you dinner was at half past seven. Your punctuality leaves much to be desired."

"We will discuss my punctuality or the lack thereof later, in private," she said, her heart pounding. "You may present your friends to me now."

* * *

Lady Tremaine couldn't quite keep straight who was an Astor, who a Vanderbilt, and who a Morgan. But it didn't matter. She had fortune, which they admired, and title, which they coveted. Her temperament fitted in perfectly with the energetic, purposeful, ambitious upper crust of the American aristocracy; her independence earned her the approval of the wives, several of whom were sympathetic toward the suffragists.

The men gawked, alongside Camden.

There'd been much surreptitious necktie-loosening when she—*later, in private*—unmistakably commanded him to shag her blind. The sexual energy she exuded was palpable; the response it provoked in him was downright atrocious. No other women came anywhere near him for the remainder of the evening; even the unsighted could see that he was hanging on to civilized behavior by the skin of his teeth, that if they didn't make themselves scarce, he'd commit public coitus right before their eyes—with his own wife.

In the end she did something almost as shocking. At precisely eleven o'clock, she disengaged from the guests and placed herself at the center of the drawing room. "It has been lovely meeting the very best society of New York, I'm sure. But if you will forgive me, it's been a long journey, and I feel myself no longer quite equal to company. Ladies and gentlemen, my repose beckons. Good night."

And with that, she left, the intricate train of her gown swaying majestically, leaving behind a speechless crowd, the ladies fanning themselves much too vigorously, the men looking as if they'd sign away half of their companies if only they could follow her out on the heels of her black suede evening slippers.

"Alas," said Camden, keeping his tone light. "It seems I have utterly failed in my husbandly duties of guidance and discipline. I shall henceforth devote the greater part of my time and energy to that eminently noble endeavor."

Half of the women blushed. Three-quarters of the men cleared their throats. The leave-taking began in the next minute, and the drawing room emptied at record speed.

Camden raced up the stairs, charged into his apartment, and threw open the door to his bedchamber. She lay prone across his bed, her cheeks in her palms, studying his copy of the *Wall Street Journal*—completely naked. Those legs, that sumptuous bottom, the curvature of her breast squeezed round and tight against the underside of her arm, and all that beautiful hair spilled across her back. Carnal desire, already simmering, exploded in him.

She tilted her head and smiled. "Hullo, Camden."

He closed the door behind him. "Hullo, Gigi. Fancy seeing you here."

"Well, you know how it is. Investment opportunities, et cetera, et cetera."

"Took you long enough," he growled. "I was about to hire dognappers."

She licked her teeth. "Am I worth the wait?"

God above! He could barely remain standing. "You were unspeakably brazen before my guests. I'm afraid you have laid waste to my staid, upstanding reputation."

"Have I? I'm terribly sorry. I must learn to be a better wife. If only you'd give me a little more practice..." She turned onto her back and slid a knuckle across her lower lip. "Won't you come to bed and make me pregnant?"

He was on that bed and inside her in a fraction of a second. She was all hellfire and heavenly suppleness, clutching at him, her legs wrapped tight about him, her unabashed gasps and moans driving him mad with desire.

He shook, shuddered, and convulsed, his vaunted control in pieces as he came endlessly, well on his way to making her pregnant.

"Will you remonstrate me for my lack of punctuality now?" Gigi said later, still mostly breathless, lying with her head on his arm.

"That and your utter want of respect toward the beauty and splendor of the public rooms of my house."

"I like them. They quite suit my parvenu tastes." The private quarter, which housed his Impressionist collection, was by contrast cool and serene. "I was looking for something to say that would immediately establish my English eccentricity."

"I think you've succeeded beyond all hope," he said. "They will prattle of this night for years to come, especially if you go into confinement nine months from today."

She smiled to herself. "You think you are so virile."

"I *know* I'm so virile." He kissed her earlobe. "Let's just hope the second time's the charm."

She didn't immediately catch the significance of his words. When she did, she found herself scrambling to a sitting position. He'd obliquely referred to her first pregnancy, which had ended in a miscarriage. But she had never spoken of it, not even to her mother. Had hidden it, along with her ravenous love, in the deepest recesses of her heart, a secret prisoner in the dungeon, whose clanking chains and whimpers of despair only she heard in the witching hours of the night.

"You knew," she whispered.

She shouldn't be so surprised. It was silly to believe her mother wouldn't have found out about it—and that once she did, she wouldn't have told Camden in the hope of forcing a reaction from him.

"Only years after the fact. I got quite drunk the day I learned of it. I believe I smashed my entire model ship collection." He sighed, smoothing a strand of her hair between his fingers. "But perhaps that was out of jealousy, since your mother mentioned the miscarriage in the same breath she invoked Lord Wrenworth's name."

She lay down again, facing him. "You? Jealous? You are with a different woman every time I turn around."

"Guilty as charged in Copenhagen. But I didn't sleep with anyone in Paris."

What she really wanted to know was what he'd been doing with the former Miss von Schweppenburg. But his extraordinary claim about Paris perked her ears nevertheless.

"Who was that woman calling on you late at night, then?"

"A rising actress at the Opéra. I hired her to knock on my door and sit in my apartment for a few hours, so that you'd assume the worst and hurt as much as I did. But I didn't touch her, or any other woman. I was faithful to you, for what that's worth, until I learned that you'd taken a lover already."

That would make him celibate for at least two and a half years after he'd left her. "Why? Why were you faithful to me?" she marveled.

"Oh, I had no time. Within weeks after my arrival in America I'd taken on such astronomical loans I could scarcely eat or sleep for fear of defaulting. I was up at five every morning and never went to bed before one." He grimaced a little at the memory, then smiled at her. "You could also say I had no intention. I wanted *you*. I wanted to stomp back into your life one day, twice as wealthy as you, if possible. I imagined decadent, histrionic reunions and wasted a river of sperm masturbating to these fantasies."

She knew what the word meant—it was what the Muscular Christians were trying to prevent, through a regimen of rigorous sports that would leave English men and boys too exhausted for anything but dead slumber—though she was sure she'd never heard it spoken aloud before. She'd thought it a dirty word, but the way he said it, as if it were the most natural thing in the world, made voluptuous images dance before her eyes.

If she weren't already naked, she'd rip off her clothes and throw herself at him. She took one of his hands and rubbed the moist inside of her lower lip against the calluses of his palm. "Tell me one of those fantasies."

He leveled a dirty look at her. "Only if you promise to act your part in it."

She bowed her head with becoming humility. "Well, I did tell myself that I would be the most obliging wife who ever lived."

He smiled wickedly, pulling her to him. "Oh, this is getting better and better."

In between fulfillment of his inventive—at times highly unorthodox—fantasies, Gigi and Camden talked about the children they would have and all the things they couldn't wait to do together. At Christmas they'd visit his grandfather in Bavaria. Come spring she would show him the gorgeous West Country of England and Wales. And in summer, if she wasn't already too far gone in her pregnancy, they'd sail the Aegean and the Adriatic on the *Mistress*.

"Take me somewhere to ride," she said. "I haven't been on a horse since you walked out on me the first time."

"I've a country house in Connecticut, on a pretty piece of land. We'll sail up tomorrow."

Thinking of the arrangements made her remember Beckett. "Your butler ... do you know that—"

"I was the one who told him to go far away. We were both shocked when three years later he came for a position I'd advertised. He immediately begged pardon and turned to leave. I stopped him. To this day I don't really know why." Camden shrugged. "By the end of the year, he'll have worked for me for seven years."

Whatever his reasons, she was grateful. "It's a well-run house," she murmured. "And what of his son?"

"He was in a Liverpool jail for a year or two, then went to South Africa when gold was discovered. He married last year."

She breathed a further sigh of relief. It was most agreeably humbling to learn that her sins hadn't stopped the earth from spinning or other people from getting on tolerably with the rest of their lives.

He traced her spine from her neck down to her tailbone and back again. "Tell me about Lord Frederick. How did he take your decision not to marry him?"

"With much better grace than I deserved, to be sure. I only wish I could arrange for him to be happy always. But don't worry," she added hastily. "I will leave him alone to live his own life. I've learned my lesson."

"Hmm, have you?" He kissed her shoulder. "That's what you said the last time we were in bed together."

She turned onto her back and placed his hand between her legs. "Feel for yourself. Nothing there anymore between you and me."

She lost count of how many times they made love. Too much and still not quite enough. Some time in the small hours of the night, he ran her a bath and laundered her thoroughly, making her giggle and squeal with all the naughty things a playful man could do with a willing woman, a tub of hot water, and a piece of fragrant soap.

When it was his turn to wash, she looted the kitchen for food. He was in his dressing gown toweling his hair dry when she returned, carrying with her a haunch of roasted pheasant left over from the dinner, a half loaf of bread, and a bowl of morello cherries.

"My God," he said, tossing aside the towel to take the tray from her. "I had no idea you did things other than turning profits and enslaving men."

She laughed as he set the tray down atop the large cedar chest at the foot of the bed. "Allow me to shock you by knitting you a pair of socks this Christmas, then."

He smiled, tearing off a chunk of bread. "Then I shall be forced to build you a rocking chair. Alas, my carpentry is quite rusty."

Tenderness, that most alien and disconcerting of emotions, swelled and billowed in her. She picked up a cherry and stared down at the soft, bright-red fruit. "I love you."

The last time she'd declared her love he'd thrown it right back in her face. She waited uncertainly for his response. She didn't even have to wait a second. He leaned over and kissed her on the mouth. "I love you more."

All the sugar in Cuba couldn't compete with the sweetness in her heart. "More than you love the grand duchess?"

"Idiot." He ruffled her already bedraggled hair. "I haven't loved her since the day I met you."

"But I saw her today, in your automobile. The doormen at the hotel said she's been seen in your automobile every day. And your driver said he was coming back for her at eleven o'clock at night."

"Incorrect. He is going to meet her and the children at eleven o'clock tomorrow morning, to take them to the train station. She has some relatives to visit in Washington, D.C."

"Then you haven't been having an affair with her?"

"I last kissed her in 1881, and I don't miss it." A sly smile curved his mouth. "So that explains your very delectable aggression. Perhaps I should keep her around, to always ensure your prompt ardor."

"Only if you want Freddie to set up a canvas in our parlor."

"Won't bother me, as long as I can still have you on the piano." He grinned. "I can never look at the damned thing without seeing you draped over it in all kinds of lascivious ways, your sweet bum up in the—"

She threw the cherry at him. He caught the fruit and ate it. "I almost forgot," he said, walking to a writing desk in the next room. "Look what news was delivered to my doorstep this afternoon."

He brought back a telegram. She wiped her hands on a napkin and took the telegram from him.

dear sir stop his grace has persuaded me to the altar
stop we wed yesterday stop will shortly depart for
corfu stop yours most affectionately stop
victoria perrin

Gigi covered her open mouth. Her mother. A duchess. The Duke of Perrin's duchess, no less. She'd suspected something, of course, but this—marriage—this was something else entirely.

"Do you realize what this means?" said Camden.

"That she'll take precedence over both you and me now?" Gigi shook her head in both delight and stupefaction.

"That the Duke of Perrin will find himself a grandfather in nine months."

She laughed hard. The image of the Duke of Perrin suddenly becoming anyone's grandfather was much too delicious. She pulled Camden close and kissed him. "Do you know that you are the love of my life?"

"Always did," said her husband. "But do you know that *you* are the love of *my* life?"

She set her head on his shoulder and rubbed contentedly. "Now I do."

About the Author

Sherry Thomas arrived on American soil at age thirteen. Within a year, with whatever English she'd scraped together and her trusty English-Chinese dictionary by her side, she was already plowing through the 600-page behemoth historical romances of the day. The vocabulary she gleaned from those stories of unquenchable ardor propelled her to great successes on the SAT and the GRE and came in very handy when she turned to writing romances herself.

Sherry has a B.S. in economics from Louisiana State University and a master's degree in accounting from the University of Texas at Austin. She lives in central Texas with her husband and two sons. When she's not writing, she enjoys reading, playing computer games with her boys, and reading some more.

Visit her on the web at www.sherrythomas.com.

Don't miss

Delicious

BY

SHERRY THOMAS

Available at your favorite bookseller
in August 2008

Read on for an exclusive sneak peek!

Delicious

BY SHERRY THOMAS

On sale August 2008

England
November 1892

In retrospect people say it was a Cinderella story. Notably missing was the personage of the Fairy Godmother. But other than that, the narrative seemed to contain all the elements of the fairy tale.

There was something of a modern prince. He had no royal blood, but he was a powerful man—London's foremost barrister, Mr. Gladstone's right hand—a man who would very likely one day, fifteen years hence, occupy 10 Downing Street and pass such radical reforms as to provide pensions for the elderly and health insurance to the working class.

There was a woman who spent much of her life in the kitchen. In the eyes of many, she was a nobody. For others, she was one of the greatest cooks of her generation, her food said to be so divine that old men dined with the gusto of adolescent boys, and so seductive that lovers forsook each other, as long as a crumb remained on the table.

There was a ball, not the usual sort of ball that made it into fairy tales or even ordinary tales, but a ball nevertheless. There was the requisite Evilish Female Relative. And most important for connoisseurs of fairy tales, there was footgear left behind in a hurry—nothing so frivolous or fancy as glass slippers, yet carefully kept and cherished, with a flickering flame of hope, for years upon years.

A Cinderella story, indeed.

Or was it?

It all began—or resumed, depending on how one looked at it—the day Bertie Somerset died.

The kitchen at Fairleigh Park was palatial in dimension, as grand as anything to be found at Chatsworth or Blenheim, and certainly several times larger than what one would expect for a manor the size of Fairleigh Park.

Bertie Somerset had the entire kitchen complex renovated in 1877—shortly after he inherited, and two years before Verity Durant came to work for him. After the improvements, the complex boasted of a dairy, a scullery, and a pantry each the size of a small cottage, separate larders for meat, game, and fish, two smokehouses, and a mushroom house where a heap of composted manure provided edible mushrooms year round.

The main kitchen, floored in cool rectangles of gray flagstone, with oak duckboards where the kitchen staff most often stood, had an old-fashioned open hearth and two modern closed ranges. The ceiling rose twenty feet above the floor. Windows were set high and faced only north and east, so that not a single beam of sunlight would ever stray inside. But still it was sweaty work in winter; in summer the temperatures inside rose hot enough to immolate.

Three maids toiled in the adjacent scullery, washing up all the plates, cups, and flatware from the servants' afternoon tea. One of Verity's apprentices stuffed tiny eggplants at the central work table, the other three stood at their respective stations about the room, attending to the rigors of dinner for the staff as well as for the master of the house.

The soup course had just been carried out, trailing behind a murmur of the sweetness of caramelized onion. From the stove billowed the steam of a white wine broth, in the last stages of reduction before being made into a sauce for a filet of brill that had been earlier poached in it. Over the great hearth a quartet of teals roasted on a spit turned by a second kitchen maid. She also looked after the *civet* of hare slowly stewing in the coals, which emitted a powerful, gamy smell every time it was stirred.

The odors of her kitchen were as beautiful to Verity as the sounds of an orchestra in the crescendo of a symphony. This kitchen was her fiefdom, her sanctuary. She cooked with an absolute, almost nerveless concentration, her awareness extending to the subtlest stimulation of the senses and the least movement on the part of her underlings.

The sound of her favorite apprentice not stirring the hazelnut butter made her turn her head slightly. "Mademoiselle Porter, the butter," she said, her voice stern. Her voice was always stern in the kitchen.

"Yes, Madame. Sorry, Madame," said Becky Porter. The girl would be purple with embarrassment now—she knew very well that it took only a few seconds of inattention before hazelnut butter became black butter.

Verity gave Tim Cartwright, the apprentice standing before the white wine reduction, a hard stare. The young man blanched. He cooked liked a dream, his sauces as velvety and breathtaking as a starry night, his soufflés taller than toques. But Verity would not hesitate to let him go without a letter of character if he made an improper advance toward Becky, Becky who'd been with Verity since she was a thirteen-year-old child.

Most of the hazelnut butter would be consumed at dinner. But a portion of it was to be saved for the midnight repast her employer had requested: one steak au poivre, a dozen oysters in Mornay sauce, potato croquettes à la Dauphine, a small lemon tart, still warm, and half a dozen dessert crepes spread with, *mais bien sûr,* hazelnut butter.

Crepes with hazelnut butter—Mrs. Danner tonight. Three days ago it had been Mrs. Childs. Bertie was becoming promiscuous in his middle age. Verity removed the cassoulet from the oven and grinned a little to herself, imagining the scene that would hopefully ensue should Mrs. Danner and Mrs. Childs find out that they shared Bertie's less-than-undying devotion.

The service hatch door burst open and slammed into a dresser, rattling the rows of copper lids hanging on pin-rails, startling one of them off its anchor. The lid hit the floor hard, bounced and wobbled, its metallic bangs and scrapes echoing in the steam and smolder of the kitchen. Verity looked up sharply. The footmen in this house knew better than to throw doors open like that.

"Madame!" Dickie, the first footman, gasped from the doorway, sweat dampening his hair despite the November chill. "Mr. Somerset—Mr. Somerset, he be not right!"

Something about Dickie's wild expression suggested that Bertie was far worse than "not right." Verity motioned Edith Briggs, her lead apprentice, to take over her spot before the stove. She wiped her hands on a clean towel and went to the door.

"Carry on," she instructed her crew before closing the door behind Dickie and herself. Dickie was already scrambling in the direction of the house.

"What's the matter?" she said, lengthening her strides to keep up with the footman.

"He be out cold, Madame."

"Has someone sent for Dr. Sergeant?"

"Mick from the stables just rode out."

She'd forgotten her shawl. The air in the unheated passage between kitchen and manor chilled the sheen of perspiration on her face and neck. Dickie pushed open doors: doors to the warming kitchen, doors to another passage, doors to the butler's pantry. Her heart thumped as they entered the dining room. But it was empty, save for an ominously overturned chair. On the floor by the chair were a puddle of water and, a little away, a miraculously unbroken crystal goblet, glinting in the light of the candelabra. A forlorn, half-finished bowl of onion soup still sat at the head of the table, waiting for dinner to resume.

Dickie led her to a drawing room deeper into the house. A gaggle of housemaids stood by the door, clutching each other's sleeves and peering in cautiously. They fell back at Verity's approach and bobbed unnecessary curtsies.

Her erstwhile lover reclined, supine, on a settee of dark blue. He wore a disconcertingly peaceful expression. Someone had loosened his necktie and opened his shirt at the collar. This state of undress contrasted sharply with his stiff positioning, his hands folded together above his breastbone like those of an effigy atop a stone sarcophagus.

Mr. Prior, the butler, stood guard over Bertie's inert body, more or less wringing his hands. At her entrance, he hurried to her side and whispered, "He's not breathing."

Her own breath quite left her at that. "Since when?"

"Since before Dickie went to the kitchen, Madame," said the butler, without quite his usual sangfroid.

Was that five minutes? Seven? She stood immobile a long moment, unable to think. It didn't make any sense. Bertie was a healthy man who experienced few physical maladies.

She crossed the room, dipping to one knee before the settee. "Bertie," she called softly, addressing him more intimately than she had at any point in the past decade. "Can you hear me, Bertie?"

He did not respond. No dramatic fluttering of the eyelids. No looking at her as if he were Snow White freshly awakened from a poisoned sleep and she the prince who brought him back to life.

She touched him, something else she hadn't done in ten years. His palm was wet as was his starched cuff. He was still warm, but her finger pressed over his wrist could detect no pulse, only an obstinate stillness.

She dug the pad of her thumb into his veins. Could he possibly be dead? He was only thirty-eight years old. He hadn't even been ill. And he had an assignation with Mrs. Danner tonight. The oysters for his post-coital fortification were resting on a bed of ice in the cold larder and the hazelnut butter was ready for the dessert crepes beloved by Mrs. Danner.

But his pulse refused to beat.

She released his hand and rose, her mind numb. With the exception of the kitchen regiment, the staff had assembled in the drawing room, the men behind Mr. Prior, the women behind Mrs. Boyce the house-keeper, everyone pressed close to the walls, a sea of black uniforms with foam caps of white collars and white aprons.

To Mrs. Boyce's inquiring gaze, Verity shook her head. The man who was once to be her prince was dead. He had taken her up to his castle, but had not kept her there. In the end she had returned to the kitchen, dumped the shards of her delusion in the rubbish bin, and carried on as if she'd never believed that she stood to become the mistress of this esteemed house.

"We'd better cable his solicitors then," said Mrs. Boyce. "They'll need to inform his brother that Fairleigh Park is now his."

His *brother*. In all the drama of Bertie's abrupt passing, Verity had not even thought of the succession of Fairleigh Park. Now she shook somewhere deep inside, like a dish of aspic set down too hard.

She nodded vaguely. "I'll be in the kitchen should you need me."

* * *

In her copy of Taillevent's *Le Viandier*, where the book opened to a recipe for gilded chicken with quenelles, Verity kept a brown envelope marked "List of Cheese Merchants in the 16th Arondissement."

In the envelope was a news clipping from the county fish wrapper, about the Liberals' victory in the general election after six years in opposition. In a corner of the clipping, Verity had written the date: 16.08.1892. In the middle of the article, a grainy photograph of Stuart Somerset looked back at her—local boy made good.

She never touched his image, for fear that her strokes would blur it. Sometimes she looked at it very close, the clipping almost at her nose. Sometimes she put it as far as her lap, but never further, never beyond reach.

The man in the photograph seemed to have scarcely aged in ten years, perhaps because his was an old soul, that he'd always been mature beyond his years. He was handsome, dramatically handsome—the face of a Shakespearean actor in his prime, all sharp peak and deep angles. And in his eyes was everything she could possibly want in a man: kindness, warmth, honesty, audacity, and love—love that would tear down this world and build it anew.

From afar she'd watched his meteoric rise—one of London's most sought-after barristers, and now, with the Liberals back in power, Mr. Gladstone's Chief Whip in the House of Commons—quite something for a man who'd spent his first nine years in a Manchester slum.

He'd accomplished it all on his own merits, of course, but she'd played her small part. She'd walked away from him, from hopes and dreams enough to spawn a generation of poets, so that he could be the man he was meant to be, the man whose face on her newspaper clipping she could not touch.

Stuart Somerset lived, not in his constituency of South Hackney, but in the elegant enclaves of Belgravia. From his visit to the house of his fiancée, he returned directly home, and went for the decanter of whiskey that he kept in his study.

He took a large swallow of the liquor. He was a little more affected by the news of Bertie's death now than he had been an hour ago. There was a faint numbness in his head. It was the shock of it, he supposed. He hadn't expected Mortality, ever present though it was, to strike Bertie, of all people.

Two shelves up from the whiskey decanter was a framed photograph of Bertie and himself, taken when Bertie had been eighteen and he seventeen, shortly after he'd been legitimized.

What had Bertie said to him that day?

You may be legitimized, but you will never be one of us. You don't know how Father panicked when it looked as if your mother might live. Your people are laborers and drunks and petty criminals. Don't flatter yourself otherwise.

For years afterward, whenever he remembered Bertie, it was Bertie as he had been that precise moment in time, impeccably turned out, a cold smile on his face, satisfied to have at last ruined something wonderful for his bastard-born brother.

But the slim youth in the picture, his fine summer coat faded to rust, resembled no one's idea of a nemesis. His fair hair, ruthlessly parted and slicked back, would have looked gauche in more fashionable circles. His posture was not so much erect as rigid. The square placement of his feet and the hand thrust nonchalantly into the coat pocket meant to indicate great assurance. As it was, he looked like any other eighteen-year-old, trying to radiate a manly confidence he didn't possess.

Stuart frowned. How long had it been since he'd last *looked* at the photograph?

The answer came far more easily than he'd expected. Not since That Night. He'd last looked at it with *her,* who'd studied the image with a disturbing concentration.

Do you hate him? she'd asked, giving the photograph back to him.

Sometimes, he'd answered absently, distracted by the nearness of her blush-pink lips. She'd been all eyes and lips, eyes the color of a tropical ocean, lips as full and soft as feather pillows.

Then I don't like him either, she'd said, smiling oddly.

Do you know him? he'd asked, suddenly, and for absolutely no reason.

No, she'd shaken her head with a grave finality, her beautiful eyes once again sad. *I don't know him at all.*

*Stories of passion and romance, adventure and intrigue,
from bestselling author*

Julia London

The Devil's Love
____22631-4 $6.99/$10.99 in Canada

Wicked Angel
____22632-1 $6.99/$8.99

The Secret Lover
____23694-8 $7.50/$9.99

The Rogues of Regent Street:
The Dangerous Gentleman
____23561-3 $6.99/$9.99

The Ruthless Charmer
____23562-0 $6.99/$9.99

The Beautiful Stranger
____23690-0 $6.99/$8.99